A Few Simple Murders

Deadly Talons – Book One

PADRAIG O'HANNON

ISBN: 1542429854
ISBN-13: 978-1542429856

padraigohannon@gmail.com

Books by Padraig O'Hannon:

JOHN COSTA MYSTERIES:

Murder in County Tyrone (The Irish Mysteries, Book One)

Child of a Cruel God (The Irish Mysteries, Book Two)

Death on the Lagan (The Irish Mysteries, Book Three)

A Few Simple Murders (Deadly Talons, Book One)

To my amazing father.

*Thank you for always being an inspiration
and an unfailing role model.*

Prologue

My name is John Costa and I'm a lawyer turned private investigator, at least that's what I tell everyone these days. I started my professional life as a crusading fix-the-world young assistant district attorney living in the Midwest United States. I was good at it, but became disenchanted when guilty people walked free thanks to plea deals and other legal maneuvering.

I left to start my own law firm and after a few high profile wins, started to get the reputation as the guy to go to when your life was on the line. It was lucrative, too. Add an unexpectedly large inheritance, and I quickly had more money than I knew what to do with.

It was in the early days of ubiquitous internet wifi, and many, including me, knew none of the dangers of unsecured public networks. I frequented a coffee shop with just such a network, laptop in hand and unafraid to do my banking and other financial transactions. Little did I know a major hacking group was targeting me for identity theft.

It was about that time that a young red-haired woman burst

into my life. On a dreary, rainy day she hacked my accounts and secured them before the real identity theft could take place. She contacted me and arranged a meeting where I could retrieve my new passwords. Thinking she was extorting me, I sent the police.

Captain George O'Neil, a friend when I was an ADA, an adversary when I was a defense attorney, summoned me to the police station to press charges. I can't imagine how the world would've turned out had he not encouraged me to hear the young woman's story.

My first glimpse of Jillian MacDonald, the woman I now fondly call Mack, was of a rain-soaked waif handcuffed to a table in an interrogation room. In spite of her disheveled appearance, her vibrant red hair and almost otherworldly green eyes that twinkled with intellect captured my curiosity. Over the next twenty minutes, I learned more about computers, networks, and security than I ever dreamed possible. I left that day with my money and identity intact.

I also left with Jillian in-tow. I ended up taking her home, meeting her father, and treating them both to dinner. Not only did I make two life-long friends, but also developed an appreciation, if not outright awe, of her towering intellect.

Her father, her sole surviving parent and one of the finest people I've ever had the pleasure to know, only lived a few years past our meeting. Before he passed, he asked me to take good care of his daughter. I accepted this as a sacred vow, sending her to college and then to graduate school. But always, she returned as if she had taken a similar oath to an unseen, unknown entity, to watch over me. It was a good thing, too, because I needed it.

My legal career was foundering, and of my own doing. Successfully defending the guilty was lucrative, but didn't let me sleep at night. Only copious amounts of Guinness and Irish Whiskey could accomplish that. Eventually, I closed my firm and took a job doing contract legal work at a local company. It was at Mack's urging and done mostly to keep me out of trouble. It was there that I first caught a glimpse of Angela Grady.

The young, slender Irish woman, only a few years older that Mack, captured every facet of my imagination. I deemed her hopelessly out of reach, but that didn't stop the gnawing of curiosity and desire from lurking in the background. It raged in secret until several strange twists of fate demanded otherwise.

When new evidence in an old crime, a deadly bombing in Northern Ireland, surfaced, I became far more entwined with Angela than I ever dreamed possible, including a whirlwind romance that ended abruptly with the United States Marshals taking her away for extradition.

Unable to let it go, Mack and I relentlessly researched the case and learned the truth. Our investigation acquitted Angela and convicted her mother of the bombing. The truth can be a funny thing, though, and in this case, it convicted Angela of being an accomplice. Both ended up in prison and I ended up back in America with a broken heart.

Two short years later, I was back in Ireland after Angela's mother escaped from prison. In an unlikely twist, a senior official from the Police Service and I joined forces to pull off a harrowing rescue of Angela from corrupt assassins within the special prison where she was being held. In collaboration, we won a deadly race to a fortune in diamonds that, had it fallen to her mother, would've undoubtedly been used to wreak untold havoc. In the ensuing chaos, Angela saved my life but suffered a mortal wound in the process. She died in my arms just as medics arrived.

Angry and hurt, I continued my quest, destroying large swaths of her mother's terrorist organization and eventually facilitating her recapture. Victorious but broken, I returned to America. The entire time, Mack was there, tirelessly at my side providing technical wizardry far beyond the capabilities of a mortal. More than that, though, she provided the precious gift of friendship.

Memories of Angela's death continue to haunt me. They're hazy, disjointed, and changing. Perhaps this is from blood loss due to injuries I received or it's my brain's way of trying to deal with things.

I don't know. Either way, I don't have any closure. Tantalizing clues that maybe, improbably, she survived continue to pull at my soul.

That brings us to the present. Mack and I are back in the Midwest and trying to get our fledgling investigative agency off the ground. I'm also trying to rebuild my life. It's Wednesday and that's the night a group of friends gathers at O'Brien's pub to play traditional Irish music. With the events of recent years, I've been a stranger at the weekly jam session. I play the violin – badly – so my musical contribution is never meaningful, but the camaraderie is as important as the tunes. Besides, Mack hounds me relentlessly every Wednesday to go. She says it's good for my soul, and she's so rarely wrong about such things, who am I to argue?

One might ask how a man whose name could easily have been Giovanni Costaglioli, had my father had his way, is a regular at an Irish session? I guess I took after my mum's side of the family. She was born and raised in County Cork, Ireland.

So sniffles be damned! I'm off to play some music.

CHAPTER ONE

I was almost home when my phone rang.

"Mister C.! Barry's been killed!" Laura McConnell said, fighting back tears.

"I just saw him, and he seemed fine," I said, pulling my car off the road. "What on earth happened?"

"I don't know," she sobbed, "but the police are here, and they're saying he was murdered. They want to talk to everyone who was at the Irish music session tonight."

"I'm sure they do," I said.

"I'm a bit surprised you answered. I thought you'd be home and in bed with your phone off."

"That was the plan," I sighed, blowing my nose. "There was some road work that slowed me down, then I stopped off for a bottle of nighttime cold medicine. I'm running more than an hour behind, all told."

"I wouldn't have called you, but they were quite insistent…"

Dammit. This was not how I wanted my Wednesday to end.

* * *

I could see the flashing lights of the police cars a block away from O'Brien's pub. As I neared, I could see that the activity centered on a nearby alleyway. Finding a parking spot well out of the way and grabbing a handful of tissues, I made my way to the entrance.

"This is terrible," Laura cried and trembled as she embraced me. "He's been coming here as long as I can remember."

Barry Myers had been a long-time patron of the pub and an integral part in starting the Wednesday night Irish music session. Less than an hour ago, we were playing tunes together. Now, he was gone.

"Do we know any more?"

"No," she said. "The police are interviewing us, but nobody's been told much. Can I get you anything?"

I shook my head, fighting off a sneeze. Before I could rejoin my fellow musicians, a familiar voice commanded my attention.

"John Costa!"

"George O'Neil," I said, clasping his outstretched hand. "I'm surprised to see you here."

"I heard the call come in," the police captain said, resting his imposing hand on my shoulder. "When I realized it was your place, I figured I'd better check it out in person."

"I don't own O'Brien's Pub anymore, George. Laura is the owner now," I said, tilting my head in her direction.

"But you're the one with the reputation, like it or not."

"Not," I said, repressing another sneeze. "What the hell is going on?"

"Barry Myers—you know him?"

I scowled. "What kind of question is that, George? Of course I know him, and you knew that before you asked!"

"Always the damned attorney," O'Neil grunted.

"Always the damned cop," I replied. "You'd think less of me if I didn't keep you honest," I said.

"Word has it that you and your pal Jillian have opened an investigative service. A millionaire attorney turned private eye—now there's something you don't see every day."

"And again, you knew that before you asked. What's really on your mind, George?"

"Take a walk with me, John," he said, motioning for me to follow. "Any chance of seeing you in the courtroom again?"

Dammit. I didn't feel like small talk. I wanted to go home and get to bed, but O'Neil had other ideas. A powerful man, in every sense of the word, he tended to get his way.

"The District Attorney," he continued, oblivious to what was surely noticeable scowling, "would certainly be delighted to have you on his staff. They're stretched to the limit, and many of the attorneys are new and inexperienced. You'd be a godsend, John."

My career as a litigator started in the District Attorney's office, when I was young and still filled with idealistic notions. They had all faded long ago, dulled by plea bargains, clever defense lawyers, and a hollow feeling that justice was missing from many, if not most, of the outcomes. I didn't miss it; not for a moment.

"I'm sure that would be preferable to having me on the other side of the courtroom," I said, referring to my successful, lucrative, but equally unsatisfying time as a defense counselor. "Your cousin would agree, undoubtedly."

George O'Neil and I had known each other since my days as an Assistant District Attorney, and he was none too happy when I decided to leave public service for my private practice. That all changed when his cousin, a police officer new to the force, was involved in a shooting on a stormy night. It resulted in homicide charges. The case was grueling and appeared lost, but through perseverance and meticulous attention to detail, the tide turned. The victory, my highest profile trial at the time, brought a steady stream of lucrative cases and good publicity.

"I expect so," he replied, chuckling. "You only saved his life, freedom, and career. Nothing much, right?"

The case was the last time I left a courtroom feeling good about myself. All that followed, lucrative and undefeated as it was, failed to satisfy.

"I'm not biting, George," I sniffled. "I'm happy as far away from a court of law as possible."

"So you continue to tell me," he said, allowing a narrow smile to reach the corner of his mouth. "I owe it to the world to try, though."

* * *

We walked north from O'Brien's toward my usual parking spot and approached the alleyway where the police activity centered.

"John, just how well did you know Barry?"

I folded my tissue, shoving it into my pocket. "Not well at all, beyond seeing him at the pub from time to time. He was a regular at the session, so I've seen more of him in the past nine months. I think he did something in manufacturing, but I don't know the details."

"Your fellow musicians told me you left the session early tonight. That's a bit unusual, isn't it?"

I stopped, abruptly, the insinuative tone of his voice making anger bubble inside. "Kiss my ass, O'Neil. I'm going home."

He continued, unperturbed. "I only ask because everyone we've interviewed mentioned that it was unusual for you to leave early."

"Did they mention my cold and my sneezing?" I growled. "You can talk to my damned attorney if you're going to make veiled threats. Am I free to go?"

O'Neil was impervious to my protestations. "The witnesses also reported that Barry left shortly after you did, seemingly in a hurry. One of them said Barry mentioned your name on his way out."

His reputation as an interrogator was widely known, but I wasn't having anything to do with it. "Good night, George," I said, turning to leave. His massive hand on my shoulder stopped me.

"You're not a suspect, Costa, although that could easily change. We've already looked at the video from the pub's security system. You walked past the alleyway," he said, pointing to the intersection, "and on to your car. The cameras show you driving south, passing the pub's entrance about fifteen seconds before Barry emerged. So unless there are two bastards in this world as ugly as you, or you've somehow perfected teleportation, you couldn't have been anywhere near the crime scene. Now, how about you cut me a damned break, counselor?"

I scowled at him, but lacked the energy to launch into the verbal tirade that was dancing around in my brain. A sneeze derailed any chance I had for a snarky retort.

"Bless you" he said. "That cold sounds nasty. It probably isn't letting you get much done around the office. How's business, anyway?"

"We're busy as beavers," I answered.

It was a convenient half-truth, and O'Neil, the consummate cop, knew it instantly.

"A lot of husbands who can't keep it in their pants, eh?"

"It pays the bills," I muttered. This was a bold-faced lie. Our fees to expose philandering spouses barely covered the expenses to pay Tom and Zonk, our front-line investigators. My business partner and closest friend, Jillian MacDonald, or Mack as I liked to call her, stayed busy, but I was covering her salary out of my pocket, not from the company coffers. Our cases, such as they were, didn't begin to challenge her formidable skills as a researcher or computer expert.

This reminded me of the growing, gnawing guilt that tugged at me with relentless zeal. Mack passed up a once-in-a-lifetime opportunity to work as a cyber crime analyst with the Police Service of Northern Ireland in favor of our business venture. As each day passed, it seemed destined to be an ill-fated business misadventure.

"No it doesn't," O'Neil said, his substantial hand squeezing my shoulder. "I'm sorry how things ended for you in Northern Ireland, and I'm sorry I've not been around more. I know a bit of what you're going through, from when my wife passed. It sucks. There's no other way to put it. "

"Are you my shrink now, George?"

He pulled me in, pretending to punch me in the stomach. It was a good thing it was in jest; O'Neil's massive fists would likely cause significant damage. "That's the kind of counseling I give, buddy! I'm just letting you know you've got friends, and some of us are worried that you're getting way too cozy with the bottom of a whiskey bottle and empty pints of Guinness again."

"I'm fine," I protested. "I've got a project that helps keep me busy."

With one glance, I could tell he knew what the project was. I could also tell that George, like Mack, thought it was a pathetic waste of time. Hell, they were probably right. It was a futile effort and was prolonging my own suffering.

Logic told me the harsh truth: Angela Grady, the woman I loved, died in my arms in Northern Ireland more than a year ago. A few inconsistencies in the official record, confusing memories and some tantalizing hints that her death might have been an elaborate ruse, spurred my latest Quixotic obsession. Oblivious to the fact that every clue either led nowhere, or to a conclusion I didn't want to accept, I soldiered on, all against the well-intended advice of those near to me.

"Well," he said, briefly pulling me back to reality, "we all do what we need to, I suppose. How many nights last week did you drink yourself to sleep?"

I didn't know, and I didn't care. And why should I? If anyone had the right to passionately embrace a bottle of whiskey, it was me, dammit. Drinking silenced the foolish optimist hiding within, the driving force behind my futile search. Drinking also brought sleep, and sleep brought the blissful dreams of Angela; dreams so real it hurt when they faded into the obnoxious light of day.

"Just killing off these damned germs," I said, blowing my nose. "Why the hell am I here, anyway?"

"Because I know you, John. The minute you get home, you're going to ask Jillian MacDonald to start looking into Barry Myers' life. I can't stop you from making inquiries, but I can sure as hell charge you with obstruction if you find something relevant and fail to share it. This is, after all, an active investigation. Follow?"

I nodded.

"I know full well you've got sources inside my department, so it isn't like you're not going to know any of this."

He lifted up the police tape, bringing me closer to the crime scene.

"And because you're involved..."

"Dammit, George," I said, stopping abruptly, "the only thing I want to be involved with is my bed. If I'm feeling frisky, maybe I'll have a passionate affair with two tablespoons of nighttime cold medicine."

6

He motioned me forward. A few paces later, our steps slowed. "We can tell from the surveillance footage that he left the pub in a hurry, likely to try to catch up to you. He stopped, rather abruptly, turning into the alleyway. As you can see, he didn't make it very far." O'Neil pointed to a bloody spot on the pavement a few yards from the intersection. The darkness of the alleyway would have obscured the scene, save for the illumination provided by lights imported by the police. It wasn't hard to see why the killer picked this location.

"Who found the body?"

"A car turned into the alleyway to turn around, spotted the body, and called us."

"Any signs of a struggle?"

"No. He either knew his attacker or didn't feel threatened."

My eyes narrowed, studying the scene. "If he was in a hurry to talk to me, why stop to talk to someone here?"

"It had to be someone or something he deemed more urgent than catching up to you. You don't have any idea what he might have wanted?"

"No," I sighed. "We saw each other every week at the session and exchanged pleasantries. That, and a few random discussions of Irish music was about it. There's usually some chit-chat that goes on after we're done, but Barry was never much for that."

"Did he know about your adventures in Northern Ireland?"

O'Neil was referring to the unlikely and sad odyssey, centered on the lovely Angela, that had consumed the last four years and drastically altered the direction of my life. It was also why I drank—well, at least one of the reasons. "Of course. Everyone at the pub knows about that. What are you getting at?"

"Nothing in particular; thinking out loud, mostly. So you don't know if he was in some sort of trouble?"

I shook my head.

"The crime scene and forensic teams are still doing their thing so we can't get any closer. Does this mean anything to you?"

He showed me a sealed plastic bag holding a bloody metal blade, well over a foot in length.

"That's a nasty thing," I said. "I can't say I've ever seen anything quite like it. Is that the murder weapon?"

"We're not entirely sure," he said, frowning. "Not that it's necessarily relevant for anything but the final coroner's report."

"I don't follow you…"

"The blade was definitely involved. We don't know yet if the stab to his gut killed him, or the bullet between the eyes did. We need to know for the final report, of course, but for practical purposes, it doesn't really matter which one came first. The end result was the same."

"Someone wanted to be sure of their work." I stared at the bag. "That's an odd knife."

"It's odd because it isn't a knife; it's a bayonet. Specifically, this is designed for the Mosin Nagant M91/30."

"The what?"

"A Russian infantry rifle from World War II. This is a spike bayonet. Look at the shape, John. It's designed to create wounds that bleed heavily and are hard to treat. It isn't really designed to be used by hand, but our perpetrator was able to improvise a way. The tip has been filed sharp, as have the sides, but only for the first twelve inches or so. The rest has been dulled."

"Probably to make it easier to grip," I said. "A rather unusual choice of weapons, don't you think?"

"Undoubtedly. In spite of it's age, neither the rifle nor the bayonet are uncommon, though. You could probably go to your local gun shop or sporting goods store and have your pick of a dozen. Hell, I've got a couple of them as part of my collection."

I ran my fingers through my hair. Something wasn't adding up. "So Barry was lured into the alley, shot, and stabbed—or stabbed, and then shot? No struggle. No witnesses. Is that your theory?"

O'Neil nodded. "For the moment. We still have officers canvassing the area to see if anyone was a witness, but we're not hopeful. All of this took place after hours for most of the businesses around here."

"No cameras?"

"None that we know of. The cameras at O'Brien's Pub captured the main street, but not the alleyway."

I sighed. "Definitely reduces the possibility that this was a random act of violence."

"I can guarantee that it *wasn't* random," O'Neil said, his voice exuding confidence.

"Why so certain?"

"Because of this," he said, producing a second, smaller sealed evidence bag.

I could see that it contained a business card. A momentary feeling of dread shook me. "George, I swear to God, if that note has the slightest thing to do with Northern Ireland, I'm going to go park my car on the nearest set of train tracks…"

He pulled the bag away. "I thought you adored Ireland?"

"I do. I just need a break." O'Neil probably knew it was a lie, but if he did, he didn't press the issue. Truth was, I'd drop everything in a heartbeat and fly to Belfast if there was the slightest chance of finding Angela Grady alive. But there wasn't, and somewhere deep inside, I knew it. When she crashed into my life, my intentions were noble: defend a woman wrongly accused of a terrible crime. It was far from that simple, though. The ensuing maelstrom destroyed her and damn near collected me as well. Or maybe it *had* destroyed me, and my refusal to let go served as ongoing proof. I wasn't sure it mattered.

He chuckled. "Unless the Irish changed alphabets and their language in the last few hours, I think you're safe. Take a glance."

The bag contained an ordinary business card. Cream-colored and otherwise nondescript, it contained only three lines of text.

"Russian?" I said, looking at the letters.

"Something like that" he said, offering no additional details.

"Barry had this card?"

"No. It was placed on his body post-mortem, just like the bayonet."

"A calling card," I muttered.

"Costa," O'Neil said, pulling me aside, "meet me for breakfast tomorrow morning. I'll even let you buy."

I stared at him. Dammit. There was more, and he wasn't telling me—or couldn't tell me. Worse, I was curious, and he knew it.

"All right," I said. "Ten?"

"Make it seven, at Taggart's diner."

Not only was seven way too early, Taggart's was on the opposite side of the city.

"Fine," I grunted, blowing my nose. "See you there."

CHAPTER TWO

The familiar voice of ace researcher and computer expert Jillian MacDonald, or Mack, as I called her, greeted me the moment I opened my front door. Since our return from Northern Ireland, she had all but taken over my guest room. And my kitchen. And my office. And my life. All of it was under the guise of building our business, but the truth was far simpler: she was worried about me and probably with good reason.

"You're running later than usual…" her voice stopped when she caught her first glimpse of me. "What on earth is wrong?"

"Barry Myers is dead."

"I'm so sorry," she said, hugging me. "He wasn't much older than you. Do you know any of the details?"

"He was murdered, Mack, half a block away from the pub. Someone lured him into an alley and shoved a knife in his gut."

She frowned. "That's terrible and quite unexpected for that neighborhood."

"I left early; damn near made it home before Laura called me with the news. Apparently Barry left the session a few minutes after I did. Word has it he had something to tell me, but I was already in my car and on my way by the time he came out of the door. I only missed him by a few seconds."

"What is it?" She studied me. "What aren't you telling me?"

"George O'Neil kept goading me when we spoke tonight, hinting that I was somehow involved."

"Well, given the wicked things you've said about banjo players over the years, you've likely given him probable cause."

I smiled. "You know perfectly well I've saved all my real vitriol for accordion players. But seriously, Mack, it felt like he was asking for my help—between the lines, of course."

"In an active case, especially so early on? Seems unlikely."

"There's more to it than he told me tonight. Of that, I'm absolutely certain. O'Neil wants to meet me early in the morning. I'll know more after we meet. If I'm wrong, I'll walk away."

"No you won't."

"Why do you say that, Mack?"

"I can see it in your eyes. You're curious, and every time you get curious, it gets expensive. In case you didn't hear me the last ten times I brought it up, we're still mostly in the red. We need paying cases, John, not wild goose chases."

"If you're worried about money, I can go to the bank tomorrow, and…"

"You're missing the point, oh Spendy One! Constantly funding the business from your own account is like an author that buys a thousand copies of his own book to get it on the charts. I want our venture to succeed on its own merits, not because one of the partners keeps tossing money at it."

She stopped, studying my face. "You really want to do this, don't you?"

"At least to figure out why a police captain was out investigating a homicide instead of leaving it to his detectives, and why did he keep hinting that I was involved?"

"Well, if it means that much to you, I can nose around and see what I can find. Was Barry married?"

"Umm… yeah, I think so."

"Perhaps his wife would be willing to pay us to look into his death. Or perhaps his insurance company…"

"Mack!"

"Maybe there'll be a reward…"

"Mack!!"

"Yes?"

"I'm sick, and I'm going to bed. And yes, I'm curious, and no, I don't care what it costs."

"Fine," she said, rolling her eyes, all while fighting an emerging smile. "Give me what you've learned so far, and I'll get the computers started working on it."

* * *

George O'Neil was not the least bit happy about my arrival, a full fifteen minutes late.

"Still on Irish time, I see," he said, glancing at his watch.

"I should be on sick time, or perhaps overtime. You're lucky I came here at all."

"Two eggs, over medium, white toast, crispy bacon, and home fries," O'Neil said to our waiter. "Bring my friend a spare pot of coffee," he added, chuckling.

"I'm not used to getting up this early," I grunted after placing my order.

"I couldn't possibly guess," he said, opening a creamer and pouring it into his coffee. He repeated the process until the coffee flirted with the brim of the cup and was closer to the color of cream than of coffee. "I suppose you want me to get to the point."

"It would be nice," I said, nibbling on a piece of toast.

"Does the name Rick Stevens mean anything to you?"

I shrugged. "No. Should it?"

"Probably not. We found his body about two weeks ago, dumped on an abandoned railroad siding by the old foundry. He was stabbed in the stomach and executed just like Barry Myers."

"Calling card and all?"

"And all," he said. In one stunning revelation, I understood why a police captain was out investigating a murder.

"Serial killer?" I said, barely loud enough to be heard.

"Possibly," he said, "or ritualistic, but I have another theory."

"What is it?"

"I have a friend," he said, pausing while the waiter delivered our food, "who is with the FBI. I sent him a copy of the calling card. I've known this fellow since high school, and I can tell when he's blowing smoke up my ass."

"Which happened, I take it…"

"And how. Gave me some song and dance about finding nothing on file, then he suggested I talk to someone at the University to get it translated. It's written in Bosnian. Word has it you might have some contacts that could help."

Dammit. My contacts, if I could reach them at all, were in Northern Ireland, and I didn't want to deal with the memories a call would invoke. "If you've already gotten the card translated, what do you need me for?"

"The professor we spoke to translated the card, but it doesn't make sense. It's nothing more than a child's poem about birds on a tree branch."

"Not your typical calling card, unless these murders are somehow the work of a jilted birdwatcher."

"Snarky bastard! If my suspicions are right, there is a secondary meaning to the card. Perhaps my friend from the FBI knows what it is and couldn't tell me. Either way, I have two bodies on my hands, and its just a matter of time before someone in the press catches wind of it."

"So where do I fit in to all this, George?

"I'm still trying to figure that out. Have you come up with any ideas as to why Barry might have chased after you?"

"Not a one," I said, sipping my coffee and sniffling. "What can you tell me about Rick Stevens?" I was blatantly fishing.

O'Neil surprised me by responding. "He worked as an independent contractor, but there's nothing to indicate that his murder had anything to do with his work."

"Family?" I asked, peering up from my breakfast.

A slight hesitation broke O'Neil's otherwise metronomic pace. "He has a ten year old daughter by his ex-wife. He spends a weekend with the child every month. Apart from his weekly bowling league,

Mister Stevens didn't lead the sort of life that would draw much attention. But then again, neither did Barry Myers, yet here we are."

"Don't you guys have profilers, or isn't there some FBI team you can summon for help?"

The corners of his mouth turned upward. "Certainly, and we're in contact as we speak. But it's equally important to talk with everyone involved."

I put my silverware down, emphatically. "Enough with the bullshit, George! You dragged me half way across the goddamned city to make another half-witted accusation? I'm no more involved than our waiter. Speaking of which, I need my check." I started to rise, and I signaled to the young man who was working our table.

"Sit the hell down," O'Neil growled. "Does this mean anything to you?" He handed me a business card enclosed in a thick, plastic evidence bag.

The sight of it caused me to sink into my seat.

```
John Costa
Attorney at Law
1732 East High Street, Suite 3B
```

"This is quite the relic," I said, pushing it back to him, "and not a harbinger of pleasant memories."

"How old would you say that card is?"

"A dozen years, perhaps. I moved my law offices to High Street a few years before I gave up the silly notion of being a lawyer. This was my final business card design."

"Rick Stevens had this in his wallet when we found his body. Look at it, John. It's barely worn, like it was tucked safely in a drawer for many years, not banging around in a wallet. Now... Do you care to revise your story about not knowing anything?"

"My story? No, George, I really don't. Hell, you should know me well enough to realize I'm telling you the truth." O'Neil was an expert at detecting the slightest fabrication, especially when it came to me.

"The word from Belfast is that you faced down one of their most wanted terrorists and beat her at her own mind games. Besides, you never found a lie you didn't like when you were in the courtroom. Maybe you've raised your game to the point where I can't tell your lies from your truths. The only common thread we've been able to find between the two murders is your name, and I want to know why!"

"Look, once and for all, I don't know why Barry was chasing after me, and I've never heard of Rick Stevens! Nor do I know how he got my card—I certainly never represented the man. Hell, we gave out hundreds of those damned things."

His eyes seared me. "You're not in over your head again on some crazy case you and MacDonald are working on, are you?"

"No," I said, slamming my fist into the table loudly enough for people at a nearby booth to look at us.

"Would it surprise you if I told you I knew exactly where Stevens got your card?"

My reply was a silent, icy stare.

O'Neil continued, unperturbed, his eyes squarely focused on me. "He got it from Jennifer Adams."

The unpleasantness that fluttered through my insides at the mention of her name must've culminated in a visible flinch, because O'Neil's expression softened almost immediately. My reaction, awful and genuine, answered his question.

"Word has it that you two were hot and heavy back in the day."

I would have been perfectly happy to never again hear that vile harpy's name, let alone talk about her. Time had hidden the wounds she left, but the pain lingered. "I was hot and heavy, George. She wasn't."

Hell, that was the understatement of the millennium. I was ready to buy a ring; she was leading me on, placating and manipulating, all while looking for someone else, whom she eventually found. She delivered the devastating news in a short phone call from a distant city. I spent the next few months in blind denial, to which she replied with heartless indifference and silence.

"When was the last time you heard from her?"

I sighed. "Seven years, maybe more. She sent me an email and a friend request on a social media site. I summarily deleted it, and that was that."

"I'm sorry to bring her up out of the blue like that, but I needed to know."

"You needed to know? If I was involved in a murder or two? If I had rekindled things with Jennifer, and she manipulated me into a simple matter of manslaughter? I knew you were an asshole, George. I guess I didn't realize the spectacular dimensions of the chasm."

"I never suspected you of the murders, Costa, but I wasn't sure if you were working on a case that somehow tied all this together."

"Well, now you have your answer," I growled, standing. "I've lost my appetite."

"Don't forget about the bill," he said, smirking. "I promised I'd let you buy."

I plunked two twenty dollar bills on the table. "If that doesn't cover it, call the cops on me, asshole."

"Don't forget to get that Bosnian poem translated for me. You'll find a picture of it in your email."

I stomped out of the diner, seething.

* * *

The long drive home gave me additional opportunities to fume, enough so that I missed several turns and quickly found myself heading into a more rural area. I was also oblivious to the impending arrival of a winter storm and the sharp drop in temperature that accompanied it.

My efforts to orient myself back to, more or less, the right general direction to return home landed me on an unfamiliar, winding road. As I worked my way westward, rain mixed with bits of ice started to fall. This, too, failed to register, as I found it nearly impossible to rid my mind of damned Jennifer Adams.

I wasn't speeding, but the combination of poor conditions, unfamiliarity with the road, and a slightly distracted mind made what happened next nearly inevitable. As I crested a gentle hill, the road turned sharply.

I turned the wheel, but the laws of physics had other ideas. The brakes proved equally futile, and the car left the road, crashing through some underbrush before crumpling around the trunk of a large tree.

Dammit.

CHAPTER THREE

I was out of the car and on my phone with the insurance company long before the first passerby arrived. I tried to assure the nice man that I was uninjured, but he insisted on lingering until help arrived.

It was probably a good thing that he did. He carried several road flares in the trunk of his car, and they likely prevented additional accidents. Even the tail of the responding police car gave a brief wiggle as it hit the slippery section of the road.

"I guess I don't need to ask what happened," he quipped, stepping out of his car cautiously. "Are you okay, sir? EMS will be here in a bit to check you out."

"I'm fine," I said, handing him my license, registration, and insurance card. "Just a bit shaken. The seat belts and the airbags did their job."

He glanced over at my car. "Yes they did, Mister Costa. Do you have a tow truck on the way?"

"Already in the works," I sighed, looking at the mangled remains of my vehicle.

"Yep," the officer said. "It's totaled for sure. I'll need to get your statement for my report."

* * *

Mack arrived as I was stuffing the last of my belongings into plastic grocery bags.

"You beat the tow truck here," I said, trying to make light of the situation.

She was having none of it. Her green eyes studied me, up and down, before collecting me in a firm embrace.

"Easy, Mack!" I said. "You're going to break my damned ribs."

"Sorry," she whispered, easing her grip, "I just worry about you."

"I'm fine," I protested. "You'd be proud of me—I actually let the paramedics give me a once-over before I called you."

"Perhaps," she said, kissing my forehead, "you're getting a modicum of wisdom in your old age."

"Stranger things have happened. Let's get this stuff loaded and wait for the tow truck in your car. I'm damned freezing."

* * *

The drive home after the long-delayed arrival of the tow truck was silent until Mack spoke.

"What really happened?" she said, easing to a stop at a red light. "The police might have bought that story about a slippery patch of road, but I know you're much too good of a driver to make a mistake like that."

"My mind was distracted, and I didn't detect the ice until it was too late. Simple as that, Mack."

"Did they write you a ticket or anything?"

"No. I think once the officer learned that I had breakfast with Captain O'Neil, he felt doing anything else would be cruel and unusual punishment."

"It didn't go well, I take it?" she asked, accelerating gently as the light turned green.

"There was another murder, Mack. About two weeks ago, there was another murder. Same weapon, same calling card left on the body."

"Well, that certainly explains why a police captain was out with his investigators," she said, deftly negotiating a slippery turn. "They got a serial killer on their hands."

"Possibly. O'Neil didn't offer up much in the way of theories apart from repeatedly insinuating that I was involved or that, perhaps, we were working on a case that is somehow related."

"Nonsense," she said, wrinkling her nose. "I'll have Zonk double check to be sure, but we don't have much going on right now. Why would he think you're involved?"

"Not only did Barry come chasing after me, but the first victim, a man named Rick Stevens, had one of my old business cards in his pocket. I've never heard of the guy, but I sure as hell know his girlfriend—Jennifer Adams."

"Well, that certainly explains your distracted mind," she said. "I bet that was a hell of a way to start your Thursday!"

Mack knew a few superficial details of the emotionally devastating events surrounding my erstwhile romantic entanglement with Miss Adams. "I could think of better," I grumbled. "Pull in here, will you?" I said, pointing to a sign.

"Here? What for?"

"I need to buy a new car."

"You're going to do no such thing today! I'm going to take you home, and you're going to rest. You can deal with vehicle nonsense tomorrow. Besides, you have a car."

I found her last comment puzzling, but lacked the energy or willpower to mount a discussion about it.

"Fine," I sighed. "Home sounds good, now that you mention it."

* * *

Mack watched me like a hawk the moment we set foot in my house, fussing over my every move. Worse, she quizzed me repeatedly on my meeting with O'Neil until I finally found a way to silence her.

"I recorded the whole thing, you know."

A wry smile graced the corners of her mouth. "Well, why didn't you say so?"

"It was more fun watching you squirm," I said, winking and handing her the memory card from my recorder. "Bring me a pain killer or two while you're at it. I'm getting a bit of a headache."

The respite was short-lived, as she returned, laptop in hand, to review the footage.

"I was hoping to take a bit of a nap," I said, swallowing the tablets she handed to me.

"I want you to take it easy, but you're not leaving my sight."

"Why not?"

"Because you might have a concussion. You were in a car wreck a few hours ago, and you're exhibiting some of the symptoms."

"I don't have a concussion, Mack, or any of the symptoms. The paramedics checked me, you know."

"You're the one with the headache…"

"Yes, from being mercilessly grilled."

"And confusion…"

"I'm not confused about anything."

"You wanted to stop at a random dealer and buy a car when you've got a perfectly good one."

"I don't have a car, and I need one," I growled.

"And irritability! Another symptom!"

"Mack!"

"Bluster and boom all you want, John Costa, but I'm not going anywhere."

I sagged back in my chair, resigned to my fate.

* * *

The arrival of our researcher, a curly-haired young man we nicknamed Zonk, eased what was shaping up to be an uncomfortable battle of wills. I wanted to sleep and forget about the day, but Mack was having none of it. Thus far, she was comfortably winning, peppering me with questions every time I started to drift off to sleep.

Zonk was in his element tailing philandering spouses and snapping pictures, but clearly aspired for more compelling cases. When confined to more traditional modes of research, he produced adequate results, but at a pace that Mack invariably found too slow. They were apparently in the throes of trying to find any and all dirt on Barry Myers when my ill-timed accident triggered Mack's inner mother hen, halting their progress.

"Your friend, Mister Myers, wasn't a very interesting fellow," he said, flopping into a nearby chair. "He worked for a company that, from what I can tell, doesn't do anything other than ship things. His house is typical and of average value for this area. No back taxes due, nothing fishy."

"Life insurance?" I asked.

"I only looked at public records, Mister Costa. Miss MacDonald was going to look into some of the financial aspects."

I jumped in before Mack could say anything. "She didn't get any of it done, Zonk. She was far too busy fussing over my nonexistent concussion."

The glare from Mack's eyes silenced me before I could say anything else.

"Next time, I'll let you slip into a coma, Sir Ungrateful! I'll have you know I was working with some of my contacts within the police department."

"And?" I said, leaning forward on my chair.

"They're being pretty tight lipped. Partially because they don't want people in a panic over the prospect of a serial killer on the loose, but also because they've got next to nothing to go on. Whoever killed these men knows what they're doing and almost certainly was known personally by both victims. There was no sign of a struggle in either situation."

"Has any sort of connection been established?" I asked, pouring some coffee.

"Other than you? No, and they're spinning their wheels trying to find one. I think they were banking on you having some relevant information. One interesting tidbit did come out of my afternoon conversations, though."

"Oh? What's that?"

"Barry's wife has been less than cooperative. They're chalking it

23

up to the shock of the whole thing, but if it continues, she's going to slip into being a suspect, merely by default."

"Barry didn't talk much about his wife. I seem to recall that she came to hear our music session once, maybe twice, but I think she waited for him outside in their car most of the time. For that matter, Barry didn't talk much about anything, except Irish music, that is."

"Anyone care if I call it a night?" Zonk interjected.

"No worries," said Mack. "We'll get back to things in the morning."

Mack waited until the front door closed in the distance. "Do you want me to call Tom in on this one? Zonk's going to be in over his head, if he isn't already."

"This one? Weren't you the one worried about getting paying cases, controlling expenses, and all that?"

"I was, and I still am, but you told me that expense didn't matter to you."

"So why the change of heart?"

"Because in everything that I've heard so far, nobody has stopped to consider the possibility that *you* are the target. You made more than your fair share of enemies as a prosecutor, no doubt. What if one of them has an ax to grind with you?"

"I suppose it's possible," I said.

"Put Zonk on your old case files. He can cross reference them with anyone who has been released lately. I'll call Tom in to handle the more sophisticated stuff."

"Isn't he hiking with his girlfriend or something?"

"No. That was his plan originally, but they broke up a couple of weeks ago. I have it on good authority that he's at home nursing a broken heart."

It was a feeling I knew all too well. "Call him in if you think he's up to it."

"I think at this point he'll probably welcome the company. Just go along with whatever story he wants to tell us—he's still nursing a bit of a bruised ego."

"Got it." I rose, stretching. "Mack, I'm getting really tired. Is it okay if I go to bed now?"

"Of course," she said, "but I'm going to keep an eye on you throughout the night, just in case."

"I'm fine, Mack. Honestly. I think, for once, *you're* the one who's worrying too much."

"Well, if I am, I will sincerely apologize first thing in the morning. For tonight, however, you're just going to have to deal with it."

CHAPTER FOUR

Coffee was my first order of business after a thoroughly dissatisfying and restless night. Mack, true to her word, had lorded over me, nudging me awake and forcing conversation every hour or two. It felt like every fifteen minutes, and I got progressively more irritable with each disturbance. Eventually, she relented, and my last three hours were spent in brief, but blissful, silence.

The accident hurt a little more than I was willing to admit, and I discovered newly aching muscles and joints, seemingly with every move. I washed down a pair of extra strength anti-inflammatory tablets and ambled slowly to my office.

Mack was already hard at work, looking fresh and energetic. She glanced up, offering only a wry smile as a greeting. At least my cold seemed marginally better.

"How the hell do you do it, Mack?" I rasped, my voice still not quite ready to work. "I feel like a damned zombie, and you're up and at it."

"I can sleep when I'm dead," she said, her eyes never leaving her computer monitor. "I've assembled a list of things for you to do today. You'll find it on your desk."

I nodded, still foggy. "Wait a minute! Don't you owe me an apology or something."

"Probably," she said, her attention still directed at the screen.

I stood silently for a moment. She stopped and looked up, her expression dripping with indifference.

"I sincerely apologize for not wanting you to slip into a coma and die. Does that meet your criteria, oh jaded one?"

I responded with a gently raised eyebrow.

"Besides, you also owe me an apology," she said.

"How so?"

"Your recording of your conversation with George O'Neil ended after the first few minutes. You forgot to erase the old recordings like I told you to, and it ran out of space."

"Dammit..."

"Water under the bridge. Now then..." She allowed her voice to drift off as her finger tapped the freshly penned list that occupied a prominent position on my desk.

Taking another deep swig of coffee, I reluctantly settled into my chair and reviewed the list.

The second item on the list elicited an immediate protest. "No way, Mack. No! I'm not going to do it. I can't!"

"You can, and you will," she said, stopping whatever she was working on. "You need a car; you have a car; it's as simple as that."

It was anything but simple. "Can't I just borrow your car, or can you at least drive me to a dealership?"

"Let me see," she said, pretending to contemplate my questions, "no, and no."

"But Mack... it's *her* car."

"No, John. It *was* Angela's car. Now it is your car. It's yours in every sense of the word. You bought it for her, and the probate court ruled you her sole beneficiary. That makes it yours. Your car."

"It just isn't that easy..."

She turned her attention to me, her expression softer than expected. "I'm not as cruel and heartless as maybe you think I am. When my father died, I saw him everywhere, or at least I wanted to. I'd go by places where he used to hang out, half expecting to see his car parked in the lot, or see him out talking to a group of his pals. I see you doing the same thing. You try to hide it and pretend it isn't happening, but I still see it. A car of the right color passes us, and you give it an extra look to see if maybe, just maybe, Angela is driving it—two or three extra looks if it's the right manufacturer. I see the hopefulness flash in your eyes, and my heart aches for you every time I see your expression fade into disappointment, because I remember how it felt."

I sighed, taking one last drink from my coffee mug. I guess I hadn't been as subtle in my hopeless search as I gave myself credit for. She continued.

"At some point, we have to…"

I interrupted before she finished her thought. "I know. I know. We have to move on."

"No. That isn't what I was going to say. Frankly, I'd like to slap whoever came up with that awful phrase. We never move on. How could we? We never stop loving the people we lose in life; we just find new and different ways to remember and cherish them. It isn't about their possessions, it's about how they touch our spirits, how our souls were made better because we were blessed to have time, however brief, together."

She rose and walked over to my desk.

"When I was in school, my father would write me notes from time to time. Sometimes I'd find them in my lunch, others when I got home. It didn't matter what the situation was, happy or sad, somehow, he always knew just the right thing to say to me: *I'm proud of you; It was only one exam, there will be others; Don't change for anyone - the right people love you for who you are.* I saved every note he ever wrote to me. After he died, I saved his favorite pen, guarding it like the crown jewels. I even tried writing with it a bit. Not only didn't it fit my hand or write all that well, it held none of the magical words he was able to summon from it. But John, it wasn't the pen. It wasn't the notes, or even the words. It was how they made me *feel.* The pen is just an implement that holds ink, the notes will yellow and fade, the words might fade from my memory, but how they touched my soul? That I'll never move on from, and I don't want to. That's the gift that endures."

I became aware of a tear rolling down my cheek. I had known

Mack's father for the last few years of his all-too-short life and considered him a remarkable man. It came as no surprise that his daughter was wise, well beyond her years.

"Exactly how did you come to be so damned smart, Jillian MacDonald?" I said, wiping away the tear.

"Good Scots-Irish genetics, I expect," she said, fluffing her long, red hair. "I'll drive you wherever you want to go today. I understand if you're not ready to deal with the car."

"No," I sighed. "I know a mechanic who owes me a favor or two. I'll give him a call after I'm done with the first item on my list."

* * *

I hadn't heard Kelly Hamilton's voice in over nine months, nor had I missed hearing it. It wasn't that I disliked her—quite the opposite, in fact. Unfortunately, her heavy Northern Irish brogue summoned far too many unpleasant memories. She, too, had been caught in the maelstrom that surrounded Angela.

The bright, plucky member of the Police Service of Northern Ireland floated somewhere between an analyst and a field operative. Unafraid to stretch the law to, and likely beyond, the breaking point, she was a reliable conduit into some of the seedy, criminal underbellies that graced Northern Ireland.

"Mister Costa! I haven't heard from you in a month of Sundays, as the saying goes. I hope you're calling to arrange a holiday to come see us here in Belfast. A lot of folks here miss you, myself included!"

"I wish that was the situation, Kelly," I said, "but I'm afraid this call is business, more or less."

"Well, I suppose a business call is better than no call at all. How can I help you?"

"I was hoping you could put me in touch with Adnan Jasik."

Mack and I had worked with Jasik, the shadowy Bosnian, during our time in Northern Ireland. In spite of Kelly's assurances, I found the man scary and never quite understood his relationship with law enforcement. He seemed to float somewhere between informant and agent. Ultimately, my misgivings were wrong. Not only was the information he provided crucial in solving our case, but I credited him with saving our lives at least one time that I was aware of, possibly more.

The line remained silent. "Kelly? Are you still there?"

"Yes," she replied, her voice dropping in volume and pitch. "Adnan missed his last two check-ins. Normally, it wouldn't concern me, knowing how he is. However, when we're actively working on something, he's as dependable as they come. I'm not really at liberty to tell you anything else."

"I understand."

"If you don't mind me asking, is there anything I can help with?"

"I was hoping that Adnan could translate something written in Bosnian for me. We already have a literal translation. I need to know if there's any sort of hidden or colloquial meaning to a short poem."

"Pardon me for saying this," she said, "but you don't strike me as the type that would be studying the finer points of Bosnian poetry. I don't think you'd reach out to a man like Adnan were that the case. What aren't you telling me?"

I laughed. "I swear you and Mack must've been sisters separated at birth. I can't keep a secret from her, either. If I tell you, you have to promise to keep it quiet. If this gets out, and I'm discovered to be the source, we'll lose our credibility within the local police."

"I understand, and of course, you have my word."

"A man I know was murdered the night before last. The killer left a small card containing a Bosnian poem on it. Someone at a local university translated it, but it's nothing more than a child's poem about birds. I'd like to know if it has a hidden meaning, especially since my friend was the second person killed in the exact same manner."

"Serial killer?" she whispered. "No wonder everyone is being careful."

"Entirely possible, and apparently I'm somehow linked to both of them. The first victim, killed about two weeks ago, had one of my old business cards in his wallet. The second played Irish music with me every Wednesday. The local police thought maybe Mack and I were working on something, but that isn't the situation."

"Two weeks ago, you say?"

"For the first victim? Yes, at least according to my sources."

"Are you comfortable sending me the poem? When Adnan checks in, I'll give it to him."

"Yes, with the same caveats as I mentioned earlier."

"Understood."

There was a subtle, unexpected hesitancy to her voice. "What is it that you're not telling me?" I asked.

"I expect it is completely coincidental, but two weeks ago is right about the time Adnan stopped checking in," she whispered.

* * *

My friend and expert mechanic, Mark Dengel, picked me up in front of my house. He was smiling and talkative, partially because my business represented a lucrative cash payday, and partially because we had been friends for many years.

Mark was the poster child for why I felt so frustrated with America's ill-conceived and deeply flawed *War on Drugs*. He was utterly harmless, but a series of misdemeanor convictions for the possession of trivial amounts of marijuana left him largely unemployable, in spite of impeccable skills and credentials. Instead of steady, gainful employment, he made ends meet by working odd jobs, often compensated poorly and under the table.

The truth was far more complicated than his love for an occasional puff of *wacky tobakky*, as he called it, and well outside the latitude granted to judges under our harsh drug laws. His wife suffered from raging fibromyalgia, and his beloved leaf was one of the few sources of relief that actually worked for her.

He prattled on during the entire trip to where Angela Grady's vehicle was stored. I smiled and nodded frequently, commenting where I could, but my thoughts were elsewhere.

* * *

The lights in the storage unit flickered to life. The climate-controlled facility, recommended to me by Mark, specialized in storing vehicles. I could only imagine what treasures lurked behind some of the other doors and how out of place Angela's simple sedan would look.

"Do you want me to open the garage door?" I asked, pointing to the buttons that controlled it.

"Hell no—too damn cold out there. There's plenty to do before we're ready for that," he said, pulling the cover off her vehicle.

I tossed him the keys, and he started working. I would have been flooded with memories, and likely struggling to deal with them, had he not been narrating nearly every task.

"Tires look good. No dry rot or anything," he announced. "I bet you paid to have this checked periodically, didn't you? Even the inflation looks good—within one PSI of spec."

I shrugged. I didn't remember paying for anything beyond storage, but four years had elapsed since I drove the car here.

"I see you unhooked the battery like I told you to," he said, poking his head out from under the hood. He handed me an electrical plug. "Plug this in, will you?"

"Sure," I said.

"Gotta give the battery a bit of juice," he said, before turning his attention elsewhere.

A short period of silence followed, and I quickly found myself missing his flowing narrative. "What are you doing now?" I asked, peeking into the engine compartment.

"I'm going to pull all of the spark plugs and shoot a bit of oil into each cylinder. When the battery looks healthy enough, I'll crank the motor a few revolutions, but with the plugs still out to help get the lubrication back into her. Dry starts are tough on a motor."

I pretended to understand. Somehow, I had missed out on cars while growing up. Many of my friends took great pride in their vehicles, souping them up in any number of ways, but for me, cars were more of a pedestrian, functional affair.

"Interesting," Mark said, pointing to the meter on the gadget I had plugged in for him earlier.

"What is it?"

"Your battery charged really quickly. Either it held its charge pretty damn well, or my charger is broken. Guess there's only one way to find out!"

He fiddled around under the hood for a bit, then reached in and turned the key. The motor spun, although the sound it made was foreign to anything I'd ever heard from a car before. He repeated the procedure several more times before disappearing under the hood. I didn't know if the sound was good or bad, but his expression seemed optimistic.

"Go ahead and open the outside door," he announced a short time later, emerging from beneath the hood and putting his coat on.

I did likewise before pressing the button. The cold, outside air swirled into the storage unit as the door opened. Mark didn't wait for it to open all the way before ducking under it and returning with a gas can.

"Should be enough fresh stuff in here to get you to the gas station we passed on the way here," he said, emptying the container into the tank. "Help me give the car a push. She's going to smoke a bit when she starts."

I climbed into the driver's side and immediately had to adjust the seat so that I had enough room. Together, we pushed the car out of the storage unit.

"Give it a try," he said, "but don't gun the motor. If it wants to stall, let it."

I took a deep breath and turned the key. The engine stumbled a bit, but quickly came to life, belching an impressive cloud of blue smoke. After running roughly for a few moments, the engine settled into a quiet, smooth idle.

Mark tapped on the driver's side window. "Just in case, I'll follow you to the gas station, then home."

CHAPTER FIVE

"You did it!" Mack said, smiling broadly. "Was it therapeutic?"

"I don't really know," I answered. "Mark talked so much, it kept my mind well away from things. Besides, I had something else on my mind most of the time."

"Oh?" she said, opening a toaster pastry.

"It seems that our esteemed Bosnian friend, Adnan Jasik hasn't been checking in with Kelly Hamilton lately, starting right around the time of the first murder here."

"Yeah, I know," she said. "Kelly called me shortly after you two got done talking this morning. We talk fairly regularly, but this one felt more like a subtle interrogation than the normal chit-chat. The conversation bore an odd resemblance to your encounter with Captain O'Neil. Kelly seemed convinced we were, in fact, working on something. I tried to assure her we weren't, but I'm not sure she believed me."

"Did you check to see if Tom or Zonk stumbled onto something in the routine course of investigating a cheating spouse or insurance fraudsters?"

"I checked—nothing in the pipeline right now. Speaking of

34

which, have you heard from Zonk today?"

"No. I'm going to get some lunch then talk to Barry's widow. I can swing by Zonk's apartment on the way, if you'd like."

"I'm probably just being paranoid, but I'd feel better if you did."

* * *

The drive back from the storage facility offered no opportunity for me to acclimate myself to Angela's vehicle. Between Mark's lengthy list of things to listen for, and my unfamiliarity with the various controls, it was all I could do to arrive home without mental overload.

The drive to Zonk's apartment was strangely peaceful. After a few additional adjustments of the seat and the position of the vents, I quickly settled in. I reached over to turn on the radio, only to be surprised by what came out of the speakers. Traditional Irish music, from a CD I created for her, greeted my ears. I chuckled gently and allowed my imagination to run wild. I swore her gentle, soft scent still lingered in the vehicle.

There were no signs of life at the apartment, but this wasn't necessarily unusual. Zonk was known to keep unusual hours, often playing computer games until the wee hours of the morning—even stretching to multiple days at times. We didn't require him to keep regular hours unless a case demanded it. He was, however, good at letting us know his schedule, bizarre as it often was, so today's silence was decidedly not the norm.

After pounding on his door to no avail, I inquired of several neighbors. None had seen him since the previous evening.

"No signs of life over here, Mack. Anything on your end?"

"No word. I've tried his cell phone numerous times, as well as all the online accounts I'm aware of. Even his guild hasn't heard from him since last night."

"His what?"

"Guild. Think of it like a gaming club. Honestly, I'm more concerned that they haven't heard from him than I am that we haven't. They're family to him."

"Does he have any real family in the area that we can call?"

"Not that I know of, John. He's mentioned his mom a few times, but she lives in another state, and I don't think they're particularly close. I'll see if I can track her down."

"I'll call O'Neil, too. They can't do anything officially until forty-eight hours have passed, but given the situation, maybe he can make a few calls. Any word from Tom?"

"I talked to him a bit ago. He'll be in tomorrow. If we haven't located Zonk yet, I'll have him start on your old case files."

"Good call, Mack. I'm off to talk to Barry's widow."

I hopped in my car, and the world suddenly took on an all too familiar feel: that I was being watched, followed, or targeted.

* * *

"Barry mentioned you on a few occasions, Mister Costa," Maureen Myers said, her voice low and thick, undoubtedly affected by nearly continuous smoking. Her complexion and the pungent odor of smoke left no doubt.

"I'm sorry for your loss."

"Don't be," she said, offering me a chair. "I couldn't care less that the worthless bastard is gone. Sure isn't going to change much in my life. Bourbon?"

"No, thank you."

"Wasn't quite what you expected to hear, was it?"

I shook my head.

"Would it help if I played the grieving widow?"

"I don't know, but I do recommend, strongly, against telling the police what you just told me."

"I'm not going to tell the police a damned thing. Did they send you around to try to trick me into something?"

"No, I don't work for the police, but what we talk about isn't protected by confidentiality either. That means that if I'm called to testify, I'd be compelled to answer questions."

"Testify? To what? You make it sound like I'm a damned suspect or something."

"Spouses are always on the list, and the more silence you feed to the police, the more they're liable to spend time trying to figure out how you did it, instead of finding the real killer. It isn't right, but it's how they work at times."

"Yeah," she smirked. "I'm going to sneak up on Barry and kill him." She pointed to a cane and a walker near her chair. "Glaciers move faster and more elegantly than I do."

"Perhaps you hired someone," I offered.

"Paid someone to kill Barry?" She cackled as she tossed me her checkbook. "We've got about fifteen hundred dollars in the bank. Most of Barry's check goes to pay our two mortgages. Most of what's left goes to this."

She slid open a drawer full of medications.

"The doctors want me to take all of these," she said, passing her hand over the drawer, "but the bastard bureaucrats at our insurance company will only pay for three of them."

"Did Barry carry a life insurance policy?"

"If he did, I don't know about it. He was always so damned secretive about everything. Why, exactly, are you here?"

"I'm trying to figure out who killed Barry."

"What does it matter to you?"

"I left the session early the night he died. Witnesses said he left shortly thereafter and mentioned my name in the process. I only missed him by a few seconds. I'm curious as to what he wanted from me, and I thought maybe he might have mentioned something to you."

"Like I said, he mentioned you a few times, but nothing recently."

"Any mention of trouble? Someone mad at him? Threats? Problems at work?"

"No, not like I think he would have told me."

"I'm sorry to ask this, but is there any chance he was having an affair or seeing someone on the side?"

"Barry?" She laughed to the point of coughing. "Not a chance. You're talking about one of the most boring men to ever grace the planet, Mister Costa. His life consisted of his job followed by an evening in front of the television. Every so often, he'd watch television *and* play that damned banjo," she motioned to an instrument hanging on the wall. "I had to badger him half to death to get him out of the house and to your session on Wednesdays. It was damn near the only time he got out, other than to go to work."

"What did Barry do for a living, Mrs. Myers?"

She motioned at a small desk across the room. "Open the top drawer. His business cards are in there. You can pop over to where he worked and get the entire forty-nine cent tour. He had some sort of fancy title, but he worked in a warehouse."

I slid the drawer open and retrieved a business card. I noticed something else while I was fetching the card. "There's a revolver in here, Mrs. Myers."

"That old thing belonged to his father. I don't think Barry even knew how to use it."

"Mind if I take a look?"

"No. Just don't shoot yourself. I'm not in any condition to clean up the mess."

Not wanting to disturb or create any fingerprints, I grabbed a paper napkin from a nearby stack, and carefully slid the firearm into better view. I released the cylinder, allowing it to pivot away from the gun's frame. Not only was the firearm loaded, but each cylinder contained modern defensive ammunition, the type designed to stop threats quickly and in a devastating fashion.

"This firearm is loaded, Mrs. Myers. Would you like me to safely unload it for you?"

"Loaded!?" Her surprise seemed genuine. "Yes. Take the damn thing with you if you want. I don't want a loaded firearm in my house."

With her permission, I searched the desk and found the box of ammunition. I removed the rounds from the gun's cylinder, returning them to the box.

"The gun is unloaded," I said, handing her the box of ammunition. "I can't take it with me. It might be somehow germane to the case, and I don't want to tamper with evidence. I strongly recommend you don't, either. I do recommend locking the desk and keeping the ammunition separate from the firearm. Guns can't load themselves."

I wasn't convinced that she was going to take my advice, but all I could do was offer. "Has crime been a problem in this neighborhood recently?" I asked.

"No. Never has been."

"Mrs. Myers, are you *sure* Barry wasn't in some sort of trouble? Money? Anything you can think of, even if it seems insignificant?"

"I really don't know," she rasped. "He never mentioned anything, and his demeanor hadn't changed recently. Same old boring Barry."

"That's a serious firearm, and it's new, not old. It was loaded with powerful defensive ammunition and kept in close proximity to where he spent a lot of his time. To me, it feels like he was expecting trouble."

"Look, I don't know how many ways to say it. I don't goddamn know! Get it?"

"If you think of anything, give me a call. I'm trying to find who killed my friend—who, by the way, was your husband—not get a convenient conviction."

"I'll consider it, if you're willing to do me one small favor."

"What do you have in mind?"

"If your curiosity happens to take you by Barry's place of employment, stop by his office and pick up his things for me. I'm not really able to drive much anymore, and the police have our damn car impounded for evidence. I don't know what they think they're going to find. The stupid thing is ten years old, but at least it's paid for. About the only thing around here that is," she grumbled, lighting a cigarette.

* * *

I was on the phone to Mack as soon as I left Maureen Myers' house. "Something isn't adding up."

"Oh?"

"His widow, who isn't even pretending to grieve, claims that Barry hasn't been up to anything out of the ordinary lately—no change of demeanor, no conversations about problems, nothing. Yet do you know what I found in his top desk drawer?"

"What?"

"A brand new .357 Magnum revolver, loaded and ready to go with some pretty serious self-defense rounds."

"Sounds like Barry was expecting trouble."

"My thoughts exactly. Maureen wasn't exactly forthcoming, but I think you and Tom should start pursuing the financial angle. She's on a dozen meds they are paying for out of pocket, and I wouldn't be surprised if she spent a few hundred dollars a month on cigarettes."

"Maybe Barry ran a-foul of a loan shark; someone who didn't tolerate late payments."

"My thoughts exactly. Maybe Rick Stevens, the first victim, was in a similar situation. Hell, if Jenn Adams had her claws into him financially, there's no telling how much the poor man might have owed."

CHAPTER SIX

Morning arrived, and we still had no word from Zonk in spite of repeated attempts to contact him. A call to O'Neil proved equally fruitless. He had managed to inquire at local hospitals, but beyond that, he lacked the available staffing to pursue the matter until if officially became a missing persons report.

I gulped down my coffee and headed toward Barry Myers' employer.

* * *

The business name was anything but imposing, but the address on Barry's business card led me to a sprawling warehouse. The receptionist, a friendly, stylish brunette, asked me to wait while she summoned someone from the Human Resources department.

I didn't expect to get much from the visit, especially since I lacked any standing beyond being a friend of the deceased. I was pleasantly surprised within moments of my arrival.

"Clarissa Jones," a woman said, extending her hand.

"John Costa."

"Maureen Myers called us yesterday to alert us that you would be coming around to collect Barry's things. I understand that you're a lawyer?"

I had, apparently, been appointed Maureen's lawyer without my knowledge or consent, but I decided to go with it. "I am, although I work more in the investigative field these days."

"She mentioned something about that," she said, showing me into her office. "When we receive Mister Myers' death certificate, we will start the process of filing his insurance claims. You'll be provided the necessary documentation to discuss these matters directly with our insurance carrier, should the need arise. He will also be receiving one more full paycheck for the previous pay period and a partial one for his final week of work."

"You mentioned insurance claims…"

"Yes. We provide all our employees insurance equal to one years' pay as part of our benefit package. Barry, I mean Mister Myers, opted for additional coverage, bringing his total coverage to three times his annual salary, or about four hundred and fifty thousand dollars."

It took all of my willpower to avoid an astonished expression. It was clear that Barry was anything but a warehouse worker.

"I'd like to collect his things, but I'd also like to talk to some of his coworkers and friends. In addition to helping Mrs. Myers with her legal matters, I'm also eager to solve the situation surrounding his death. Doing so will expedite payment of claims and so forth."

"Understandable. With his wife's health issues, I'm sure she's quite eager to have these lingering questions answered. I'm going to get someone from our security team to show you around."

* * *

I waited in a small conference room until I was joined by a short, energetic young woman who introduced herself as Ashley Vinton.

"You picked a good day to come around, although I wish it was under different circumstances," she said.

"Agreed."

"The police talked to most of us already. I'm not sure there's

42

much else to tell."

"My focus is slightly different. I'm looking out for the best interests of Maureen Myers, and knowing the details of the case seems to be the best way I can accomplish that. For example, the sooner the case is settled, the sooner insurance payments will be made available to her."

"I understand. How much do you know about Quantelle Logistics, Mister Costa?"

"I'm sorry, but honestly, not a thing."

She laughed. "Don't be too hard on yourself. We're probably the biggest company that nobody has ever heard of. We're primarily a logistics and fulfillment company, although we have diversified a bit at several locations. Follow me."

She escorted me through several narrow hallways before we passed through a doorway and into a wider, general corridor.

"Our office staff work up here in the front. HR, Accounting, IT, Finance, and so forth. Unfortunately, Barry's office is all the way on the other end of the building. I hope you're wearing comfortable shoes; we're in for a bit of a walk."

We turned left into a wide, branch hallway and passed through a set of double doors. Beyond was a sprawling warehouse. Row after row of shelving stretched into the distance.

I stopped, shocked by the expansiveness of it. "Wow," I muttered. "It didn't look anywhere near this big from the road."

"It's really something, isn't it? From here, you can only see about a third of it," she said. "The layout blocks us from seeing the rest of the fulfillment and shipping areas, and there is another alcove off to the left and around the corner. We have facilities like this all over the United States, and we're starting to build an international presence. We're mostly in Europe at the moment, but we're starting to develop our markets in the far east as well."

"It looks like a warehouse, but far more complicated."

"Quite an understatement! Let's say you wanted to open a store that sells audio equipment. What would you have to do?"

"I'd have to get a storefront, hire people to sell, have inventory on hand. The normal stuff."

"Exactly. And if you wanted to sell stuff anywhere in the United States?"

"Phones, shipping, a bigger warehouse…"

"And have it to your customers in a few days, free of charge?"

"I'd go broke on the shipping fees," I said, laughing.

"That's where we come in. Our inventory becomes your inventory. We handle all the storage, shipping, inventory, and so forth. Need to get speakers to Wyoming in two days? We figure out the best way to get it there. Instead of paying a fortune to ship them two thousand miles, we have it on a truck from one of our regional facilities."

"The folks working in this part of the facility assemble the orders, check to make sure everything is complete and correct, and get them to the shipping docks. From there, we have contracts with multiple, big national carriers to handle the rest."

She motioned for me to follow her up a long, tall staircase. It led to an upper floor that covered only a portion of the total warehouse footprint. It was filled with rows of machines and people busy operating them.

"Our facility handles engraving for most of the eastern United States," she explained. "Everything is computerized, so a skilled operator can run up to four machines simultaneously."

"Barry was involved in this?"

"Not this part of the business," she answered.

The second floor only covered a small portion of the warehouse, but afforded a view of the expansive floor below. Even from our elevated position, not all of the facility was visible. As impressive as all of it was, I wondered why Ashley was giving me the grand tour instead of taking me directly to Barry's work area. It became obvious as we rounded a corner, entering an area of cubicles nestled within the bustling work area.

"There's a daily meeting between the logistics team and the engraving team," she explained. "Hopefully, they're still here so you can meet them."

As luck would have it, we were slightly late. Barry's manager had already left the meeting area, but several members of his department still lingered.

My first conversation was with a dark-haired woman, likely of an age near mine. "We're still in a bit of a state of shock," she said. "Barry was a quiet man, so not a lot of people really got to know him. Once you did, though, he was very nice."

"Have you noticed any change in his demeanor lately?"

"Nope. Not a thing. Same old Barry."

"Did anything seem to be bothering him?"

"If it was, he didn't show it. I understand his wife has some medical issues, and I know those weighed on him, but that wasn't exactly news."

"Was he having a problem with anyone at work?"

"Barry?" She laughed. "No. He did his thing and went home. He didn't get angry, and people didn't get angry with him. He was really a nice man, which is why this is so puzzling to all of us. Who would want to hurt Barry?"

"What exactly did he do here?"

"Barry was our process optimization and systems expert. Sam, his boss, can give you a better description, but Barry designed most of what you see around here."

Conversations with two other members of Barry's team all echoed similar sentiments. His co-workers generally liked him and appreciated his work, but few of them really knew him.

Ashley popped her head into the conference room. "I've located Sam," she announced. "He's in a meeting, but he'll step out to meet with us. Sorry, but we're going to have to walk back the way we came. He's in the front part of the building."

"No worries."

* * *

"John Costa! Small world, isn't it?" a man's voice said.

"You two know each other?" Ashley said, beaming. "Isn't that fun?"

Fun wasn't exactly the word I had in mind. I hadn't seen or thought of the tall, superficial, smirking idiot I knew as Sam Thomas for nearly five years. It could've been fifty years, and it still would have been too soon to cross paths again. Now I had to smile, shake the man's hand, and pretend the loathing I felt for him didn't exist.

"We worked together, briefly, in a past life," Sam said. "I was a manager, and John worked in our legal offices doing—I'm not exactly sure what you did, to be honest."

"As little as possible." My quip elicited the expected fake laughter from Sam. "Fraud investigation," I said, turning serious. "I'm good at finding and exposing fakes."

When I first met Angela Grady, she was living with Sam. Their relationship was, by all accounts, flawless. He was tall, chiseled, and handsome; she was the pretty blonde trophy hanging off his arm. I'd pegged the man as a phony from the moment I met him, but dismissed it as raging jealousy.

Ultimately, I was proven right, at least as far as his relationship with Angela was concerned. When her legal problems surfaced, Sam abruptly bailed on her, leaving her with an empty apartment she couldn't afford. When she finally reached out to me for help, she was weeks away from being broke and homeless. Hell, maybe he was the smart one after all—Angela had nearly pulled me down with her—but I couldn't find forgiveness for him.

His face turned serious. "I'm sorry to hear about Angela. I feel a little guilty about bailing out on her the way I did, but when that cop showed up accusing her of a terrible crime, I sorta freaked out."

Part of me wanted to give him the benefit of the doubt, and it was at war with the part that wanted to punch him squarely in the face. I did neither, merely nodding as he continued talking. He seemed to fidget more than I remember, but previously I had only despised him from afar. Perhaps it was nervousness from my presence, or perhaps it was something else. Either way, if he was working on a noose, I wasn't going to limit his supply of rope.

"My girl just surprised me a few months ago," he said, pulling a picture from his wallet. He handed me a picture, taken, I presumed from the outfits and the surrounding decor, during the prior year's Christmas season. Enveloped in his arms was an Angela Grady lookalike. "Penny just gave birth to our first child about a month ago. Talk about a life changing event!"

"Congratulations," I said, forcing a broad smile. I really wanted to get her contact information and send her my condolences. Not only had she saddled her child with his undoubtedly hideous DNA, but he was *precisely* the type of man who would turn her into a single mother the moment he realized that a child was cramping his style.

"News of Barry really put a damper on an otherwise festive season," he said.

"What can you tell me about Barry's work?" I asked, trying to leverage his talkative spirit.

"Barry designed everything from the warehouse layout to the software that controls how orders flow through our systems. The man was a genius, really. Quiet, kept to himself for the most part, but an absolute genius. I think it is fair to say that his contributions directly led to our growth over the past few years. Without them, we'd still be shipping stuff all over the place and wondering why our customers aren't happy with our services."

"Impressive. We played music together nearly every Wednesday, but he never really talked much about his work."

"Barry never talked about much of anything," Sam said. "He had a sick wife, that much I know, and I think caring for her took a lot out of him."

"Any recent issues at work? Performance problems? Attendance? Attitude?"

"None. He seemed to be himself, at least as far as any of us could tell, not that I'm sure we would've known. He didn't exactly wear his feelings on his sleeve, if you know what I mean."

"Do you know if he was having any financial difficulties? Did he ask for a raise recently?"

"He got a raise and a bonus about five months ago as part of our normal review process. Both were fairly significant. If he was having problems in that area, he didn't share them with me."

"Do you mind if I collect his personal belongings?"

"Of course not. I've got another meeting to go to, but Ashley can take you to his desk."

CHAPTER SEVEN

"I was serious about those comfortable shoes," Ashley said as we retraced our steps back into the warehouse portion of the building. Instead of climbing the stairs, we turned in the opposite direction. "Please stay between these lines," she instructed, pointing to lines painted on the floor.

"What do they mean?"

"They are areas designated for pedestrian traffic. There are large forklifts operating here, and the drivers know to use extra caution around these lanes."

"It doesn't seem very busy over here," I commented as we walked. I could hear the sounds of forklifts operating in the distance, but we seemed to be walking away from them.

"We stagger our shift changes and adjust shift durations to reflect demand. The software that controls the order flow knows when an area is changing shifts or performing maintenance, and prioritizes orders and items that can be filled in other zones."

"What about the lights?"

"The system knows when an order is being filled in a given area of the warehouse and turns lights on accordingly. It also senses motion, so the lights will stay low unless they're needed. Not only is the system good for the environment, it saved us thousands of dollars last year."

"Clever."

We walked silently until the sound of a forklift's horn caught our attention. The driver signaled to us, and we stopped.

"Lance says the lights in zone sixteen aren't working. It's awfully dark back there, so it might be better if you routed through seven."

"Okay," Ashley replied. "Are we clear to cut through?"

The man said something on his radio, but I couldn't make out what it was. "Yeah, Lance approved it. You've got another ten minutes, probably more, before anyone will be over this way." He tooted his horn and drove away.

"We normally don't do this," she said, "but there won't be any forklifts operating here for a while, and we've got clearance from the floor manager, so it will be okay. Besides, you're with a security officer, and I promise not to tell."

She crossed the painted lines, taking us down a corridor formed by ceiling-tall pallet racks.

"I feel like such a renegade," I whispered.

As we walked between the racks, I became aware of the sound of an approaching forklift. Ashley heard it, too.

"Odd," she said, pulling a small radio from her pocket. "Lance, do you copy me?"

The radio was silent. She called again, but I didn't hear if she received a reply. From behind us, a forklift turned into our aisle.

At first, I thought the driver was possibly oblivious to our presence, but that notion was quickly abandoned. With its tines raised to the height of my chest, the forklift accelerated.

Still distracted by her silent radio, my guide was slow to respond to the threat. "Ashley!" I screamed.

The vehicle was much faster than any of the others of its type I had observed zipping around the warehouse. Even though we were close to the end of our aisle, we would not be able to make it in time. The velocity of the approaching forklift was simply too great to allow such an escape.

Ashley's first step was good. Young and athletic, she leapt to her right, grasping one of the vertical supports and pulling herself up.

I was on the other side of the aisle and took the only escape route available to me. On the floor level to my left, the removal of a pallet had created a small crevice, and I dove for it.

As I started my escape, I noticed some erratic behavior by the forklift. Instead of hurtling directly toward us in a straight line, it seemed to twitch slightly, like a race car on the verge of an accident. I didn't have time to observe the results. As I dove to safety, banging my ankle solidly against a metal shelf in the process, I heard a loud crash, followed by the sound of metal grinding against cement.

I turned to look behind me just in time to see the forklift, now on its side, careen into the pallet rack on the opposite side. I had seen enough videos of warehouse disasters where shelves fall like dominoes, to understand that we were far from being out of danger.

I scampered from my hiding spot in search of Ashley. I spotted her on the floor a few feet in front of the overturned forklift.

"Costa!" she screamed, trying to pull herself up. Obviously injured, she was unable to rise.

The impact from the speeding forklift had buckled one of the pallet rack's vertical supports. Extending nearly to the ceiling with four layers of shelves, each fully laden, the unit racked precariously. I ran for Ashley as a pallet from one of the upper shelves crashed onto the derelict forklift.

Fueled by adrenaline and pure terror, I had no time for propriety or manners. I tossed the petite young woman over my shoulder, unceremoniously akin to a sack of potatoes, and sprinted out of the aisle. I found one of the thick, vertical columns that supported the warehouse roof and eased her onto the floor, positioned so that the steel girder shielded her back from the listing shelf. It would also protect her from any more rogue forklifts. I glanced around, but saw none.

The pallet rack shed more of its contents onto the floor below as the unit slumped around the damaged support. Fortunately, the side-to-side listing stopped, and the danger of a domino-effect collapse faded.

Now, however, we had another problem. I detected the smell of something burning. A glance back to the overturned forklift confirmed my fears. Something had ignited a small fire, and it was quickly threatening to get serious.

Ashley shouted something into her radio. She yelled something to me, but I couldn't make out what it was as I sprinted toward the nearest fire extinguisher. As I removed it from the enclosure that housed it, I heard a bell ringing continuously in the distance. People were running toward us, but the growing fire didn't afford me the luxury of waiting for them.

Dodging the fallen debris, I found the source of the fire. I pulled the pin and squeezed the handle. The extinguisher released its cloudy torrent. I heard the sound of other extinguishers discharging from the opposite side of the wreck, and the fire was quickly eliminated.

I found Ashley where I had left her, and immediately turned my attention to providing first aid. Below her left knee, her leg, obviously broken, hung at an unpleasant and unnatural angle. I wrapped her with my jacket in hopes of avoiding the onset of shock.

"Hurts like hell," she said, pointing to her leg.

"People are on their way," I said. "Just stay calm."

"Broken for sure," she grunted, "but the rest of me is in one piece. Thanks for pulling me out of there."

"My pleasure," I said. It would have been easy to underestimate the young woman's fortitude, especially with the streaks of purple that accented her blonde hair, but her ability to stay calm under pressure was impressive.

"Give me your business card," she said, pulling a pen from her pocket and motioning urgently.

I had come well prepared, and pulled a card from my shirt pocket. In a shaky hand, she scribbled something on the back before handing it back to me. "Call me," she whispered. "Now get that damn card back in your pocket."

Puzzled, I complied.

As people approached, I intercepted them. "We're going to need an ambulance. She's got a broken leg." A man tried to call on the radio, but when he failed to reach anyone, he dialed 911 on his phone. The others joined me in attending to Ashley, keeping her calm until medics arrived.

I waited until the paramedics finished their work, then went on the offensive. "I want to speak to your head of security, right now," I growled to anyone who would listen, "and I'm not leaving until I get some answers."

I pulled my cell phone from my pocket and dialed. "George? John Costa here. I'm at the Quantelle Logistics facility on Ramey Drive. Send some units over here. Someone just tried to kill me. Yes, I'm as serious as a heart attack."

The people around me grew silent as they exchanged glances of disbelief.

* * *

Brenda Simmons, the head of security, massaged her temples before running her fingers through her mid-length brown hair.

"I can't even begin to apologize enough," she said. "We've never had anything like this happen before—nothing remotely like this. Our biggest problem is warehouse theft, not attempted murder. Are you sure I can't get you some ice for that ankle?"

The pain in my ankle, up to this point, was masked by a fierce run of adrenaline. Now, as the rush faded, throbbing and swelling commenced.

I was about to answer when George O'Neil's voice interrupted me.

"What is this nonsense I hear, Costa?" O'Neil was accompanied by three uniformed officers and two in plain clothes, presumably detectives.

"Someone tried to kill me, George."

"Sadly, it seems to be true," Brenda added. "We've got the entire thing recorded on our security system cameras."

"Go seal off the area and start doing your thing," he said to his crew. "I'm going to review the footage."

The recording showed events largely as I remembered them, but added clarity to the final moments that I couldn't see while fleeing the oncoming vehicle.

"It appears that the vehicle isn't quite stable when operated at full throttle," O'Neil commented. "He seems to start having control issues right about here," he said, stopping the playback. "You two were smart to jump to opposite sides of the aisle, too." He advanced the recording slowly. "It looks like there is a moment of hesitation, then he over-corrects in an effort to strike you."

"Look at how he jumped off the lift, George," I commented, watching the driver's elegant, controlled exit, in spite of a vehicle that was unstable and moving rapidly.

"I see it," O'Neil muttered. "Either this bastard is lucky, or he's had some training. Combat training or martial arts come to mind when I see this. He lands like a freaking ninja!"

"He sprints off to the left, into the area where the lights weren't working," Brenda added, and out one of our emergency egress doors. "It triggered an alarm, but the situation with the forklift demanded our presence more than a door alert."

"It isn't a bad image," O'Neil said, "especially in poor lighting conditions, but certainly not enough to make a facial identification, especially with the hat he's wearing. Where does the door he used lead?"

"It leads to a narrow strip of grass, ten yards or so, with a fence beyond."

"How high?"

"Six feet."

"Given the way that guy made it off the forklift," I added, "the fence probably didn't provide the slightest obstacle."

"Are there any exterior cameras that might have captured his image?" O'Neil asked.

"Not over there," Brenda sighed.

"I'll need copies of all this," O'Neil said. "Maybe our boy will show up on one of your other cameras."

"Already in the works," Brenda said, "and my security staff will review the footage as well."

"It just occurred to me," I said, standing and regretting my decision to do so almost immediately, "Ashley's radio didn't seem to be working."

"We'll collect it and examine it," said O'Neil.

"Our maintenance department is reporting that they are still having issues with their radios in that part of the building even as we speak," Brenda added.

"We're going to need to collect statements from everybody," O'Neil said. "It seems obvious that this wasn't a simple on-the-job accident."

"Of course," Brenda said, her fingers massaging her temples.

George O'Neil looked me over before asking, "can I get a look at that ankle?"

I nodded, rolling up my pant leg. A nasty looking black and blue bruise was covering a significant portion of my ankle.

"You might want to get that thing X-rayed," he said. "Even if nothing is broken, it's going to hurt like hell. Miss Simmons, do you have a first aid kit handy? I'd like to wrap Mister Costa's ankle."

"Oh! Yes, of course. Excuse me for a moment."

It seemed out of character for George O'Neil to give a damn about what, I'm sure, he deemed to be a minor discomfort. The real reason for his concern became apparent as soon as Brenda Simmons left the room. He showed me the screen of his phone, where a single text message awaited.

```
The forklift was altered.

The circuit that limits the current to
the motors was bypassed.

Without this governor in place, it can
travel much faster than usual.
```

"Somebody knew you were coming, my friend, and there was something here they didn't want you to find," O'Neil whispered.

"I'd already talked to all his co-workers," I said. "We were on our way to collect his personal effects so I could return them to his wife."

"I think we need to take a good look at Barry's office," O'Neil said.

CHAPTER EIGHT

Walking all the way back to Barry's office wasn't the most pleasant thing I'd ever experienced, but it was probably the best thing for my throbbing ankle. The more I walked, the looser it felt and the less it hurt.

Brenda handed O'Neil the master key that would open all of the office doors, save those belonging to Human Resources. Within ten seconds of turning on the lights and glancing around the room, O'Neil was on his radio.

"Get up here to Barry Myers' office and dust for prints."

"What is it?" I said, seeing nothing out of the ordinary in the room.

O'Neil removed a pen from his pocket and pointed to a faint scratch in the paint on Barry's desk. To me, it looked indistinguishable from normal wear and tear, but I wasn't trained in the art of police work. He quickly donned a pair of blue gloves and gently pulled on one of the drawers.

"Son of a bitch," he grumbled.

"What is it?"

"Miss Simmons, find out if Barry Myers kept his desk locked."

57

Brenda dialed her phone. I overheard her asking for Sam Thomas. A pause and then a brief conversation followed before she spoke. "Yes. Barry kept his desk locked at all times, at least according to his supervisor."

"Double son of a bitch. All right. Everyone out. We've got another crime scene."

"How can you be so sure?"

"Because, Mister Costa, this may come as a shock to you, but this isn't my first case. The scratches are from a screwdriver, inserted at precisely the right spot to defeat the locking mechanism. The desk opens faster that way than if you have the key for it. Whoever opened it was in a hurry."

"They knew exactly what they were looking for, too, and where to find it," I added, quietly.

O'Neil turned to me, eyebrow raised. "Why do you say that, Detective Costa?" he said.

"The office is immaculate—not a single thing out of place. Whoever it was took the time to push the drawers closed, probably in hopes that nobody would notice."

"You should'a been a cop, Costa," he chuckled. "Every so often, I think there's hope for you."

* * *

At O'Neil's request, I lingered at the periphery of the investigation. It was clear that Quantelle's legal department didn't want me around, especially when the conversation turned to the possibility of corporate espionage. George shot them down, summarily. I mumbled something vaguely threatening about filing my own set of lawsuits, and things suddenly returned to being artificially cordial.

"Costa," O'Neil said, pulling me aside. "Who knew you were coming here today?"

"Maureen Myers asked me to pick up Barry's personal items, so she knew. But honestly, it seems that damn near everybody here knew I was coming. She called the Human Resources department to tell them to expect me."

"That's what I was afraid of. They're being pretty tight-lipped about what Barry might have had in his desk. I guess I can't blame them."

"My understanding is that he wrote most of the software that runs this place, but they made no secret of that fact, at least not to me."

"You're free to take off, John. In fact, it might be best if you did. I don't think Quantelle's lawyers are entirely comfortable with your presence."

"They're looking out for their intellectual property. They're not my client, and I haven't signed a non-disclosure agreement, so I understand their hesitancy."

"We have to consider the possibility the entire episode with the forklift was a distraction and that the contents of Barry's desk, whatever the hell that might have been, was the real target. At the same time, it could have been you. Do you want me to send cars around your house to check on things from time to time?"

"No. I'll hire some security." I looked around and when satisfied nobody was listening I whispered, "it might not be a bad idea to keep an eye on the young woman that went to the hospital. Call it a hunch, but I think she knows something."

* * *

"You were certainly gone a while," Mack said.

"It was an eventful visit," I said, pouring myself a Guinness.

"Starting a bit early, aren't we?"

"I think I'm well within my rights, especially since my quick visit to pick up Barry's things turned into a case of attempted murder."

"Oh?" she said, raising a skeptical eyebrow.

"Someone tried to run me over with a forklift, thank you very much. The security guard that was taking me to Barry's office broke her leg. That wasn't the worst of it, either! Of all the people in the world, I ended up running into Sam Thomas."

"*The* Sam Thomas?" she asked, raising her left eyebrow.

"Yep," I said, consuming most of my Guinness in a single, deep quaff. "He was Barry's supervisor."

My face must have been flushed, or on its way there, because Mack touched my arm, gently. "Let it go," she whispered.

"He was awfully nervous and fidgety when I was talking to him."

"It would be more interesting if he wasn't," Mack said, sipping lightly from a bottle of water. "I'm sure you were the last person in the world he'd want to see, given your history."

"You're probably right," I sighed. "To add insult to injury, I wasn't even able to collect Barry's things."

"Why?"

"Someone broke into his desk before we could get there. Quantelle's lawyers stepped in and politely shooed me away. I bought myself a few minutes by threatening to sue, but I could tell they didn't want me there. The company cited intellectual property concerns, but I'm not buying it. They ship boxes from here to there. I understand that somebody needs to do it, but it isn't like they've invented a wonder drug? What could they have that is so damned important?"

Mack's expression turned distant. She left the room without speaking, only to return a few moments later with one of her laptop computers.

"I seem to remember an article from a month or two ago in one of the magazines I subscribe to." Her voice drifted away as her attention turned to her screen. After several silent minutes, she spoke.

"Here it is! I knew the name was familiar. Take a look."

I peered over her shoulder at the magazine article: an interview with Quantelle's CIO.

"I didn't pay a lot of attention to this article when it came out, beyond passing curiosity," she said. "Logistics isn't exactly a field that I'm interested in, but any time cool technology is yielding great dividends for a company, I at least give it a look. For about the last six months, Quantelle Logistics has been the darling of their industry."

"How so, Mack?"

"They've been beating the big boys at their own game and doing it handily. Enough so that some competitors have complained that they are receiving special inside information—cheating, in other words."

"They ship stuff. They ship it quickly. I get it, but where does this supposed inside information come from and how does it help them?"

She peered at me, annoyed. "When an item goes in to high demand, what happens to it?"

"The price goes up?"

"And?"

"Available quantities go down?"

"Yes. You've got it."

"Basic economics. But where does Quantelle fit into this equation?"

"In the past nine months," she said, tapping her screen, "there have been six high-profile incidents where all of the major suppliers and retailers ran out of a hot item, with one notable exception."

"Quantelle?"

"Quantelle, and they profited mightily from their seeming good fortune. Their CIO did the magazine interview to counter some claims they benefited from inside information or were engaging in some unethical practices. He cited a new, predictive software application as being responsible for their good fortune. I remember reading the article. It was plausible, but very short on details."

"The way people made it sound, Barry was the genius behind all this. Is some sort of shipping and ordering program worth stealing? Is it worth killing over?"

Mack shrugged. "Considering we're coming up on the holiday season, it could be. If Quantelle repeats their past successes during the peak season, it could be worth millions. Maybe hundreds of millions."

"I suppose we need to start investigating them."

"It's going to be a challenge. They're privately held and don't share information freely."

"See what you can do. Any word on Zonk?"

"He's fine. He'll be here tomorrow."

"Where the hell has he been, Mack?"

"He was with friends, apparently, playing a new online game. He just lost track of time."

"Call him and tell him not to come in tomorrow!" I said, jumping out of my chair.

"You're not going to fire him, are you?"

"Not exactly. You just reminded me of something, though. I saw a sign that Quantelle Logistics is hiring for the holiday season. I'm sentencing our friend Zonk to some hard labor; he's going to apply for a job! Maybe he can learn something from the inside. Just make sure he knows not to mention me or this firm in any way, even in passing."

"Are you sure he's ready for something like that?"

"No, I'm not sure, but he's been wanting better assignments. Let's give him one. Brief him of the risks, and make sure he knows that it is completely optional. No hard feelings or repercussions if he passes."

"I'm still not sure…"

"Oh, and see if you can find anything on Sam Thomas." I was met with a scornful look. "What? I just have a gut feeling."

"Are you sure it isn't irrational hatred?"

"Nope."

* * *

Mack was clearly unhappy with me, and it was too cold to retreat to the back porch, so I sequestered myself in my bedroom, well out of the line of fire.

I picked up my cell phone and dialed Jerry Keynes. Jerry was a veteran of an untold number of covert operations during his career in the intelligence community. After leaving the agency, exactly which one I wasn't sure, he settled into the role of an information broker. His list of contacts and informants seemed limitless. His services invariably came at a premium cost, but were always worth the money.

"Welcome back to the States, Jack!" Jerry said. After years of chain smoking and incessant coughing, he managed to kick the habit. His voice sounded so strong and clear I almost didn't recognize it.

The surefire giveaway was that he called me Jack. He was the only one to call me by that name, which he claimed was short for Jackass. Given my propensity for expensive and heartbreaking debacles, often fueled by ill-founded, rash decisions, the moniker wasn't entirely unfair.

"You sound good, Jerry."

"You don't."

"It's been a long day. Someone tried to impale me with a forklift."

"How long have you been back in the States, Jack?"

"Nine months, give or take."

"I'm surprised it took this long," he said, laughing at his own joke. "What do you have yourself into this time?"

"I'm not really sure," I said, briefing him on the goings-on of the past week. "At the least, I could use some security guards. I know it isn't cheap, but I'll pay for it."

"You've got it. I can tell from your voice that there's more."

"You know me too well, Jerry. There is, but I don't even know what to ask for yet. Perhaps see what you can find out about Quantelle Logistics."

"Join the club," he said.

"How so?"

"I know of at least four companies with pockets far deeper than yours that would love to have the answer to that question."

"Well, if you can't do that, maybe you can look for dirt on a few of their employees. Mack isn't happy with me for doing this, but I'm running with a hunch here."

"For once, I can see her point."

Jerry had never explained to me exactly why he distrusted Jillian MacDonald, but it was a recurring theme in nearly every conversation.

"You've been saying that for over ten years, Jerry, and I'm still waiting for something bad to happen. So far, she's managed to help me build a fortune, keep a fortune—in spite of myself— and save my life on at least two occasions."

"I don't know," he grumbled. "When something seems to be too good to be true, it usually is."

I wanted to let the subject drop, but Jerry had other ideas.

"One of these days, she's going to clean you out, and you're going to wonder what the hell happened. Trust me; I've been there."

"If she was going to do that, she's had every opportunity in the world to do so. You're just sore because she keeps proving you wrong."

"You know what scares me about her? Whether you realize it or not, she's the type of woman who wants to get married. You think life's going to be all happy and fulfilling, then you sign on the dotted line, and everything goes to hell."

"You don't believe in marriage, do you, Jerry?" I chuckled.

"Oh, I believe in it. I also believe in the bubonic plague. I've got three ex wives who still have their claws stuck in me as proof. I think the only thing keeping me alive is the big fat check I write each of them every month. If not for that, I'd be in the damn morgue, and you'd be investigating which one of them pulled the trigger—probably all three," he laughed.

"Speaking of which, the police have a couple of bodies on their hands. One of the victims worked at Quantelle Logistics. It might be relevant in some way," I said, desperately trying to change the subject.

"Wait a minute? This is intertwined with the two copycat murders?"

"Possibly."

"Jack, Jack, Jack... It just figures that you've managed to get yourself in the middle of it. Whatever is going on, the police are being very tight-lipped about it, but there are rumors of a serial killer circulating within certain circles. I know they've reached out to the feds, but my sources there aren't talking, either."

"A serial killer seems to be within the realm of possibility. Look, I'm not in the middle of this unpleasantness of my own volition—if I'm really there at all. If I send you a couple more names, can you at least try?"

"Usual fee?"

"Of course, Jerry."

"Send me what you've got."

CHAPTER NINE

"Zonk agreed to what you suggested," Mack said, clearly unhappy with his decision.

"You explained the possible risks, didn't you?"

"The part about his possible death? Yeah, I think I mentioned that a few times."

"Then he made his decision," I said.

"He made the decision he thought would please you, especially after he arbitrarily blew off work for a few days. He knows he's lucky not to get fired, so I doubt he felt like he had much choice."

"Eric Csonkos can take care of himself, in spite of your opinion to the contrary. I can, too, for that matter."

"Suit yourself," she said. "You know my opinion on the matter. What's the game plan, oh wise one?"

"Tom's going to go through my old case files, and you're going to work your wizardry in whatever area and manner you see fit."

"What about you?"

"I'm going to help out where I'm needed."

"You should probably start by figuring out what's burning in the kitchen."

"Dammit. My toast! Mack, you were standing right there. Why didn't you say something?"

"You can take care of yourself, remember?" she said, sticking her tongue out at me.

* * *

The burned toast was a harbinger of the day to come. Tom quickly bogged down in my case files, mostly due to their woeful lack of organization. By lunchtime, we had barely scratched the surface. The mid-afternoon arrival of a lengthy list of people against whom I had won convictions as a prosecutor wiped out any hint of progress we were feeling.

Jerry's security team arrived and with them, the invoice for his services. The toe-curling amount did nothing to improve my mood. Neither did my call to Maureen Myers.

"I'm disappointed," she said, her voice sounding husky and filled with smoke, "that you were unable to bring me Barry's things from work, not that I expect him to have had anything of value. The worthless piece of crap probably didn't even have my picture in his office."

"I apologize, Mrs. Myers, but the police discovered that Barry's locked desk had been tampered with and immediately locked me out. In case you didn't know, somebody tried to kill me yesterday while I was there attempting to do you a favor. You're more than welcome to find someone else to go pick up your husband's personal items from his work."

"Do you know what boring Barry did with his free time, other than watch the TV and plunk away on that banjo of his?"

"I can't imagine," I said, getting more annoyed by the moment.

"He would sit at his desk in the basement with his damn computers. Hours at a time, he'd be down there, doing whatever it was he did. I used to ask. He'd either ignore me or tell me I was bothering him. Whatever it was, the fool had nothing to show for it, at least not that I could see."

"I'm rather busy today, Mrs. Myers. What, exactly, are you

getting at?"

"You're the only person I've told, Mister Costa. Maybe there's something interesting on there. Maybe not. Maybe he was down there watching porn all the time—hell if I know or care. But you're the curious type, and if I were in your shoes, I'd want to know what was on those computers."

I quickly went from annoyed to downright angry. She was playing with me, and I didn't appreciate it. At the same time, she had read me like a predictable romance novel. "The police might consider what you're doing withholding evidence and obstruction of justice."

"I call it leverage, and I have precious little of it. So are you going to help me or not?"

"What, exactly, do you want? No damned surprises, either, Mrs. Myers. I hate surprises."

"Get me Barry's things from work, that's the first thing. The second thing: get me every damned penny of insurance that bastard had, assuming he had any at all, and get it soon. Without it, I won't be able to afford my meds, and I'll be dead in a year or two, not to mention losing the house. I'm sure, by your high-rolling standards it isn't much, but its all I've got, and I'd like to keep it. I'm figuring I might need a lawyer to fight for it, so why not go with the best?"

"First off, I never agreed to be your attorney, Mrs. Myers. Secondly, I don't actively practice any more, and thirdly, even when I did, I didn't argue insurance cases."

"Good is good, and Barry said you were the best. He might have told me other things, too, but I won't tell them to anyone but my attorney."

Dammit. I wanted to punch something, but she was right: she had leverage. "All right, Maureen," I said, "I'll play along for now, but any more games and I'm out. Understood?"

"Fair enough," she said.

* * *

Between the call to Maureen Myers and a stark lack of progress, the afternoon descended into a tense stalemate. Mack was giving me a thorough and, in my opinion, undeserved cold shoulder. Tom spent more time organizing my files, split between computerized records and physical copies, than doing actual investigating. He feigned patience, but his comments grew increasingly sharp as the day progressed. By late afternoon, I'd had more than enough.

"We're done for the day," I announced. Tom, relieved, headed home. Mack pretended not to hear me and continued, unabated.

"Mack?" I said, skulking into our office.

Silence.

"Truce?"

She stopped typing and stared at her monitor for an awkwardly long moment. "The sovereign nation of Mackistan will negotiate your surrender on one condition."

"What does the nation of Mackistan demand?"

"That we get the hell out of here and have dinner. Not at some greasy burger joint, and not O'Brien's, either. I want to get dressed up and have a proper dinner. No televisions, no sports, no bands. A proper dinner."

"Any place in particular you had in mind?"

"South Avenue," she said. "I'll start getting ready."

"Why did I know, somehow, that is what you were going to say?" Dammit.

* * *

I hadn't set foot in South Avenue in years, in spite of being its majority owner. I had invested in a business venture with two friends from college, providing the lion's share of funding to launch the venture. I stayed in the background, allowing them to handle the day to day operations as they saw fit.

Whatever they were doing was working. From the moment it opened, it earned rave reviews and continued to remain on the short list of the city's best. The waiting list for a table typically stretched several weeks into the future, but I always had a table waiting on demand.

I spent a silent moment eying an empty table nearby. It wouldn't stay empty long, of course, but for the moment, it was occupied by my memories. On my first, and only, visit to South Avenue, I brought Angela Grady. I stared, replaying the magical evening in my mind.

The gentle touch of Mack's hand on my shoulder brought me back to reality. "Happy memories are good," she said, her voice barely above a whisper, "but we can't ignore the present to live in the past. Do you like my dress?"

"It's quite lovely, Mack." Stunning would have been a better word. Somewhere along the line, mostly lost on me, she had blossomed from a little lost waif into a beautiful woman.

"Not bad for a nerd, huh?" she said, winking. "Getting dressed up isn't really my thing, but this isn't too bad, although these damn shoes are killing me!"

And a nerd, she was, which is what made our trip to South Avenue so unexpected. Peace negotiations, such as they were, usually ended with a trip to a local computer store or electronics supplier. I found myself at a loss for words until our server rescued me by taking our drink order.

"Have you ever had really good wine, Mack?"

"I don't think so, but I'm willing to try if you promise not to go nuts and spend a thousand dollars on a bottle. I'm not sure I could even tell the difference. However, if you're bound and determined to spend money on me, I could really use a new motherboard and processor for one of my image processing computers."

"As you wish," I said. "I'll be sensible in my selection."

She eyed me suspiciously during the entire process of ordering. "I want to talk about Zonk," she said.

"I thought we had agreed upon a truce."

Her eyes narrowed as she studied my reactions. "Something's not right here. You're supposed to be the one worrying about everything, and I'm supposed to be the calm one."

Mack was right when she claimed my true skill in life was worrying. "You're not willing to accept my new, relaxed style?"

"I know you too well. You're as fond of Zonk as I am. You wouldn't arbitrarily send him into harm's way unless…"

I interrupted. "I had a fair amount of quiet time this afternoon,

Mack. Nobody would talk to me, so I used the opportunity to do some research. Did you know that Quantelle Logistics has one of the best industrial safety records over the past three years? In fact, they earned two awards, one this year, one last, for their work in this area."

"You're trying to change the subject…"

"From all indications, they are a well-run company. They were the local business of the year last year, and two years ago they won awards for exceptional charitable work in our community."

"You're trying to change the subject," she growled.

"There's a decent chance that Quantelle Logistics is a victim of industrial espionage, and the attack on me was a diversion."

"Okay. Who are you, and what have you done with John Costa?"

"What did you work on today, Jillian?"

"All right. If you don't answer my question, I'm going to drink the entire bottle of wine when it gets here, then I'm going to demand you dance with me, right here, right now, in front of everyone."

Mack was bringing out the heavy ammunition. I wasn't a skilled dancer by any stretch of the imagination, but for her it was a totally foreign language. She not only lacked moves, but she lacked rhythm. Alcohol would only serve to intensify her ineptitude; combined with a lowering of inhibitions, the threat was very real.

"All right," I said. "I didn't expect the sovereign nation of Mackistan to make a surprise attack."

"Spill it, Costa!"

"I hired some security for us. That much, you knew. What I didn't tell you was I also hired one of Jerry's experts to apply at Quantelle and keep an eye on Zonk. Now, I think I'm owed an apology…"

"I can't control what you think," she said, fighting back a smile. "You know, for the first time in recent memory, you got more done today than I did. I started to look into Rick Stevens, the first victim. My police contacts are being unusually tight-lipped."

Sensing the hostilities were fading, I settled back into my chair. "What do we know about him?"

"Honestly, we don't know much. He worked as an independent

contractor, but I don't know exactly what he did or if he did any work for Quantelle." A smirk formed. "It might be worth checking with Barry's widow to see if either of them happened to know him, since you two are so chummy."

"Thanks for reminding me," I grumbled. "I need to call O'Neil and see when they're going to let me collect Barry's things. Maureen claims that Barry told her things, but she won't even give me a hint until I deliver his things. I really want to get my hands on his computers."

Mack's face lit up. "Now we're getting somewhere!"

"Perhaps," I said, gently tempering her enthusiasm. "Not only do we not have the computers, we don't know if there's anything on there that will help us. It could all be a game to leverage me into pressing for the insurance money. She plays stupid about the whole thing, but at the same time she's awfully eager. I guess I can understand it, given her health issues. The life insurance Barry carried through his employer should keep her comfortably in her home for a while. I don't see why they would be reluctant to pay it, but then again, I haven't read the fine print on the policy."

"Oh, I bet you're looking forward to doing that, aren't you?"

"Just like I look forward to a root canal. This is why I didn't get into insurance or contract law. It's far easier to sort out the laws that apply to a few simple murders than it is to deal with the most *straightforward* contracts. Damn. I wish I had a paralegal!"

"Why not hire one? It might get you off the hook with Maureen Myers and save you all that lovely insurance work."

"That's a really good idea, Mack. I'll find a younger man, one who's in good shape and wears his shirts unbuttoned one hole too far. That should keep Mrs. Myers preoccupied long enough to allow me to work on the case."

"Either that, or you'll earn a world's record for the shortest employment of a paralegal."

CHAPTER TEN

George O'Neil released the crime scene first thing in the morning, and I was there almost immediately thereafter to collect Barry's personal items. Complete with my towering bodyguard and an armed, off-duty police officer, nobody at Quantelle Logistics offered the slightest hint of resistance.

Much as his widow predicted, Barry's office was largely devoid of personal items, but it did include several pictures of her. Under the watchful eye of Brenda Simmons, I packed most of his items into a paper box. The few that would not fit found a home in a plastic grocery bag.

Before I could leave, I was asked to make a detour to the company president's office. Wanting to keep things cordial with the company, I accepted.

* * *

Drew Scanlon, the Quantelle president, shook my hand. "I believe you've already met our chief counselor." He motioned to the slender, grey-haired man standing to his right.

I nodded. "Only in passing," I said, shaking the man's hand.

"Please, Mister Costa, have a seat," he said, motioning toward a comfortable looking chair. "I apologize that I was not available when all the unpleasantness happened, but I was traveling and didn't arrive until after all of the excitement ended. First and foremost, I want to pass along condolences to Barry Myers' widow from all of the Quantelle family."

He was obviously well-practiced and smooth, but he seemed genuine. I nodded silently in response.

"We're also shocked and horrified by what happened to you when you visited. In addition to the investigation by the police, we are conducting an internal assessment of the situation, what went wrong, and how it can be avoided moving forward."

He handed me a small box.

"Our team wanted to offer you a small token of our appreciation. We understand you came to the assistance of our security officer when she was injured."

The box contained a pen, a pen holder, and a wooden base containing a tablet. An engraved strip of gold-colored metal bore my name.

"Thank you," I said, closing the box, "but this wasn't necessary." They were clearly engaged in egregious ass kissing, likely in hope of avoiding a lawsuit. The promised procedural reviews reeked of a witch hunt, likely designed to pin the blame on Ashley.

He smiled a lot and continued talking, but I tuned him out, waiting for a lull in the monologue.

"Just so we're on the same page," I said, interrupting another canned line of bullshit, "we both know that I have multiple events that I consider actionable. Now, I know you have a team of lawyers and deep pockets, but I have the luxury of time and absolutely zero legal fees. So cut the crap. You don't want me to sue your company, and you're lining up a cast of characters to throw under the bus to play the victim—simple as that."

He stopped, maintaining his composure. "I see your reputation for directness is well earned. What type of settlement do you have in mind?"

Finally, I had some leverage. "For starters, I expect no opposition to the claim I will be filing on behalf of Barry's widow to your life insurance carrier. I expect his life insurance policies to be paid, and paid as quickly as possible."

"Done, and we will work with our carrier to minimize any delays to Maureen Myers' claim."

"Secondly, I expect no repercussions against Ashley Vinton. She acted in an exemplary manner and should be treated as such. I expect her medical bills, including any rehabilitation, are fully covered, with no out-of-pocket expense—and she gets her full pay through all of it."

"Of course," he said. "Our company prides itself on how we treat our employees. You have my personal assurance that her job and income are safe. I'm quite impressed with your concern for her well-being, Mister Costa. She must've made quite an impression."

I ignored his attempt to steer the conversation. "Earlier, you mentioned an internal investigation. I expect to have full access to this process."

The lawyer, who had previously been expressionless, tensed at my words.

"While I understand your position, I am concerned that parts of our investigation will likely include information proprietary to our company."

"Then have your legal team draft a suitable nondisclosure agreement. I have no interest in anything but solving Barry Myers' murder and the attack against me. For example, I want to know what went wrong with the lighting system, who had access to it. I want to know how a forklift could fall into the hands of a non-employee. I want to know why the radios weren't working in that area and who might have had access to render them inoperable. Of course, I want copied of all of the video footage from that day."

"I understand, but I will have to discuss this matter with our legal counsel."

"We would," the lawyer interjected, "expect certain legal concessions were we to provide the level of access you request."

"Of course. I have little interest in litigation. If we reach an understanding and suitable sharing happens, I will be glad to hold your organization harmless. After all, accidents happen, even at an organization as safety conscious as Quantelle. On the other hand, if I get stonewalled, it will give me time to sharpen the blade of my legal arguments, which, I assure you, will cut deeply."

"I don't respond well to threats, Mister Costa" the president said.

"I don't respond well to attempted murder, Mister Scanlon" I growled.

* * *

My previous calls to Ashley Vinton had gone unanswered. Much to my relief, a text message awaited.

```
Sorry for not returning your calls. The break
is worse than thought and needed surgery. I
will be out of the hospital in a day or two,
and will call you when I get home.
The police are here, but I didn't feel safe
until your security person arrived. She's
absolutely terrifying, but in a good way. I
hope you are taking similar precautions.
```

* * *

Maureen Myers was in a noticeably better mood when I arrived, although I thought I detected hints of alcohol on her breath as she spoke.

"I just got a call from Quantelle," she said. "Apparently, you lit quite a fire under them. I'm told old Barry had four hundred thousand in coverage. Imagine that! Worthless old fool turned out to be good for something after all."

"May I *please* suggest you stop talking like that, even to me. The police are undoubtedly searching for someone with a motive, and with the life insurance benefit in the picture, I'm sure you've moved to the top of the list."

"Like I care what the police think," she growled. "Let them think whatever they want. Do you think Barry had any other money he didn't tell me about?"

"I suppose it's possible. Quantelle will facilitate getting you copies of any benefits he had through his work. It seems likely that he had a retirement account, since that is one of the benefits Quantelle advertises on their web site."

"Really? Do you know how much it is and how soon I will get the money?"

"No and no. This isn't my specialty, Maureen. I think you should consider hiring someone who knows the laws around inheritance, taxes, and insurance better than I do."

"No. You'll do," she said.

"I honestly don't understand why you're so set on working with me. I'm out of my area of expertise, and I don't actively practice law any more."

"You don't really want to represent me, do you?"

"No. I really don't."

"Well, that's why I want you. I figure anyone honest enough to answer that question the way you did is the person I want. Besides, I know a thing or two about you. I didn't even know Barry had any life insurance, but some other bastard would probably be scheming how he could get half of it as his legal fee. That four hundred grand is pocket change to you, buddy, even after you gave away half your damn fortune. So I figure you've got no incentive to rob me."

Not only did she have a point, she had done her homework. When I learned that a significant portion of my inheritance, although legal, had originated from a relative involved in an unsavory business enterprise, I donated it to charity. I would have shed my entire fortune until Mack intervened, protecting me from myself.

"Fair enough," I said. "But you've not given me any incentive to continue to hold up my end of the bargain. Toss me a bone, would you?"

"Care to join me in a drink?"

"Not really. Still a bit early for me, and I have to drive."

"Suit yourself," she said. "I'm going to drink a toast to old

Barry's demise!"

"I'll see myself out," I said, uncomfortable with the situation.

She laughed. "You want a bone? Here. See what you can do with this, Rover." She reached into a small drawer and produced a smart phone.

"What's this?"

"Barry's phone. He didn't take it with him to the pub that night."

"Was that unusual?"

"Damn straight it was," she said, guzzling her drink before pouring another. "He never went anywhere without it, but he did on Wednesday night."

"If we're able to get into this, what are we likely to find?"

"Damned if I know. Just make sure you get it back to me when all of this is over so I can sell the damn thing. While you're at it, find me a buyer for that damned banjo of his, otherwise I might have to stick it in the fireplace and send it on its way to meet Barry."

"I don't recommend you do that," I said. "His instrument is fairly high end; it's worth thousands."

"Then find me a buyer. If you're good and quick, I might even tell you what he said to me about the phone."

"When did he say it, Maureen?"

"Wednesday, before he left to play music."

"Come on! Tell me!"

"Now, now, Fido. You fetch me some banjo money, and I'll tell you."

I was beginning to develop a fervent dislike for Maureen Myers, but I packed up Barry's banjo and skulked out, tail between my legs. I could swallow my pride in exchange for information, at least for the time being.

* * *

"Mack, see what you can do with this," I said, handing her the phone.

"Nice!"

Her response confused me. "What's nice?"

"The phone. It came out two months ago and has been getting rave reviews. I was going to get one, but decided to wait until the prices dropped."

"I would expect you to always have the latest, greatest thing, Mack. I'm surprised."

"There's always something new and better coming out. The trick is timing, oh surprised one. Who does this belong to?"

"Barry Myers."

Her expression changed, almost immediately.

"What is it, Mack?"

"Didn't you say Barry was paying two mortgages and covering a lot of prescriptions for his wife?"

"Yes, but he made decent money. I'm honestly a little puzzled where all of it went, given the age and condition of his car and house. Why?"

"This phone is sold directly, not through carriers. There's no getting it for free; you pay for the whole thing up front. On top of that, this is the larger model and if my suspicions are correct..."

She paused to pry the back off the phone and inspect what she found.

"Yep. This bad boy is maxed out."

"How much are we talking about?"

"Around seven hundred bucks, plus whatever he's paying for the data plans."

"Plans? Plural?"

"Yes. This is a dual SIM phone, and he's got both slots occupied."

Mack could tell that I was getting lost in her explanation.

"The phone has two identities," she explained. "It can make and receive calls or texts on two different numbers, two different carriers, and two different technologies. Did Barry travel overseas a lot?"

"I suppose it is possible. Quantelle does have branches in Europe, but it wasn't mentioned to me when I talked to his coworkers."

"A dual SIM phone is incredibly convenient in that situation. *You* have one."

"I do?"

"Yes, you do. You used it in Northern Ireland, but your phone still worked when you came home. Interesting... These SIMs are both domestic carriers. Maybe my theory of overseas travel is wrong. I'm going to dig into this now unless you have any objection."

"None. Old Rover here is going to lie down for a nap."

"Huh?"

"Never mind, Mack. Just some egregious mistreatment at the hands of my so-called client. I made the mistake of asking her to throw me a bone, and she started calling me Rover. Fido, too."

Mack smiled. "Well, hopefully I'll find something you can sink your teeth into. Just give us a howl if you need anything, Barky McWoofington."

"Mack!"

"Oh, can you fetch me an energy drink?"

"Mack!!"

CHAPTER ELEVEN

"I hope you have good news, Mack," I said, sipping my morning coffee.

"Nothing yet," she said, pouring herself a cup. "These things take time, especially with newer technology. Not as many of the exploits and weaknesses have been published, so I'll have to find them myself."

"Rats. I was hoping you had something. I feel like we're spinning our wheels."

"Well, there is one person who should be able to shed some light on the situation: Jennifer Adams."

"Oh, hell no," I said, nearly spitting my coffee all over the table. You call her, or Tom can call her, but I'm not."

"I already did," Mack said, "but she refused to talk to anyone but you."

I buried my head in my hands. It was bad enough merely hearing her name after all these years. The thought of talking to her was downright repugnant.

"I'm not an expert at reading voices or anything," Mack said, stealing a piece of my toast, "but she sounded scared."

"Tell her to fly somewhere she thinks is safe. The South Pole comes to mind. I'll even buy her damned ticket. One way, of course."

Mack sat down, studying me as she spoke. "She really hurt you badly, didn't she?"

"Yeah, I guess you could say that. I've told the story to a few people, but it hurts so damn much that I stopped, largely for my own mental health."

"You don't have to tell me," she said, gently touching my arm. "I can try calling her again."

"No," I said, sighing, "she's my headache to deal with. Besides, when she has her mind set on something, it is usually impossible to sway her."

"Sorry to change the subject," Mack said, her eyes drifting away from me, "but what the hell is that thing?" She pointed toward the banjo case leaning against the corner. "It looks like a case for an oversized thermometer."

"Interesting description," I said, fighting back laughter. "It is Barry's banjo. Maureen Myers wants to sell it, and I'm the one who's supposed to find a buyer for it."

"Why you?"

"Well, partially because I know some local musicians, but mostly because she's reveling in the fact that she can pull my strings. When I get her the money for the banjo, she gives us another snippet of information."

"Well, the answer to that is easy," Mack said, leaning back in her chair. "You buy it. That way you get tossed the next bone, and you don't have to mess around with finding a buyer. A bigger question in my mind is why she's doing what she's doing. Why not just tell you what she knows?"

"Leverage and a serious case of paranoia, I imagine. What's worse, she doesn't seem the least bit upset about Barry's death. It's all about getting money, from any and every possible source. She's even eager to sell his cell phone."

"Absolutely none of this makes her look guilty," Mack quipped, rolling her eyes.

"Almost like she's going out of her way to make herself the prime suspect. Unless..." My voice drifted away.

"What?"

"Sorry. I zoned out for a moment. Unless there's some reason she wants or needs to be at the top of the suspect list."

"Perhaps to shield someone else?"

"Could be. Or she could simply be nuts. If you or Tom has a chance, it's probably worth looking into her, too. Family, friends, anything."

"It'll be me," she chuckled. "Tom is about a quarter of the way through your files now. He's used some colorful and unflattering words to describe your organizational skills. Probably best not to heap anything else on him at the moment."

"Duly noted." I took a deep breath. "Wish me luck," I said, standing. "I'm off to call Satan, herself."

* * *

It wasn't only the pending call to Jennifer Adams that nagged at me. Maureen Myers spoke of four hundred thousand in coverage, but the human resources representative at Quantelle quoted a higher amount. Perhaps it was a simple matter of rounding or misspeaking, but the discrepancy warranted investigation. My client, reprehensible as she was, deserved to know the exact amount. Pondering it was also an easy way to avoid the inevitable. Taking a deep breath, I dialed Jennifer's number.

"You called," she said.

Two short words were all it took for the unpleasant past to rush over me and to immediately regret my decision to call. The younger, idealistic me that had fallen for the beguiling Jennifer, a confident woman who seemed to have all the answers, was still there. But he wasn't bright-eyed and idealistic any more; he was bitter and jaded.

Fallen didn't quite capture the sentiment. I was full-throttle, ass-over-tea-kettle in love with her. There was a time when it seemed she shared my passion, but it was merely a hopeful illusion. She pulled back, talking a lot about change and introspection And me? I foolishly waited, passing every line of bullshit she spewed through a filter of unbridled optimism.

Perhaps she thought she was, somehow, sparing my feelings, by stringing me along. Perhaps she enjoyed having a foolish puppy dog on her leash. Whatever it was didn't matter. I had failed to read the signals or discern the actual meaning of her half-truths. When she said she wasn't ready for a relationship, she meant she wasn't ready for one *with* *me.*

"I did."

An awkward pause followed. This, too, triggered sorrowful memories. She hadn't the decency to end our relationship, such as it was, in person. Instead, she thrust the dagger from afar, ringing me from ninety miles away to tell me of the new relationship she was about to embark upon. It turned out to be nothing new. As I later learned, she had been seeing the other man for at least six months.

I recalled that, in the moment, I muttered a few words of defeat, but managed to temper the verbal torrent that raged within. She even had the nerve to ask me if I hated her, but I couldn't summon the words that desperately needed to be said. Rather, I replied with some of the same milquetoast doublespeak she had fed me for months. In so doing, I not only lost my chance for catharsis, but likely doomed a string of hopeful suitors to the same broken heart she served me. My inability to deliver a venomous reply seemed to vindicate her actions, or so I imagined. But hate her, I did, or maybe I hated myself for being hopeful. Either way, time had only applied bandages and cosmetics to the wounds. They still growled with the same pain today as they did many years before.

"I spoke to your assistant."

"She's not my assistant, she's my business partner."

"She sounds very nice," Jenn said, her words arriving hesitantly.

Fishing, after all these years? More likely, she was trying to make pleasant conversation, but I didn't care. I just wanted to be rid of her. "She mentioned that you wanted to talk to me about Rick Stevens."

"I do," she said, "but not over the phone. I have a few things I want to give you."

"This is all pertaining to his death?"

"Yes."

"If it's evidence, you should give it to the police." I hoped she'd take my advice and vanish from my life, once and for all. Such luck, however, wasn't in the cards.

"I can't, and I don't have time to explain right now. Can you meet me at the Northwinds Outlet Mall?"

A sick feeling rumbled through my stomach. I had no desire to see her, but knew that there was no choice if I wanted to learn more about Rick's demise. "Yes, I suppose so. When would you like to meet?"

"Can you be there in an hour?"

"Sure, if I leave now."

"Good. See you there."

I tried to ask at which of the myriad of stores to meet, but she had already hung up the phone.

* * *

The specter of the upcoming holidays was looming, reflected by the woeful parking situation at the outlets. Not only was I not sure where she wanted to meet, but I couldn't find a decent parking place to save my life.

My bodyguard was none too thrilled about the crowds, voicing his concern over my well being. I was less worried about physical threats than I was about the prospect of meeting Jennifer Adams.

After circling several times, I found what looked like the type of store she might choose. It met all the criteria: large, lots of traffic, had a cafe within known for its coffee, and was stocked, floor to ceiling, with cheap, imitation crap that looked expensive. My bodyguard cracked the only hint of a smile I'd ever seen from him when I muttered something to that effect as I parked my car.

We made the brisk walk across the parking lot and entered the store. There wasn't much for us to do other than mill about and hope that we were in the right place. After about ten minutes, I made my way to the cafe. Much to my surprise, several spots were available. I picked one from where I could survey the entryway.

As I sat, my memories followed the inevitable course back to our parting. I believed her hollow talk of friendship and tried to keep in touch for a few months. I was met with merciless silence. My efforts were halfhearted, at best. Maybe it was fortunate, after all, that she cut ties, but I never saw it that way.

"John?"

I glanced up to see Jennifer Adams approaching my table. She looked trim and in shape, but time and, I theorized, too many days in the sun, had taken their toll on her skin. Most noticeable, however, was her hair. Once shoulder-length and curly, it was cut short and was uneven. It looked suspiciously like she might have cut it herself, or perhaps allowed someone unskilled to try their hand at cutting hair. The color was different, too, her normal dark brown traded for blonde with cheap-looking blonde highlights.

She hovered at an awkward distance, seeming to be uncertain whether to offer a handshake or a hug. I offered neither, simply motioning for her to sit down.

"Thank you for meeting me," she said, talking more quickly than I remembered. "I want to make this as quick as possible."

"Me, too," I muttered. I wasn't sure she heard me over the din of the cafe.

"I'm sorry to dump this on you, but I couldn't think of anyone else."

"Why don't you start from the beginning," I said.

"I started working with Rick about eight years ago. A year later, we were in a relationship and have been ever since."

It was all I could do to avoid making a snide comment. I clenched my jaw as she continued.

"Rick was a good man, he really was. But in recent months, I started to notice a change in him. He seemed nervous, started drinking more, and had trouble sleeping. He eventually admitted to me that he had gotten himself mixed up with some bad people. I don't think he set out with that in mind, but it just sort of happened."

"What kind of bad people?" I asked, settling back into my chair.

"I don't know exactly, but I'm fairly sure they were foreign. Russian, perhaps. We started getting phone calls, then visits. The more they showed up, the less he slept."

"Do you think these men had something to do with his death?"

"I'm certain of it, and I told all of this to the police, but they didn't seem to be overly interested in my theories. Anyway, in the days leading up to his death, he hardly slept at all. He told me if anything happened to him to get the hell out of town and hide. That's when I gave him your card. I'd read some articles online about you and thought maybe you'd be able to help him. He vanished shortly thereafter."

"Do you have any idea what he was mixed up in?"

"No, but I'm sure it had something to do with his work. Here," she said, handing me a small satchel. "I pulled all the records I could get my hands on. Maybe you can find something."

"You need to give this to the police. It might be evidence."

"I can't. You're free to give it to them if there's anything relevant in there."

I was uncomfortable with her answer, but in the interest of my own sanity, I decided to let the subject drop.

"Do you recall if Rick ever mentioned a company called Quantelle Logistics?"

"No, he didn't, and I've never heard of them. Should I have?"

"Not necessarily. A second man, a friend of mine, was killed in the same way as Rick. It is where he used to work. I don't have much to go on, so I'm following the few clues we have."

She seemed to grow more nervous by the minute. I could tell that the news of a second death had rattled her to the core.

"What was his name?"

"Barry Myers. Are you familiar with the name, or did you ever hear Rick mention it?"

"No, I don't think so," she said, "but he came into contact with a decent number of people in his line of work."

"He was an independent contractor, right?"

She nodded. "He wasn't going to get rich from it, but it seemed to be doing well enough. You have his books among all that stuff," she motioned to the satchel. "Maybe you'll find something."

"Thanks."

An awkward pause followed.

"I'm headed out of town," she said, rising from her chair and collecting her purse. "I'm going to take his advice and keep out of sight for a while."

"Probably not a bad idea, given what you've just told me."

"I can let you know where I'm going to be if you need to reach me."

"It would probably be better if you didn't tell me. I can't accidentally tell what I don't know. One word of advice: turn off your cell phone right now, remove the battery, and then get rid of it. They are much easier to track than I ever realized."

"Thank you," she said, rising.

I watched her walk away, wishing that she was nothing more than a stranger in the crowd.

My bodyguard leaned over to me and whispered, "she's lying."

"No doubt," I replied.

CHAPTER TWELVE

The line of traffic leading back toward the city meandered ponderously through a cold rain. Progress was slow, giving me plenty of time to reflect on the revelations shared by Jennifer Adams. My bodyguard was right: she wasn't telling the truth—at least not all of it— but she was definitely scared by something. That part of her demeanor seemed genuine. Other parts seemed rehearsed.

Still, it was pointless to conjecture until we had looked through the satchel. A quick glance revealed several worn notebooks, a binder, and a stack of loose papers. I also spotted several cases containing optical disks and at least two flash drives. Hopefully, it would give Mack something to sink her teeth into.

The world was silent, save for the rhythmic drone of the windshield wipers, punctuated by the occasional sound of a distant car horn.

My bodyguard, rarely one to speak, broke the monotony. "Time shall unfold what plighted cunning hides: Who cover faults, at last shame them derides."

"King Lear?" My face was undoubtedly etched with surprise.

He nodded. "The benefits of a classical education. You're

surprised, I see."

"Of all people, I should know not to judge a book by its cover. My apologies, but it was unexpected."

A gentle smile crossed his lips. "You're not the first. My undergraduate degree is in English literature. My graduate degree is in behavioral analysis. In my line of work, it has proven to be a valuable asset."

"I'm sure being tall and ridiculously large doesn't hurt, either."

"Size and muscles are pointless without thought and wisdom to direct them. I'm brought in for special cases."

I laughed. "I'm sure Jerry considers me special, but not in a good way."

"Whatever slings and arrows are flung are done so strictly in jest. He brought me in because he knows you are a thinking man; and thinking men are harder to protect—that, and he holds you in high regard."

"He has an odd way of showing it."

The bodyguard smiled. "It wasn't hard to tell that your friend was lying," he said, changing the direction of the conversation. "Stop me if I'm speaking out of place, but it is equally apparent that you two have some unpleasant history, likely romantic. The non-verbal signals were unmistakable."

"Impressive," I said, "and quite accurate. Jennifer Adams is a manipulative shrew and a skilled liar. She *was* scared, though."

"Agreed. There are definitely elements of truth in what she told you. Her hair was cut in haste, as was her makeup. Her non-verbal signals told me she still harbors feelings for you, at least some, yet her nail polish was sloppy. So yes, she's leaving town urgently and in fear."

"I'm sorry," I said, breaking the flow of our conversation, "I'm ashamed to admit that I don't know your name."

"Kevin," he replied. "Kevin Moriarty. Perhaps when I retire from this line of work, I can finish my PhD and be called professor."

I chuckled. "Nice to meet you, Kevin. Was there any part of my conversation with Jennifer where you found her to be more dishonest than others?"

"She was uncomfortable with the meeting, in general, but I

believe that she is not telling you everything about Rick Stevens' business. Her tells—the signals when someone is lying—grew more pronounced when the conversation went in that direction. My advice, if you're so inclined, is to look at the business records with a fine-toothed comb. Miss MacDonald's skills in this area are the stuff of legend. A question, if I may?"

"Of course."

"Is Jennifer Adams the type of person who would, in spite of her feelings for you, dump a serious problem in your lap and then vanish?"

"Yes. She is precisely the type to do that."

"Then I suggest approaching the contents of the satchel with great caution. There's obviously not a bomb hidden there, at least not in the literal sense. Unlike an explosive, though, it might not be immediately evident what you're dealing with, ergo prudence."

"I will keep that well in mind."

I had more to say, but the ringing of my cell phone stopped me. The number was unfamiliar, but from Northern Ireland, so I answered it.

"I see the old dog is still answering his phone," Adnan Jasik said.

"Thank you for calling me," I said. "Kelly seemed worried about you, and I started to as well."

"The Poppy," he said, referring to one of Kelly Hamilton's many online pseudonyms, "forgot that I had a planned holiday. I was in Scotland, fishing for the Loch Ness Monster."

"Well, I'm going to assume you came up empty, because I didn't see you on the news."

"The monster managed to avoid me again this time. Perhaps one day," he laughed. "I understand you need some help."

"I do. Did Kelly have a chance to brief you."

"Yes. Two bodies. Two notes. Both killed the same way: bayonet to the stomach, bullet between the eyes."

"Correct."

"The bayonet is a Russian variety, no?"

"Correct again."

"Have the police identified the type of gun used for the kill shot?"

"If so, they haven't shared it with me."

"Ask your friend, the Captain, if the gun was a Nagant M1895 revolver fitted with a suppressor."

"What the hell is that?"

"One of the few revolvers that can be fitted with a suppressor, among other things. It was a favorite of the Bolsheviks during the Russian revolution and saw plenty of use in the Second World War as a sidearm. Not good for much beyond one, close-ranged shot. If you'd ever fired one, you'd know why."

His words left a sick feeling in my stomach. "You've seen this before, haven't you?"

"Possibly. Tell me more."

"A local professor looked at the poem and translated it, but said it had no particular meaning beyond being a child's rhyme."

"Yes. It is a child's poem about three birds."

"When the local police inquired, the FBI clammed up about it quickly, which is why I think it is important."

"It might be, or it might not be. After the fall of the Soviet Union, it wasn't long before Yugoslavia's problems started to escalate into outright war. There were at least three incidences where bodies, killed in the manner you described, were found. To this day, nobody has even stood trial, nor has there been a single arrest."

"Serial killer?"

"Quite possibly, although nobody knows for sure. Some thought it was part of the ethnic cleansing. Others thought it was retribution. What we do know is that the weapons used are always the same and there are always three victims. The poem speaks of three birds, and there are always three bodies."

"We only have two…"

"There could be another murder coming, or there's a body you haven't found yet."

I clenched my jaw. "Why the hell didn't the FBI tell us any of this?"

"What's there to tell? Unsubstantiated claims from wartime Sarajevo? Most Bosnians don't even know about it. The war made for bad record keeping. Do you happen to know what kind of paper on which the poem was written? If not, it is important to find out"

"What's so important about the paper?"

"I was able to get samples of the card stock used in five of the nine killings in what is now Bosnia and Herzegovina. All samples were identical and quite rare. That will tell you."

"What will it tell?"

"If you have a copy cat, or if you have a real problem on your hands. Since the conflict ended in my homeland, there have been four killings internationally that followed the same pattern, but none of them had notes printed on the original paper."

"Maybe the killer ran out of the original supply."

"Possible, but not the case. There were three murders in South America last year that met the criteria. It took some work and collection of a few favors, but I was able to verify that the poem was printed on the original paper, exactly like what happened in the original cases. I follow this closely, you see, because one of the victims was a member of my family."

"I'm sorry."

"Don't be. The man was a prick, but he was family, so I have to work on it." He laughed, but it quickly faded. "I hope you have a copy cat on your hands. Because if not, you've got a serious problem. I paid, personally, to have a profile worked up. I'll send it to you, along with what we know of the previous killings. Maybe they will help."

* * *

"You look none the worse for wear," Mack said, "although all of this took longer than I expected it would."

"Traffic," I said. "Our meeting was tense, but cordial, likely because we stayed away from the past and kept our conversation strictly business, such as it was."

"What's in the satchel?"

"Some paperwork from Rick Stevens' business. It looks like there are a couple of flash drives in there, and a couple of DVDs as well. Approach it carefully, Mack."

"What do you mean?"

"I'm not sure, exactly, but I have the strange feeling that Jennifer might be dropping a problem right into my lap. Just treat it as a hostile witness."

"I get it. Oh! Did I mention today exactly how awesome I am?"

"I'm sure you did…"

"I got into Barry's phone."

"You broke the encryption?"

"Nah," she said. "I called Maureen Myers, and she gave me the unlock code."

"What did you have to promise to do for her?"

"Nothing. I just asked, and she gave it to me straight away."

"I guess when she was in the presence of such awesomeness, she had no choice," I said, rolling my eyes.

"I don't think she cares for men very much, to be honest with you. But I tend to think it had more to do with yours truly," she said, fluffing her hair. "It was either that, or that I mentioned you had a buyer for the banjo."

"Mack!" I glowered at her. "Exactly how much did your mystery buyer offer for the banjo?"

"Fair market."

"How soon?"

"Later today."

"Mack!! I don't want a damned banjo."

"But you *do* want what is on Barry's phone. Besides, it might be nice for you to learn how to play it—then you can stand under my window and serenade me."

"Only if it's the window of a freighter taking a long, slow trip to the South Pole."

"A cruise! How thoughtful! But if I'm on the South Pole, you won't find out what is on Barry's phone," her voice lilted.

"Dish it, Mack."

"When you get back. You've got a banjo to buy."

CHAPTER THIRTEEN

My traffic woes continued, unabated, the entire way to Maureen's house. It didn't help that she demanded payment in cash. My stop at the bank only served to delay me more. By the time I rang her doorbell, my jaw was tired from clenching, and a headache threatened.

"Come on in," she bellowed.

"You really shouldn't leave your door unlocked," I said, "especially living alone."

"Big time lawyer advice! No wonder you crooks charge so much. Did you bring it?"

"Yes, Mrs. Myers. I brought the money."

"Come on in to the kitchen," she said, slowly rising from her chair. "You can count it for me."

Reluctantly, I followed her, taking the seat offered to me at her modest kitchen table. As requested, I counted the cash—twice, for good measure—before handing it to her.

"Thank you," she said, drawing deeply on her cigarette. "Any word on the insurance money?"

"As I've said before, these things take time. There are processes that have to be followed, and some of them are complicated by the fact that he was the victim of a homicide. I understand your urgency, and am pressing wherever and whenever I can."

She grunted, nodding her head. "You want to see why I don't have any money in the bank?"

"I guess," I said, uncertain of where she was going.

"See that door?" She pointed toward the far wall. "It leads down to our basement. The light switch is on the wall."

"Go on," she said, in response to my hesitation. "I'll be here when you get back."

I didn't know what to expect. Neither the door nor the switch were anything special, but when I turned on the lights, I realized what she meant. Unlike the rest of the house, which was decidedly dated, the basement was finished and contemporary.

Two large gun safes dominated the shortest wall, along with a sump system, complete with a backup. Apart from an area occupied by the furnace, the rest of the basement was filled with computers, monitors, and shelves full of electronic equipment, the purpose of which I didn't understand. Function aside, it was obvious that Barry Myers had spent a lot of money to outfit his basement. Careful not to disturb anything, I returned to the kitchen.

"Impressive," I said, eyebrows raised. I have no idea what most of it is, but it is impressive."

"Hell if I know, either" she said.

"I'd like for my computer expert to get a look at this stuff. I'm sure she could tell us what all of it does."

"Are you talking about the young lady I spoke with on the phone earlier?"

"Yes. Jillian MacDonald."

"That's the one. She sounds nice, and I'd love to meet her. But, you know the price of admission, even if you do bring your lovely friend with you."

My sore jaw and aching head had officially had enough of Maureen Myers. "You know what, Maureen? You can find yourself another lawyer. I'll find out what happened to Barry with or without your help, and quite frankly, I'm sick and tired of your games."

"About damn time you grew a set," she said, drawing deeply on her cigarette. "You bring your little friend over tomorrow. Any time after about ten is fine."

* * *

Upon arriving home, I retreated to my basement music room, my one remaining island of solace. Since my return from Northern Ireland, it had gotten little use. The recording equipment, state of the art when I bought it, was now flirting with obsolescence. It didn't matter. I hadn't done a thing with it, and modernizing it wouldn't change anything.

The information Adnan Jasik promised arrived electronically and captured my attention almost immediately. Hours slipped by, until Mack ventured downstairs to check on me.

"Dinner's upstairs, although its cold by now," she said.

"Thanks. I lost track of time."

"What are you working on?"

"Adnan sent me some information, and it has had me spellbound for the last three hours."

"What is it?"

"There were nine murders during the Yugoslav war, all of which follow the same general pattern as ours. None of them were ever properly investigated, so naturally they remain unsolved. Adnan has been quietly pursuing these crimes whenever he can, but a lot of the evidence is lost. There's not even an official admission that the deaths were homicides or related, this in spite of the fact that the killer faithfully left the same calling card."

She peered over my shoulder. "Always in threes, just like the poem. Three birds, three bodies."

I nodded. "The first three victims were in Sarajevo. We know a fair bit about them because Adnan was related to this one," I said, pointing to a picture on the screen. "His uncle was ostensibly a banker, but it looks like he was the brains and money behind a fairly sizable network of sex workers, more than a few of which were under age. Adnan called him a prick; rather hard to argue with that assessment. From what I can tell, he had some friends in law enforcement that helped him skate by, including the first victim."

"Odd," Mack said. "The death of a law enforcement officer usually generates a significant manhunt."

"It might have, under normal circumstances, were it not for the war."

"What about the third victim?"

"He," I said, pointing to a picture on my screen, "ran a trucking company. It was also the only time that the killer deviated from his normal routine, if the information we have is reliable."

"What was different?" Mack asked.

"He was shot two extra times. The normal routine is a bayonet to the stomach and a bullet between the eyes. He got shot in the knee and groin. Problem is, there is no way to know if the extra shots were delivered by the killer or by someone else."

"And the other murders?"

"Whoever is responsible seems to be on the move," I replied, pointing to a different map. "Unfortunately, the records are so bad, Adnan is unable to determine which killing spree came first. No matter what, there was a long pause between killings. Then," I said, changing screens, "this happened in the Philippines in 2003."

"Three bodies, just like before," she muttered.

"Yes, but once again, very little evidence. The only thread holding them together, beyond the method of death, is the paper upon which the notes are written. According to Adnan, it dates back to the early 1970s and came out of East Germany. What is special about this particular card stock is that it bears an embossed watermark, supposedly associated with the secret police, the Stasi. From what I can tell, the paper is the only element that separates what is believed to be the real serial killer from the handful of copycats that have emerged."

"What is this?" she asked, pointing to a red dot on the screen.

"After a dozen years, there was another triple murder, this time in Argentina. Adnan, working through channels, was able to get the authorities to test the paper. It was a match."

"What do we know about the victims?"

"One of the men worked as a manager in a large agricultural company, the second was the son of a local politician, although his exact profession is hazy. The third sold cars and trucks. There is nothing to connect them, other than the murders."

Mack sank back into her chair. "The same problem we're running in to. But," she said, massaging her temples, "there has to be *something*. We're just not finding it."

"Speaking of which," I added, "we're going to pay our friend Maureen a visit tomorrow. I saw where all of Barry's money went: equipment. Unfortunately, I'm clueless as to what most of it does, but I suspect you'll be like a kid in a candy shop."

"Tom has designs on your time tomorrow, too. He's got your case files in order, and has a handful that he'd like to review with you. I don't think our killer is among them, but it is probably worth your time to take a look."

"Agreed."

* * *

I turned in early, but found myself unable to sleep. Grabbing my robe, I headed back to my music room for a quiet glass of whiskey. I had, out of habit, stuffed my cell phone into the pocket of my robe. I was surprised when it vibrated, signaling the arrival of a text message. I was doubly surprised when I saw the source.

It's Ashley V. from Quantelle. I don't suppose you're awake.

Actually, I am. I went to bed early but couldn't sleep. Is everything okay?

I'm getting out sometime tomorrow afternoon. Can you come over to my place tomorrow evening?`

As far as I know, I'm free.

With a name like Costa, I think I know the answer to this question, but do you like

Italian food?

> Sure, but please don't go out of your way.

My mother's maiden name is Peretti, and she has insisted on cooking a meal for you.

> I know better than to say no to an Italian woman who wants to cook.

Excellent. 8pm?

> Works for me.

You must've really lit a fire under Quantelle.

> Why do you say that?

The president of the company visited me today. He told me not to worry about work. Just get better, and my job will be waiting for me when I'm ready to return. Want to know the interesting part?

> Sure.

He told me I should help your investigation in any and every way possible. Two hours later, my boss showed up with the same message. Coincidence, no doubt. LOL

> Sounds like they're worried about getting sued. I hope I did the right thing pressing them about keeping you employed.

You did, and I appreciate it. I really enjoy
working there. It is a good company. I've got
to go, the nurse is about to yell at me, I
think. Bring your appetite. My mother gets
carried away with her portions.

Okay. See you then. Have a good night.

I eased my feet onto the sofa, savoring the last few sips of my
whiskey. I knew myself well enough to realize that sleep was not going
to arrive easily when my mind was unsettled. Opening my laptop, I
dove back into the information Adnan provided.

There was something that bothered me, but even after repeated
readings of the profiler's report, I couldn't put my finger on it. I put the
laptop aside and paced for a while before taking another look. The
pattern repeated several more times before I finally locked in on what
didn't add up for me: the timeline.

The profile pegged the killer as a man in his early forties, likely
from an ethnically diverse background. It theorized that he had
experienced a devastating loss, likely a close family member, when war
came to Sarajevo. The stress caused a psychological event, triggering a
periodic need to engage in his unique form of ritualistic killings. It went
on to theorize that the man had, at some point, worked with or for the
East German Stasi, although it did not offer conjecture on what role he
might have held.

It was a plausible theory in many ways, especially given some of
the horrible war crimes that happened in the area. What didn't work for
me was the serial killer's supposed age. Given that the siege of Sarajevo
started in the spring of 1992, the killer would now be in his middle
sixties. While not impossible for a man of that age, it struck me as
unlikely. My own aches and pains, in spite of my fairly rigorous exercise
regimen, reminded me that time was a relentless and unkind adversary.
Lacking the motivation to return to my room, I stretched out on the
sofa and allowed sleep to arrive.

I awoke sometime later with the distinct and unsettling feeling that I was not alone. Glancing around the darkened room, I saw nothing out of the ordinary. From out of nowhere, a hand gently touched my shoulder. Startled, I tried to move, but found it impossible to do so.

A gentle, familiar voice whispered, "Soon, my love."

I smiled, only now aware that a solitary tear was making a slow journey down the length of my cheek. I closed my eyes and allowed the pleasant dream that followed to take flight.

CHAPTER FOURTEEN

Mack seemed surprised to see me emerge from the music room. "You look awful," she said.

"Good morning to you, too. I was reviewing the profile Adnan Jasik sent and ended up falling asleep on the sofa. I hate it when I do that," I groaned. "Every muscle is complaining loudly right now."

"Maybe a warm shower will help, but don't take too long. We've got to be at Maureen's in just a little over an hour."

"Dammit. I didn't mean to sleep that long. Now, I've got to hurry. By the way, thank you for covering me up last night."

"Huh?"

"The blanket—it was a nice gesture."

"I have no idea what you're talking about, John. I really don't."

I didn't believe her, but didn't have time to debate the issue. I went to sleep without a blanket and woke up covered, having no recollection of getting the blanket out of the closet. Sure, I'd consumed several glasses of whiskey through the course of my review, but that was far less than it took to bring on forgetfulness.

"Sure, Mack, whatever. Give me fifteen minutes or so, and we'll be on our way."

* * *

Mack watched me like a hawk the entire way to Maureen's house, almost as if she was waiting for something to happen. I noticed her clear sense of relief when we arrived. I, on the other hand, had come to dread visiting Maureen Myers.

Today, however, she seemed to be an entirely different woman, warmly greeting us as we arrived. Although the house still smelled strongly of smoke, she was, for the first time since I met her, without a cigarette.

"It is so nice to meet you, Jillian," she said, extending her hand.

Mack engaged in the normal pleasantries while I tried to find a corner to hide in, awaiting the inevitable condescension I had come to know and love. Instead, she offered us tea.

For the next twenty minutes, she engaged in small talk with Mack, mostly espousing her general dislike and distrust of men. I surmised it was from an abusive relationship in her past, but had no evidence to support my theory. Much to my delight, she all but ignored me the entire time. Finally, she arrived at the salient point.

"Jillian, I understand you might be able to shed some insight on to Barry's rather extensive collection of unknown technology in the basement. Perhaps you could also enlighten me as to its value."

"Of course," Mack answered.

"You two will have to go down there without me, but take as long as you need."

* * *

"See?" Mack whispered as we descended the stairs. "She's perfectly nice, just like she was when we spoke on the phone."

"Leopards and their spots, Mack," I whispered in reply.

"Oh my!"

"Told you," I said, as the full scope of Barry's basement came into view. "The computers, I understand, but I have no idea what this stuff is," I said, motioning to the shelves of equipment on the far wall.

Mack walked over, studying each device carefully. "These are radios," she announced. "Your friend was a ham."

"An actor?"

"No," she said, looking annoyed, "an amateur radio operator."

"I thought the Internet killed amateur radio as a hobby."

"It put a dent in it for a while, but more people, especially younger people, are getting into it again. Probably because they've figured out that hackers and governments can shut down the Internet, but they can't jam every radio wave everywhere. Extra class," she said, tapping on a picture frame that held an official looking document. "That's the highest level of non-commercial radio license available. It means your friend was proficient in electrical theory, understood antennas, radio waves, and propagation. Depending on when he got his license, he might have even known Morse code. He's got some decent soldering equipment, too," she said, pointing to another unrecognizable gadget.

She turned her attention to the bottom level of a shelf, removing and opening several cases. "Wow. This is interesting."

"What is it?"

"I'd say this was part of his bug out kit. It has a transceiver capable of battery operation, a handheld radio, several rechargeable battery packs, and portable antennas. Impressive stuff, too. All new and top of the line. Interesting..."

She removed one of the rechargeable battery packs and pointed to a sticker affixed to its side. "He logged his recharging and conditioning cycles. He did it faithfully every month," she said, "but he broke his tendencies here." Her finger tapped on the last entry. "He recharged all the batteries in this pack a full two weeks prior to when he normally would. John—it was the day before he was killed. It looks like he modified the case to hold another battery pack, too."

My eyes narrowed. "He knew something and was expecting trouble. He wasn't expecting it to arrive as quickly as it did."

"He was getting ready to bug out," she said, opening another case. "This is a hardened laptop, fully charged, and with spare batteries. They use these at construction sites and in the military because they're so hard to destroy. I bet if you look in that safe, you'll find the rest of his stuff."

I nodded. "What the hell was he into?"

"We've got to convince her to let us look at those computers," she said. "There are a least six. It could take weeks to get through all of them, maybe more. We need to start now!"

"Okay," I said, "We'll try."

* * *

Maureen was more pleasant than usual, but no less firm on her demands. Until she felt financially secure, she wasn't budging. Even Mack failed to erode her will. We left, empty handed.

"Turn left up here," Mack said as we neared an intersection. "I want to see if there is an alley that runs behind her property."

"All right," I said, turning the wheel, "but I'm not sure what you expect to gain."

"Just a hunch," she said.

As Mack had hoped, a narrow alley ran parallel to the street where Maureen lived. I drove slowly, stopping as we reached her back yard.

"As I hoped," she said, pulling out her phone.

"What is it?"

"When we were in the basement, I noticed that Barry had a rotator control box as part of his equipment."

"What does that do?"

"It controls the orientation of a directional antenna, like that one," she said, rolling down her window and pointing skyward. "I'm going to take a few pictures of it, then try to figure out where it is pointed."

I hadn't really noticed the radio tower tucked into the corner of Barry's property. It was tiny when compared to the massive, tall structures erected by commercial radio and television stations, but it was more than sufficient to lift an antenna higher than the surrounding rooftops.

The antenna was unfamiliar to me, too. It looked a bit like a television antenna from years gone by, only much larger. Mack, however, seemed to understand its function, so I allowed her to proceed, unencumbered by the myriad of questions that raced around my mind.

"Okay," she said, climbing back in the car and rolling up the window. "Let's go home."

* * *

Mack was silent the entire trip home, focused intently on whatever she was doing. Immediately upon our arrival, she went to our office, providing me no additional information as to the nature of her activities.

This gave me the opportunity to finally relieve Tom, our investigator, of the albatross that was my old case files. We spent several hours reviewing the handful of candidates he had identified, finally settling on two names that were worthy of some additional consideration.

Fred Zeigler was the first name mentioned. A thoroughly reprehensible human, I had earned a conviction against him for murdering his girlfriend with a bayonet. In retrospect, the case set the wheels of my disenchantment with the legal system in motion. After committing such a heinous crime, the man should have never again sniffed the air of freedom, but that wasn't how justice played out for him. Through a plea arrangement, in trade for testifying against a drug dealer, we opened the door to the possibility of parole.

I hated the arrangement and made no secret of it. I wanted Zeigler to rot in a prison cell forever, but the testimony was deemed too valuable to miss. In spite of impassioned pleas by the victim's family, the parole board released him, two weeks prior to the murder of Rick Stevens.

The second name Tom identified shocked me. He had singled out Tamara Yost, a woman convicted of killing her husband. I remembered the case well, because I felt that justice had not been done. Tamara drove a knife into her husband's stomach, then killed him with a bullet to the brain. Those facts were not in doubt. The miscarriage, in my mind, was that she had spent ten years in an abusive marriage and finally took what she saw as the only way out. Of course, she waited until the man was passed-out drunk to do it and in so doing, sealed her fate.

I didn't consider her a threat or a plausible candidate for Barry's murderer, but it did remind me that we had all ignored the possibility that he could have been killed by a woman.

* * *

A short call to O'Neil set in motion an investigation into Fred Zeigler's whereabouts during the murders.

"It strikes me as a long shot, Costa, but I'll call his parole officer and see if Fred's been a good boy since getting out of prison. By the way, your friend from Northern Ireland gave me a call the other day."

"Oh? Which friend is that?"

"Jasik, the Bosnian man. He sent me all the stuff on his serial killer theory that he sent to you."

"Good. Are you going to test the paper?"

"Costa, do you have any idea how much it is going to cost the taxpayers to run all the tests needed to confirm the origin of the paper?"

"Cost the taxpayers? George, we have two murders on our side. I would expect it to be standard procedure to perform forensic analysis on all of the evidence found at the crime scene, not a cost-benefit analysis!"

"We analyzed both notes for DNA evidence and fingerprints. Our lab confirmed that the card stock used was the same in both notes, but that is a far cry from spending tens of thousands of dollars on a hare brained theory of a serial killer."

"Why the stonewall, George? I'll pay for the damn tests personally. In your shoes, I'd want to know what I'm dealing with. There were nine murders in Yugoslavia, three in the Philippines, and three in Argentina last year, and all of them are linked."

"This friend of yours—Jasik—how much do you trust him?"

"He's a little crazy, but he saved my life on at least one occasion in Belfast last year."

"There's a reason, you know, why international law enforcement isn't falling all over itself to catch this supposed serial killer."

"Why's that?"

"Because no government or official police agency has ever independently verified that any of the murders are related. Hell, we don't even know if the murders that happened during the Yugoslav war were the work of the same person. There's a fairly sizable contingency, hell, a majority, that believes the so-called serial killer was an invention of rogue elements during the war, likely to cover up atrocities."

"But the paper…"

"A crowd stormed the Stasi headquarters in 1990. Any number of people could have gotten their hands on this supposedly unique paper. Today, I can buy Stasi memorabilia on line. I'm sorry, John. I know you're trying to find out who killed your friend, as are we, but I don't think we're dealing with the same murderer your Bosnian pal is trying to find—if that person ever existed at all. If you still want to pay for testing, I'm sure you'll find a way, but I suggest you save your money and buy something nice for Miss MacDonald for Christmas. Like a diamond ring."

CHAPTER FIFTEEN

Ashley Vinton's apartment complex was nestled in what looked to be a quiet, suburban neighborhood. The counterintuitive numbering scheme nearly caused me to be late, but thanks to setting a brisk pace from my car to her landing, I knocked on her door precisely at 8 PM.

I didn't know the woman who answered the door, but she seemed to know me.

"Mister Costa!" she bubbled, "come in, come in."

"Mrs. Vinton, I presume?"

"Eva Peretti," she said. "May I take your coat?"

"Certainly. I brought wine," I said, glancing around for a place to put the bag I was carrying. "I didn't know what we were having, so I brought both red and white."

Eva, moving like a whirlwind, collected my parcel and disappeared into another room. She returned, moments later to take my coat. "Please," she said, motioning for me to follow.

Leaving the small foyer, we turned a corner into the living room. Ashley was seated in a comfortable chair in the opposite corner. Her leg, wrapped in a cast that looked restrictive and uncomfortable, rested on a stack of pillows atop a coffee table repurposed to serve as a footrest. Crutches leaned against the corner.

She looked tired, but I could tell that the ordeal hadn't reduced her spunk. She started to reach for her crutches when Eva interceded.

"Ash, you stay put! Mister Costa will understand if you don't stand. You need to follow the doctor's instructions."

"Of course," I said, walking over to her chair, hugging her as best I could, given the situation.

"I'm supposed to take it easy and keep it elevated," she explained. "First snow of the year, and instead of being online looking for places to go skiing, I'm stuck in front of the television."

"I've only gone skiing once," I said, "and it wasn't the most pleasant experience."

"When Ashley's leg is better, we'll have to go," interjected Eva, reappearing from another room, "all three of us. Ashley can teach you. She's quite good."

"Mother!" Ashley said, rolling her eyes.

"Seriously, Mister Costa, she is," Eva said, dragging me from the living room into the adjacent dining room. She pointed to a shelf full of trophies. "See? All Ashley's. In college, she was a few hundredths of a second from qualifying for the Olympics. I think the timekeeper cheated."

"The timekeeper did not cheat," Ashley said, "and I was a few hundredths of a second from earning a spot in the U.S. Olympic trials, not the Olympics."

"Impressive!" I said, returning to the living room. "I knew that you were athletic the way you avoided that forklift."

"The landing wasn't so good," she quipped.

Eva arrived carrying three wine glasses, two filled with red wine. The third barely had enough to taste. "Sorry, Ash," she said, handing me a full glass. "The doctors said you're not allowed to have much alcohol, but I don't think this little bit will hurt you. Let's drink a quick toast to Mister Costa."

"Make it a toast to your daughter, too. It was her quick thinking that alerted me to the approaching danger. And please, call me John."

We raised our glasses. Idle chatter dominated the next half hour until Eva announced that dinner was ready. With my help, Ashley made her way to the table, using the extra chair to prop up her injured leg.

Eva's culinary skills were remarkable, her meal rivaling the best I'd eaten on a trip to Italy eight years before. How either of them kept so trim and fit was beyond me, but perhaps they were blessed with good DNA. Pictures dating back to Ashley's childhood adorned the walls, and I couldn't detect any noticeable change in Eva's appearance over the years. Her jet black hair, curly and shoulder length, didn't betray a single strand of gray. Only a few subtle wrinkles at the corner of her eyes, likely from smiling, gave any hint whatsoever that she was over the age of forty. And smile, she did often, exuding a genuine love for life—and talk!

We were nearly to dessert when Ashley finally got a solitary moment of my time. "I'm sorry if my mother is overwhelming you," she said. "She has been eager to meet you since I mentioned our chance encounter."

"She's fine, Ashley. I don't mind."

"I didn't want the evening to slip away without telling you a couple of things. They might be important, or they might be unrelated, but it is better that you should know."

"Of course. What's on your mind?"

"Well, it may be only a rumor, but given my own observations, I think there might be some truth to it."

"What?"

"Barry Myers was awfully friendly with one of the ladies in the Human Resources department, Clarissa Jones. I think you met her when you visited."

"Do you think there was anything going on? I mean, like an affair?"

"I don't really know. It would be out of character for both of them, but I've seen stranger things happen."

"I'll investigate, but I'll do it discretely. I don't condone infidelity, but I *have* met Barry's wife…"

Ashley laughed, gently. "The second is a bit more concrete, but I don't know how much good it is going to do you to know. Quantelle takes out company-owned life insurance policies on some of its key employees. I only know this because my department is required to provide documentation on the risks in their work environment. Barry Myers was one of the employees for whom they carried a policy, and a sizable one, at that."

"How much?"

"I happened to get a glimpse of it when it passed through our office. It was ten million dollars, I believe, and that was two years ago."

"Do you know who the beneficiary was?"

"I'm sure it was payable to the company, but as to who handles the claims or payments, I have no idea. I just thought you should know. Ten million dollars isn't a trivial amount of money."

"True, but to a corporation the size of Quantelle, it might be a drop in the bucket. Still good to know, though. Thank you for sharing."

"Well, I was specifically instructed to help in your investigation in any way possible…"

"So you were!"

Ashley's mother reappeared with plans for more wine, then dessert, followed by coffee. Kevin, at his own insistence, waited in the car. I cited this in an attempt to make it an early evening, but Eva would have none of it. She marched out of Ashley's apartment, collected Kevin, and damn near dragged him in.

"Mister Costa," he whispered, "I would prefer to wait outside. If there is a threat, it is easier for me to respond if I see it coming."

"I understand, but you're risking running afoul of Italian hospitality. I don't think we're in significant danger tonight. Try to make the best of it."

"Understood."

He stayed true to his word, hanging at the periphery and eschewing alcohol. Finally, though, at Eva's insistence, he entered the conversation. It only took a few well-crafted sentences on his part for Ashley to take notice. The chemistry between them was immediate and obvious. It wasn't long before I quietly slipped into the dining room, feeling distinctly like a third wheel.

"They seem to be getting along quite well," Eva said, refilling my wine glass.

"They do," I said, smiling. "Kevin is a man full of surprises. It isn't every day that you discover your bodyguard was originally an

English lit. major. He seems to know his Shakespeare quite well, but I don't really know his prowess as a guard."

"That's a good thing, isn't it?"

"Yes, I suppose it is."

"John, be honest with me. Do you think Ashley is in danger? Was that forklift aimed at you or at her?"

"I don't know. Truly, I don't."

"If you think it is wise, I could send her to my mother's for a while, or she could visit her father, although I don't think she'd go for the latter unless things were desperate."

"She doesn't get along with her father?"

"They get along all right, I guess. The bigger issue is his new wife. She's young enough to be Ashley's sister."

"Oh my! I can see how that could be a bit awkward."

"Well, it was my ex-husband's choice. I don't know if he wanted to buy a new car, so to speak, or just take it for a test drive. It didn't matter to me; he was gone and good riddance!"

The source of Ashley's indomitable spunk was obvious.

"I got the paid-for house, the bank account, and a new car out of the deal. He got his freedom and his bimbo."

"I think he's absolutely, freaking crazy," I blurted, my tongue likely loosened by the prodigious amount of wine I had consumed.

"Thank you," she said. "I have to confess, I researched you a bit. When Ashley told me about you and her plans to invite you over for dinner, I wanted to learn what I could. You can't be too careful these days."

"Smart," I replied. "You're a good mom. I can tell that you really care."

"The divorce definitely brought us closer," she said. "I did my homework on you, and by all indications, you seem to be a good man. You have had quite a rough run of luck lately, though."

I nodded. "Things certainly didn't end the way I hoped they would. Some days, I do pretty well. Others are rough."

"Do you have dreams about her?"

Her question took me aback, to the point where I momentarily wondered if the entire evening had been a set up, orchestrated by my well-meaning researcher. My expression must've betrayed me, because she immediately touched my arm, gently.

"I'm sorry," she said. "Ashley's father was my second husband. I married my high school sweetheart. We had been together since my freshman year—and all the way through college. We graduated together and got married about a month later. Six months later, he was dead, killed in a car accident. I was depressed; then I was angry. The dreams were my only happy times."

"Sometimes, the dreams are so vivid, when I wake up, I'm confused about what was the dream and what was real. Then I find myself angry—angry that I woke up at all. Because then reality sets in, and I know that she's gone. Does it ever get better?"

"It did for me, but it took a while. Somewhere along the line, the dreams came less frequently. I started to understand that they were a blessing and not a curse. It was like he was stopping by to check up on me, making sure I was okay; that he wanted me to be happy. It seemed that all the things I wanted to tell him, he somehow knew. You probably think I'm nuts, but that's how I got through it."

"I don't think you're nuts. Anything but, actually. I'm sorry—I didn't mean to put a damper on the evening."

"You didn't. I asked, and you were honest, which I appreciate." She excused herself, returning moments later with a business card in her hand. "I'm not much for game playing or subtlety," she said, handing me the card. "My cell phone number is on the back. Let's have coffee, or dinner, if you're feeling adventurous. Or call if you just want to chat. I understand what you're going through, so no pressure, okay?"

I smiled, taking the card. "I think that sounds like a great idea. I'm working on this case, though, so if I don't call right away, don't think I've lost interest."

"Sounds like a plan!"

CHAPTER SIXTEEN

Mack was waiting for me when I returned from Ashley's apartment.

"My, but you had a late night, especially since you told me it would only take a couple of hours."

"Sorry, Mom. Would you like to smell my breath to see if I've been smoking and drinking?"

She started to make a face, but stopped, abruptly.

"What is it?" I asked.

"That look."

"What look?"

"Your look. I haven't seen that look from you in a long time." She paused, studying me.

"I didn't realize I had a look, Mack."

"The last time I saw that look... you met someone, didn't you?"

"I meet people all the time."

"That isn't what I mean, and you know it. Ashley Vinton? I know I'm always preaching that age is only a number, but... really?"

"No. Eva Peretti."

"Oh, Ashley's mother. I thought you two might get along."

115

"Wait a minute, Mack. How did you know about Ashley's mother?"

"Because I'm a woman, and I'm smarter than you."

"Did you set all that up? Because if you did, I'm not going to be happy about it."

"If I had, what would it matter?"

"It would be like a betrayal; a vote of no confidence."

"Well, if it makes you feel better, I didn't set it up. She called, mostly to check up on you. I, of course, lied through my teeth and told her what a good person you are."

"Thank you, Mack."

"When you're sober…"

"Mack!"

"And not kicking puppies…"

"Mack!!"

"I stayed up, mostly to tell you not to drink any more tonight. We need to get started first thing in the morning. Quantelle sent over their first batch of documentation, and we need to go over it. Oh, and Captain O'Neil called. Fred Zeigler has an airtight alibi for both murders."

"Oh well," I sighed. "It was a long shot, at best."

"I have some interesting information about Barry Myers. His phone is starting to reveal some secrets."

"Do any of them have to do with Clarissa Jones?"

She looked at me, her expression somewhere between surprised and impressed. "Some do. How did you know?"

"Because I'm a man, and I'm pretty damn smart, too. Good night, Mack!"

* * *

I was actually the first one to the breakfast table, in spite of Mack's insistence of an early start. She arrived some fifteen minutes later and headed straight for the fresh pot of coffee I had brewed.

"Sorry," she said. "I started working on something and wanted to get to a good stopping point."

"No worries. Here's a little tidbit to start your day: According to Ashley, Quantelle carried a company-owned life insurance policy on Barry, worth at least ten million dollars."

She wrinkled her nose. "Not common, but also not unheard of, especially given the importance of his role."

"Speaking of insurance, there seems to be a little discrepancy in the amount of life insurance, too. Clarissa Jones told me that Barry had coverage of thrice his annual salary, but when Maureen mentioned it to me, the number she quoted was slightly less. Perhaps she misspoke, but the way things are going, I'm going to check every loose end."

"I think," Mack said, refilling her coffee, "we should have a talk with Miss Jones. I was able to retrieve the logs from Barry's phone. There were quite a few calls to her work number and even more to a cellular number I'd bet belongs to her."

"Agreed."

"The second SIM was interesting, too. There were a series of international calls, made exclusively on it, never from the primary SIM. Do you want to know where the calls went?"

"Of course I do!"

"There were some that were clearly related to business. In fact, I was able to trace almost all the calls to the UK, Ireland, France, Germany, Spain, and Italy to Quantelle locations."

"Makes sense, I guess, especially since he was instrumental in setting up their warehouse flows and layouts."

"Yes, indeed, but that doesn't explain a large number of calls to Slovenia, Croatia, Serbia, Montenegro, Albania, and Bosnia and Herzegovina. Quantelle has no presence in these countries. Perhaps they are working to setup distribution hubs there."

"If they are," I sighed, "they're probably not going to be in any hurry to tell us, especially since it isn't germane to the attack at the warehouse."

"Perhaps, but then again, it might be worth asking. They were pretty forthcoming in their initial delivery."

"Oh? What did they send?"

"I was surprised, honestly. They sent me security camera footage, plus a fair bit of information on the forklift used in the attack."

She motioned for me to follow her into the office. "It's a little easier to explain with screens where we can see everything. Here," she said, tapping on some keys as an image appeared on several monitors.

"What am I looking at?"

"This is forklift B-106, the one that tried to skewer you. The old fellow went out with quite a bang."

"That's one way to look at it."

"B-106 was one of four of its type, the Hanlon Mark 1, remaining at this Quantelle location. All four are in the backup pool and are slated to be sold at the end of the year. They took delivery of newer models in July, and those have been in daily service since their arrival. B-106 and the three others like it were relegated to service only when others are down for service or routine maintenance."

"Not sure where you're going with this, but, okay."

She continued, unfazed. "The newer models are so much more efficient, that they freed up Mark 2 models for the backup pool, making B-106 and all the other Mark 1 forklifts absolutely redundant. In order to save space, B-106 and the others like it were moved to an area near the loading dock."

"So it wasn't in regular use."

"Correct. In fact, there are all sorts of problems with what happened the day you were attacked. First of all, B-106 wasn't in service and wasn't on the docket to be in service. The entire fleet of newer forklifts was in service, and the backup pool was full and working as well. But that's not the half of it."

I could tell Mack was getting excited about her findings. She continued, almost forgetting to breathe.

"These forklifts run on a bank of lead acid batteries—really big car batteries, essentially. When the decision was made to retire the old forklifts, the maintenance crews systematically harvested the best and newest of their batteries, replacing them with the worst. Quantelle provided an in-depth service report for each forklift. The battery maneuvering is recorded, right down to the serial numbers."

"So they swapped some batteries around. I'm not sure how this matters."

"Patience, oh confused one! Not only did the old forklifts get bad batteries, they weren't being charged or maintained. In other words, they sat there for months, their batteries, which were bad to start with, slowly draining the entire time. B-106 is lucky it had enough juice to make it out of its parking place without help, let alone attacking you. There's yet another oddity at work here."

"What is it?"

"B-106 was hacked so that it would go faster than its governor normally allowed. I did a little research into this, and it turns out to be a common trick people play. Thanks to a design flaw, it is easy to do. There are tons of videos all over the internet of people doing silly things with hacked Hanlon Mark 1 forklifts. The problem is, the hack not only causes instability from going faster than the vehicle really should go, it ages the motors, but most of all, it consumes the batteries far more quickly than normal operation. Long and short of it: B-106 couldn't have attacked you at the speed it did unless it had good, fully-charged batteries. But according to Quantelle's own service records, it had anything but."

"So someone figured out I was coming and put in new batteries?"

"It isn't exactly that easy."

"It's like a car battery, right? I can change a car battery." Mack scowled at me. "Okay. I can pay someone to change the car battery for me."

"You know, I keep hoping that one of these days, you'll appreciate my brilliance," she said, rolling her eyes. "The batteries come in packs. For the type of forklifts we're talking about, the pack is about the size of your car's engine, and it weighs thousands of pounds, thanks to all of the lead. It requires special equipment and skill to change one. Nobody knew you were going to Quantelle until Maureen called them late in the afternoon the day before you arrived. There wasn't time to order, receive, and prepare new batteries, which leaves only one possibility."

I looked at her, expectantly. "Continue…"

"Someone installed one of the spare battery packs Quantelle maintains. The Hanlon Mark 1 and Mark 2 models take the same batteries."

"Does their report confirm this?"

"It conveniently neglected to cover that little detail, which strikes me as intentional. It smacks of an inside job."

'That, it does, and that's likely why they've kept it from us."

"The good news is that the maintenance data includes the names of the people that performed the work, the supervisors, and so forth. I've already started making some inquiries about them. This fellow named Lance seems to be the most prevalent name."

"I remember the name," I said. "He's the one that Ashley was talking to on the radio; he gave us clearance to leave the walkway. Sounds like I should have a conversation with him, too."

"Oh! The radio! I almost forgot," said Mack. "They discovered why the radios stopped working the morning you were there. Someone stole one of their two-way radios and modified it. It was set to transmit continuously on both channels, which effectively jammed their system until its battery ran out. Quantelle turned it over to the police to examine. I wish I would've gotten a look at it first, because I'd like to know what triggered it. Didn't you say the radios were working?"

"As far as I know. There was a fellow who came by to tell us the lights weren't working and that we should take another route. His radio was functional, but when Ashley tried to call, her radio didn't work. What kind of skill would it take to modify a radio like that?"

"It would take a decent knowledge of electronics and access to schematics for the radios in question."

"Do you think an amateur radio operator would have possessed the knowledge and skill to modify the radio? Would Barry?"

She frowned. "You don't think Barry was somehow involved, do you?"

"No, I'm just trying to understand the skills needed."

"It's possible that a ham could perform the modifications. Skills vary rather dramatically from one ham to another. Some are retired broadcast professionals, others memorized the questions and passed the test. In Barry's case, given his level of license, the length of time he held it, and the equipment in his basement, I'd say there's a decent chance that it would have been within his capability."

"What about the modification to the forklift?"

120

"Even less skill required. For perspective, you might be able to do it, given enough time and practice. Maybe."

"Gee, thanks for the vote of confidence."

She winked at me.

"What else do you have?"

"They also sent us the video of the attack. It isn't as good as it could be due to the lower light, but I was able to enhance it a bit. Take a look."

She played the video on one of the large screen monitors. The events unfolded largely as I remembered them.

"I sent this to a friend of mine. She happens to be married to a forklift operator. His comment was that the operator appeared to be inexperienced operating the lift. An experienced driver wouldn't have over steered the way your driver did."

"In other words, we were damn lucky."

"Pretty much. I also did some analysis of the driver. He made quite a graceful exit."

"Indeed."

"Photogrammetry places the driver's height between five foot, six and five foot, eight. I would assume slender build, but the clothing masks a lot of the details."

"Nice work, Mack. I'm going to stop by Quantelle this afternoon and press them for more details on access to the forklift maintenance area. I also plan on talking to Miss Jones and Lance. What's his last name?"

"It looks like it begins with the letter Y, but after that, it is more or less a squiggly line."

"I'm sure they can help sort this out. Take a nap, Mack. You look tired."

"Meh. I can rest when I'm dead."

CHAPTER SEVENTEEN

The receptionist, a pleasant young woman with reddish-brown hair, chatted with me until Clarissa Jones arrived to take me to her office. We walked quietly through several short hallways before arriving. She closed the door behind us, offered me a chair, and sat down behind her desk.

"I'm afraid I owe you and your client an apology," she said. "There was a delay in the paperwork."

"My client is eager for a swift resolution of her claim."

She paused, sighing. "I guess there's no point in beating around the bush. I'm the delay, Mister Costa. When I received the forms from the insurance company, they really threw me for a loop. Honestly, I didn't exactly know what to do."

She handed me the papers, and within a few glances, it was easy to see why she was shaken. Barry Myers had listed her as a beneficiary, set to receive fifty thousand dollars, with the remaining amount targeted for Maureen.

"I'm going to have to give the forms to someone else within the company to sign, and I'm not sure what that's going to happen in terms of my employment."

"That may be the least of your worries," I said, handing the papers back to her. "This gives you motive. The police will likely consider you a suspect once this comes to light."

"I didn't know Barry was going to do this," she insisted, "and I certainly had nothing to do with his death."

"Whatever you do, don't talk to the police. When they want to talk to you, and I'm sure they will, you call this number and keep quiet." I took one of her business cards, and wrote a number on the back. "This is the best lawyer in town."

"Thank you," she said, slipping the card into her purse.

"Were you and Barry having an affair?"

My question was direct, but it didn't seem to shake her.

"No, nothing like that. I expect this is the reason he put me on his insurance policy." She handed me a picture of two children.

"Barry's?"

"No. Just the happy results of two unhappy and ill-advised relationships. Barry was my friend, Mister Costa. He was twenty years older than me, but the first time we met, it was like we'd known each other for our entire lives. We'd have lunch together every week. The only thing that stopped it was if I had a sick kid and had to miss work or he was out of town. We'd talk on the phone or by text. He'd ask how the kids were doing and if we needed anything. I'd help him select presents for his wife for her birthday or holidays. He was a sweet man, and I'm going to miss him terribly. I'd never do anything to hurt him."

I believed her. Although I didn't really know Barry outside the Wednesday music session, her description of him seemed in line with my impressions of the man.

"It sounds like you might have known him better than anyone, even his wife. Can you think of anyone who would want to hurt him?"

"I really can't think of anyone," she said, her voice falling. "He was quiet, and by all indications, did his job really well. Nobody ever had a problem with him."

"In the days or weeks leading up to his death, did you see any change in his behavior? Did he seem anxious? Was anything bothering him?"

"I didn't think much of it at the time, but the last time we had lunch, he seemed a bit distant. I suppose you could say that something was bothering him. I just chalked it up to the fact that things were getting busy at work. I figured if he wanted to talk about it, he would. He didn't, and I let it go."

"What day was this?"

"Thursday. Six days before he was killed. I hadn't seen much of him around the office the week he died, but that wasn't unusual. We didn't always cross paths in the normal course of our days."

"I have a few more questions if you're feeling up to it."

"I'll answer if I can," she replied.

"Quantelle's lawyers sent me some documentation on the forklift that was used in the attack against me There are several people mentioned, and I'd like to talk to them. Can you help set it up?"

"I'll have to run it by legal, but yes. I can do that. Who are you interested in talking to?"

"Some of the people on this report. I can't make out all the names because of the handwriting." I showed her the maintenance report.

"These two work on different shifts, so they won't be here now," she said, pointing to the first two lines on the form. "This person should be here, and this is the floor manager."

"Lance?"

"Lance Yannis, yes. You won't be able to talk to him, however, until he gets back from vacation. He's somewhere in the Southwest, I think, and won't have cellular reception most of the time. He goes on these crazy, long hikes for days on end. No thank you! But the other man you asked about should be around. Let me make sure it's okay."

I waited, silently, while she talked to the legal department. Within moments, she had her answer.

"Let's go," she said. "I've been given instructions to assist your investigation in any way possible."

* * *

"What you're looking for is over here," Walter Osterman said, motioning to an area to the left of the sprawling shipping dock. Three well-used forklifts were parked, facing the wall. "The police impounded the fourth Mark 1 lift."

"What is the condition of the battery packs in these?"

"Not too good," he chuckled, pulling a meter off his belt. Skillfully, he removed a panel from the nearest forklift and reached inside with a pair of probes. "This one will be lucky to make it to the service area without needing a push."

"How far away is that?"

"Just over here," he said, motioning to the left. "Follow me."

An interior wall jutted out from the taller, external wall, creating a series of offices. The wall extended well beyond the end of the last window, creating an area where the forklifts and batteries could be serviced.

"This is where we keep things running. We can work on everything from mechanics to hydraulics to electrical back here. Was there something in particular you wanted to see?"

"I'm interested in the battery packs. B-106 was supposed to have a weak battery, like the one you tested a few minutes ago, but it didn't."

"Yeah, that bothered me too," he said, "but it happens every now and then with all the lifts, new and old. Someone gets in a hurry and forgets to log a swap. When we got the new shipment of lifts back in the summer, we migrated all of the bad cells to the lifts we were getting rid of. Here is the pack that should have been with B-106." He motioned to a large tray of batteries connected to a device that looked like an oversized battery charger. "The police came by yesterday and tried to get fingerprints from it, but it had been handled too many times. Hell, how was I supposed to know? It was just another battery pack until I ran its tracking number and found out it wasn't where it should have been. They impounded the lift with the good pack, now I'm down one of our good spares until the replacement I ordered arrives."

"How long does it take to swap out these batteries?" I asked.

"The packs? Assuming one is available, is fully charged and watered—not all that long."

"Less than two hours?"

"Definitely, assuming you have a pack that is ready to go."

"So, it's possible that someone could have discovered I was here and changed the battery pack?"

"Sure, but I don't think it happened that way."

"Why not?"

"Because I was here all morning and would've known about it. It had to have happened sometime the day before—maybe even on one of the other shifts. Lance would be the person to talk to about that. He reviews all of the logs first thing in the morning. Probably wouldn't be a bad idea to talk to my counterparts on the other shifts, too. If the packs got swapped, it had to happen then."

"Batteries are that important?"

"Hell yes, they are. Without them, we can't run our business. It's that simple."

"We're awfully close to the loading dock, and people seem to be coming and going all the time. Is this area secured?"

"Not really, but staff is here nearly all the time."

"Nearly?"

"There's probably a couple times in a week when there is a gap in the coverage, like if a shift change happens early or late due to workload, a lift that can't make it back for service, or a team meeting—things like that."

"Anything like that recently?"

"Not on my shift, apart from the events you already know about."

* * *

"Mack," I sighed, "I don't feel like we're getting anywhere. At least this pizza is good," I said, referring to our dinner. "This isn't our usual."

"Eva Peretti recommended this place. You've been ordering from Dominic's for so long, that you've not looked elsewhere. This place is within a block of our normal spot and has quicker delivery; just more proof that sometimes the best things are hidden in plain sight."

"I'm beginning to detect a conspiracy brewing," I said, looking annoyed. "You two are in cahoots!"

"Yes, it is a grand conspiracy to get you tasty pizza and introduce you to nice people that are interested in being friends with you. My nefarious plan has been unmasked!"

Sensing that I was likely on unstable intellectual ground, I quietly let the subject drop. "Seriously, I don't feel that we've made much headway."

"I'm not sure I agree with you," Mack said, pulling the pepperoni off her slice of pizza, then eating them one by one. "You learned a hell of a lot about forklift batteries."

"God help me, if Walter would have gone on much longer, my head would have exploded! I thought a battery was a battery. Little did I know!"

"Speaking of which, I spent most of the afternoon looking at the video of the infamous forklift incident, along with some of the other security footage Quantelle sent. I took the time to enhance some of the alternate views, and I'm beginning to wonder about something."

"What's that?"

"Take a look at this," she said, motioning toward her monitor. "This is the attack, but from the opposite direction. The camera was a long way from the action, so I had to do some wizardry to stabilize it. Watch the driver's hand."

"It just looks like a mush of pixels to me, Mack."

She pointed to the monitor. "A hand," she said. "Take my word for it. Now…" she advanced the video slowly, frame by frame. "Right here. The forklift has stabilized after the initial wiggle it gave but then, a flick of the hand causes it to oversteer."

"Yes. I see that. Do you think the driver was inexperienced?"

"Could be, but we've only been looking at one possibility: the forklift was aimed at either you or Ashley."

"That's because it was, Mack. I was there, remember."

"What if the intention was never to hit either of you, but to scare you off? Or, maybe, to catch your attention? We haven't looked at it from that perspective."

I sat back in my chair, contemplating her words while sipping my Guinness. Had the theory come from anyone else, I might have summarily dismissed it. "You might be onto something," I said, "although I'm not sure where it gets us."

"There is one commonality running through all this," she said, twirling her hair. "Clarissa Jones admitted that Barry's behavior had subtly changed right before he was murdered. Same general theme from Jennifer Adams regarding Rick. Barry went chasing after you, and Rick had your card, for reasons we don't fully understand. Maybe the forklift driver needed to get your attention, and that was the only method available to him."

"I can think of better ways. A phone call comes to mind."

CHAPTER EIGHTEEN

The first report arrived from Zonk, and it was anything but enlightening. The recent events at Quantelle obviously had them on high alert. Security and safety monitors were everywhere. His solution was to apply for a later shift in the hopes that the watchfulness decreased after the muckety-mucks left the building. It seemed to make sense, so I issued my approval through our agreed communication channel.

"Call Maureen," Mack said, deeply focused on whatever she was working on.

I tried to ask some questions, but received no reply other than the constant clicking of her keyboard.

* * *

I was in no mood to deal with Maureen Myers. Our phone call, short on details, felt more like a summoning than a conversation. Reluctantly, I climbed into my car and headed to her house.

"Barry received some mail that I'd like you to interpret for me," she said, handing me a letter from a major insurance company.

I scanned the letter, extracting the salient points fairly quickly. "It looks," I said, handing the letter back to her, "like Barry had a life insurance policy with this company. Do you know where he kept paperwork for things like this? I can check."

"Probably in the left side of that desk," she said. "Take a look if you want."

Going through the drawer, I found several letters from the same company before eventually finding a policy summary.

"It looks like this policy is worth half a million dollars," I said. "I can start the process if you want."

"Of course I goddamn want," she said. "How soon will I get the money?"

True love—measured in dollar signs. "I don't know, Maureen. We have everything we need, but with the cause of death officially listed as a homicide, it may complicate things. I don't have the full policy in front of me to know for sure."

"Well, Fido, you go do your thing."

"You know, I think it's about time you stopped the nonsense and leveled with me. You say you want the insurance money right away, but the only reason you knew about the policy was from a random letter that arrived. If you had let me go through Barry's things right away, you would be closer to your precious payoff. Who knows what might be lurking on his computers downstairs, but you won't let me look at them."

She laughed. "Do you want to know what Barry told me?"

"Yes, I do."

"The last thing he said to me was that there were some problems at work, and he thought you might be able to help."

My face flushed. "That might have been nice to know before I went barging around there," I growled. "Here's what's going to happen. You're going to let my assistant go through Barry's computers, his paperwork, and whatever the hell he's storing in those two big safes downstairs, or you can find yourself another attorney."

"Suit yourself, Rover," she said. "Barry was probably researching the secret formula for infinite boredom. You might find it interesting."

* * *

"Mack, I truly don't like that woman. I don't think I've ever had a client—if you can even call her that—treat me with such utter disdain."

"Suck it up, buttercup! I'm sure you'll survive." Mack winked at me.

"What's the world coming to," I said, rolling my eyes.

"An interesting conclusion, no doubt. Speaking of which, I tracked down a couple of those numbers in the Balkans I retrieved from Barry's cell phone. I think you're going to find this very interesting."

"I'm all ears."

"Several were to law enforcement agencies. There were two that captured my attention, mostly because of the length of the conversation. One ran thirty minutes, a call to Serbia; the other, to Bosnia and Herzegovina, lasted nearly an hour."

"To law enforcement? Do you think it could have anything to do with work, such as work permits, site regulations, and so forth?"

"First thing I thought of," she said. "It's entirely possible that he called a general number and was routed to where he ultimately needed to go, but why would he do that when the right numbers and procedures are relatively easy to find online?"

"Perhaps his Internet searching skills are on par with mine."

"You've gotten better," she said, rolling her eyes.

"Yeah, thanks to my futile obsession, right?"

"I didn't mean it like that," she said.

"It's okay. Nobody has to believe me. I find it hard to believe," I said, redirecting the conversation, "that all this is a coincidence, the Bosnian stuff, I mean."

"I don't think it is coincidental at all," Mack said. "Barry's antenna was pointed to that part of the world, too. It isn't perfect, mind you. The same general antenna orientation would work for reaching Spain, southern France, and Italy. Or any place beyond—like the Ukraine, and central Russia."

"Is there any way to know who he might have been talking to?"

"Amateur operators are supposed to keep a log of all their contacts. If we can find it, maybe it will tell us something."

"Stop what you're doing, Mack. We're going to pay Maureen an unexpected visit."

* * *

Maureen Myers seemed happy to see Mack and thoroughly indifferent to my presence, a situation that I found quite satisfactory. I was terrified that she would receive the news about Barry's generosity toward his co-worker poorly. She sat quietly, reflecting on my words, before she spoke.

"The girl's name is Clarissa? No affair? Two kids? No husband?"

"Correct."

"Okay," she said, lighting a cigarette. "What else do you want?"

It took a fair bit of negotiating to get Maureen to agree to my earlier demands, but Mack finally prevailed. She headed for the basement, while I worked my way through Barry's records.

Barry was hopelessly disorganized, even by my lax standards, so finding items of interest took far longer than I expected. Nevertheless, I emerged several hours later. "I have some good news, Maureen," I said.

She greeted my words with a billowing plume of cigarette smoke, directly toward my face. It took all of my willpower to avoid coughing. Once the smoke cleared, it took equal willpower not to strangle her on the spot.

"Please don't do that again."

"You'll live," she grunted. "You said you had news…"

"I found the documentation on Barry's 401(K) account," handing her the document. "Here is an IRA he had, likely rolled over from his previous employer. Worth about three hundred thousand

132

between them."

"Cash 'em in," she said, between puffs on her cigarette.

"We need to go through the proper channels to get them transferred to you, and there may be negative tax implications. I'd really prefer if it you'd talk to a retirement professional."

"Thieves," she grunted. "I'll end up broke."

"What is the damned emergency for money, Maureen?"

"Look at my damn checking account balance," she said, pointing to her check register. "I've got three hundred dollars."

"There hasn't been a deposit recorded to this account in several months," I said, handing the checkbook back to her.

"Barry handled the deposits, and I wrote the checks."

"I think we need to take a trip to your bank," I said. "Something isn't adding up for me."

"He had a lot of our bills setup to automatically debit," she said. "Some months, there wasn't much left for anything but the essentials."

"Odd," I said, handing her another document. "This is an investment account that is in both your names. There's a bit over a hundred thousand in there."

"I suppose I have to wait to do anything with this one, too?"

"No. Your name is on the account. You should be able to do whatever you want with it, but please, don't do anything crazy. Let's go to your bank first and see if my suspicions are correct. Then, if I'm wrong, you can sell off some of this stock."

* * *

Maureen wasn't happy with the prospects of leaving Mack alone in her house while she went to the bank with me, but after some tense negotiations, she agreed.

"I want to talk to a different banker," she said, studying the first young man that offered to help us. "He's too young to possibly know what he's doing."

"I'm thirty-four years old, Mrs. Myers," he explained, "and I've been working in banking for ten years now. If you'd still prefer someone else, I can talk to my manager."

"No," I said, interceding before Maureen could say something insulting, "I'm sure you'll do a wonderful job."

Maureen glowered at me, but, thankfully, remained silent.

It didn't take long before my suspicions were proven correct. The checking account that Maureen was faithfully tracking was a secondary account. Barry's paycheck went into a larger, primary account. Studying the transactions, a pattern emerged.

"It seems," I said, "Barry was dispersing funds from his paycheck to several other accounts. There are regular transfers to savings and to several investment accounts."

Barry wasn't ever going to be rich, but all indications pointed to conservative investing aimed toward a comfortable retirement. Even Maureen's account balance wasn't accurate, the actual balance being a factor of ten higher.

"What about our mortgages?" asked Maureen.

The banker clicked his mouse a few times, and a new screen appeared on the monitor. "The primary mortgage has been paid off for about four years. The second is only a line of credit, and it hasn't been used."

"But..." she said.

"Looks like Barry was investing the money he claimed was going toward the mortgage," I interjected before she could finish. "Not sure why he felt the necessity to do that, but you're anything but broke."

The banker stepped in, doing his best to convince Maureen to start using their latest and greatest technology to track her accounts. I knew he was fighting a losing battle, but he soldiered on. Eventually we left, making virtually no progress beyond transferring some additional funds into her checking account.

"He's not trying to rob you," I said as we made our way slowly to my car. "This is a very reputable bank, you know."

"I don't trust any of them," she grunted, as I helped her into the passenger seat.

"I wish you'd consider working with a financial planner. Between the investments and the insurance policies, you've got a decent amount of money. Stuffing it in your mattress isn't a viable plan. If it makes you feel better, I can review what the planner tells you."

"I don't trust you, either," she said.

"What if Mack reviewed things. Do you trust her?"

"More than you, but that ain't saying much. Take me home, Rover."

* * *

When she finally got situated in her favorite chair, Maureen proclaimed, "This calls for a bourbon! Costa, you're going to drink with me, and so is your little friend."

Mack agreed, with unusual alacrity, especially since I knew she detested bourbon.

"I want to see if she'll let me take four of his computers," she whispered.

"To boring old Barry," Maureen, said, lifting her glass. "At least you tried, you stupid son of a bitch."

"To Barry," I repeated, quietly.

Perhaps it was just my imagination, but I thought I saw the hint of a tear in the corner of Maureen's eye.

* * *

"Mack, I sure hope these computers are worth it. I've never had to write the equivalent of a promissory note for something like this before."

"I must admit, she drives a hard bargain."

"She's unique, I'll give her that. I've never had a client that actively resisted my help with such fervor."

"You know," Mack said, her fingers massaging her temples, "we might want to start asking why. Perhaps that's just how she is, or she hates men, or whatever, but you've done nothing but work *for* her."

"True. What do you hope to get from those computers, anyway?"

"Likely, a headache. It's going to be another late night."

"Why don't you take the night off?"

"I've got too much to do. I still have to go through all the crap that Jennifer Adams gave us and now these computers…"

"Not only do you need to eat, you need to get a good night's sleep. When was the last time you slept more than a few hours."

She wrinkled her nose. "A couple of weeks ago, but…"

"I can sleep when I'm dead," I said, stealing her line. "But you also can't solve this crime when you're dead. Let's go get some dinner, and then have a nice, quiet evening that involves you actually sleeping."

"All right," she said, collecting her coat. "I can use a night off."

CHAPTER NINETEEN

Our simple, relaxing dinner turned into a much needed night out. An impromptu choice to see a movie followed by a late evening dessert run had us out until nearly one in the morning. So much for early to bed. As we turned onto my street, I noticed a strange car waiting near my driveway.

"Do you recognize it?" Mack asked, reacting almost immediately.

"No, but it looks like an undercover police car."

I was right. George O'Neil was waiting for me. "You two are certainly out late," he said, his tone anything but jovial. "Just where have you guys been, anyway?"

"Out buying your Christmas present, George. A box full of mind your own damned business."

"I'm sorry, but I've got to ask the question. Can you account for your last six hours?"

"I don't have to account for anything. What the hell is going on, anyway?"

"Jennifer Adams' body was found about two hours ago. I know you two weren't exactly on amicable terms, so I wanted to exclude you right away, before any of my superiors get any ideas."

There were times when I wished that lightning would strike her, but now that it figuratively had, it didn't bring any happiness or closure. O'Neil continued before I could say anything.

"It looked like she was on the run, from the reports we're getting. I've got detectives on their way to the scene, but they haven't reported in yet. It takes a couple hours to get there. Funny thing—she had your number in her cell phone. In fact, the last call she made on it was to you."

So much for my good advice about ditching her phone. I shouldn't have been surprised. Jennifer Adams always had everything figured out—even when she didn't. My words were little more than an annoying background buzz to her. It had never meant anything before, beyond the harbinger of doom for our so-called relationship. This time, it had likely been fatal.

"Come on in, George," I sighed. "So much for a fun, restful evening."

* * *

It was trivial to document our whereabouts. Between receipts and some frivolous pictures Mack had snapped on her cell phone, it was obvious that we couldn't have made it to wherever Jennifer was hiding.

"Jennifer had my number because she called me before she left town," I said. "She offered to tell me where she was going, but I intentionally didn't want to know."

"Why not?"

"Because she told me Rick Stevens had fallen in with some bad characters—Russians, perhaps—and she was scared. I figured that, just in case, it was better not to know. That way, I couldn't tell anyone."

"She was killed in the same way as the others," O'Neil said, "except for a few differences. It looks like she tried to run away, but someone shot her in the leg. She was also stabbed twice, rather than once."

"That's a significant change," I commented.

"It gets worse, and pardon my bluntness, but the first stab

138

wound wasn't fatal. We know because of the blood trail. The first wound was lower, to the genital region. Then came the same wounds as the other victims, with the final shot to the head. We're not sure if it was the same perpetrator or not. This one was drawn out and bloody, not the precision strikes we saw previously. Jennifer Adams suffered before she died. We don't think the other victims did."

"If Jenn ran, it seems logical that she might have recognized her attacker or at least sensed the imminent danger. Our other victims didn't see it coming."

"She just called you? There wasn't anything else?"

I could tell from his face that O'Neil already knew the answer.

"No. I met her at the mall when she was on her way out of town. I wanted to ask her questions about Rick Stevens, but she insisted on meeting in person. So I did, mostly because she wanted to give me something."

"What did she give you? Costa, if you're withholding evidence..."

"You'll do nothing, George. I'll just claim privilege and tie this stuff up indefinitely while you fight it with subpoenas."

"Okay," he sighed, "although I'm having a hard time believing you would ever accept her as a client, we'll play it your way."

"I'm proposing a trade."

"Do tell?"

"You brief Miss MacDonald on what you've learned on our murders so far, and I'll give you the satchel of stuff that Jennifer Adams gave to me. But I'll warn you—I haven't taken a look at any of it yet. For all I know, she could have stuffed it full of the love letters I wrote her back in the day."

"Well, if that's the case, at least all of us around the station will get a hell of a laugh at your expense."

"So we have a deal?"

"Deal," he grumbled.

"I hope you made copies of everything," I whispered to Mack as I headed into the office.

"Of course I did," she said, winking. "Coffee?"

"Yeah. At least my intentions for a restful evening were noble."

139

"Perhaps tomorrow," she said, smiling.

* * *

"The police are spinning their wheels for the most part," Mack said, pouring a cup of coffee. "Forensics were a bit more interesting, but it could be meaningless."

"How so?" I asked, fighting sleepiness.

"There was an inconsistency in the entry angle of the bullet to the head between the two victims. Even when taking into account the differences in their height, the angle was still different. O'Neil didn't seem to make much of it, and I can't really blame him."

"If it *did* mean something, what would it tell is?"

"That, all things being held equal, Barry was killed by a taller person than Rick Stevens. But that is holding all other things constant, such as assuming level terrain, same firing position, and the same posture by the shooter. Other than that, they're running into dead ends."

"Did they test the paper yet?" I asked, massaging my temples.

"They ordered the test, but the results aren't back yet. O'Neil seemed none too happy about expending budget on it."

"I'll make a donation to our local ballet company in his honor."

"Didn't you tell me O'Neil hates the ballet, John?"

"I did, and that's exactly the point. By the way, assuming one shooter is taller than the other, how tall would that make them, respectively, Mack?"

Mack ran her fingers through her hair. "Barry's killer would have been over six feet, and Rick's would have been five seven, or so."

"About the height of the person driving the forklift?"

She rolled her eyes. "Now dammit, I wish I hadn't said anything. This smells of a rabbit hole, and I can already tell your wheels are turning."

"It might be a rabbit hole, but if O'Neil mentioned it, it wasn't by accident. Do you know enough about where the first victim was found to be able to find it again?"

"Yes, but…"

"Get your coat, Mack. I want to take a look at the crime scenes."

"It's cold, rainy, and three in the morning," she protested

"Then there won't be people there bothering us."

"But isn't the old foundry on private property?"

"Probably. I'll go without you if you're worried."

"No," she said, getting her coat.

"You better pack heat, Mack. Just in case."

"Already a step ahead of you," she said.

* * *

I was right about one thing: there wasn't anybody around where Barry was killed. Mack was right about the cold and rainy conditions, enough so that I started having second thoughts. I'd never have the nerve to mention them, though.

I pulled my car into the alleyway, oriented so my lights illuminated the scene. "Barry's body was right about here," I said, fighting the urge to shiver. "How far away was the shooter?"

"According to O'Neil, the report placed the shooter between one and two yards from the victim," Mack said, fighting off a yawn.

"Okay. I'm going to play the role of Barry, and you're going to be the killer. You're about five foot six, right?"

"If I wear heels, yes."

"So, with me standing here, is there anything that the killer could have stood on to gain four to six inches of height? A curb? A step?"

Mack looked around. "No, nothing like that."

"How do the police think it went down?" I asked.

"Barry and his assailant had to have been close, like this," she said, stepping closer to me, "within stabbing distance. Neither victim had defensive wounds, so it is likely that whomever they were talking to wasn't considered a threat."

"Like now—perhaps someone they knew?"

"Yes, except if I catch pneumonia from this midnight foolishness, you will find me to be damned threatening."

"Duly noted, Mack. Continue."

"They're talking, and the murderer stabs the victim," she said, pretending to stab my midsection, "with speed and precision. The blood loss starts right as the blade is removed, causing the victim to sink to his knees."

I followed her instructions.

"Then, simply, the murderer steps back, aims, and fires," she said, pretending to hold a firearm in her hands.

"So," I said, still on my knees, "to gain height, you would have to lift your arms, but that would make your aim far less precise."

"I could also wear shoes that give me a few inches of height. Or Barry could have slumped more than they thought he did. All of this is terribly subjective, and probably why O'Neil didn't make a big deal about it."

"What if someone saw you, Mack? Can you run in shoes with that much lift?"

"I can't, but I'm sure that some people are able to. Can we get back in the car now?"

"Yes, I'm sorry," I said, climbing to my feet and back into the car. "Let's go."

* * *

Mack protested briefly about our next destination, but resigned herself to the inevitable. Our route took us by one of the local twenty-four hour burger joints.

"What the hell?" she asked as I turned into the parking lot. "I'm not hungry, and I'm certainly not hungry for *this* place," she said, wrinkling her nose.

"You can't tell me you haven't had a late night craving for this," I said, pretending to scowl.

"Okay. Guilty as charged, but I'm really not hungry."

"This isn't for us," I said, parking the car.

* * *

The lobby was occupied by a sole patron, a rotund man eating a generous meal that went a long way to explain his physical condition.

"Twenty-five sliders, half with cheese, half without. Fries and coffee for each. To go."

The cashier took my order, obviously surprised by its size. "We have these large containers for coffee," she offered. "Each holds about fifteen cups and will be much easier to transport."

"Two of those, plus cups will work," I said, paying and settling into my seat.

"At least you had the decency to come inside with an order like that," the man said. "I've had bigger orders working the drive-through. In fact, I think my biggest was just under a hundred dollars."

I nodded. Apparently that signaled our interest in his story, because he talked constantly until our order was ready, regaling us with stories of his time working in the fast food industry. Finally, citing the late hour, we were able to break free.

"Okay. On to the foundry," I announced.

CHAPTER TWENTY

"I'm still not sure what you're up to," Mack said, as we pulled onto the street that lead to the foundry.

"Just flies and honey, Mack. Which way?"

"Building three," she said, pointing into the distance.

We turned, driving until we were stopped by a tall chain-link fence. The gate barring our way wasn't locked, but the road beyond was littered with debris, most of which looked like it could puncture a tire rather easily.

"Hide your money under the seat," I said. "We're going on foot from here. Look on the bright side: it isn't raining anymore."

Armed with bags of sliders, fries, and coffee, we slowly made our way toward building three. As we approached, we could see the light of a fire coming from between two of the abandoned buildings.

"Which side of the building?" I whispered.

"The one opposite the light," she said. "Between two and three."

We made our way to the gap and proceeded until Mack signaled a stop.

"Here," she whispered. "I can tell this is the right place by the piping. It matches what was in the crime scene pictures."

"This terrain is very level," I said. "For some reason, I expected it to be rough."

"Great. Now, can we go?"

"Yes. We can go."

We made our way back to the gap, but instead of heading back to my car, I turned in the direction of the light.

"What are you doing?" Mack whispered.

"Investigating. Or being crazy."

We walked quietly, the entire width of building three. As we neared the end, I could hear a few voices, although I couldn't make out what was being said. Staying close to the wall, I moved closer, eventually allowing myself a short peek around the corner.

Much to my relief, there was only a handful of people gathered around a fire built in a makeshift barrel.

"There aren't many," I said to Mack, "but be ready in the unlikely situation they decide to get violent."

She nodded.

"Hello?" I called, moving slowly into view, stopping at the end of the gap between buildings three and four.

The talking stopped. "Get lost," one of the men said.

"I have food and hot coffee. My assistant and I aren't here to get anyone in trouble, we just have a couple of questions about the murder that took place."

"We don't know nothing," said another man. "Damn cops chased us out when all that happened, we're just now getting settled back in."

"I'm not going to do anything to change that," I said. "There's a cash reward if anybody saw anything. I bet the cops forgot to mention that."

A few of them spoke quietly amongst themselves.

"We still don't know nothing," the man said.

"All right, I said, "you're still welcome to the food and the coffee, just for hearing me out. Mind if I bring it over?"

"Nice and slowly," one of the men said.

"Of course."

We moved toward the fire, slowly. An overhang from the roof

of building four kept their gathering area dry. A barrier, fashioned from tarps tossed over stacked shopping carts, blocked most of the wind that swept between the foundry buildings. A stack of pallets served as fuel for their fire.

One man rose, removed his blanket, and moved toward me. He said nothing as I handed him the bags of food. He inspected the contents of each before nodding and passing them around.

"Coffee?" Mack asked, quietly.

He nodded, and she poured him a cup. After initial reluctance, others joined.

"Thanks," a woman said, her mouth stuffed with fries.

"You're welcome," I said. "We'll leave the coffee in the shopping cart and be on our way."

The man who had initially accepted our gift nodded, motioning toward the cart. I placed the containers and the extra cups and started walking back to my car.

We were almost to the gate when we heard someone following us. I turned to see a man approaching.

"You mentioned something about a reward?"

"I did. Do you know something?"

"I seen the whole thing."

"Did you tell the police?"

"No. I wanted to keep out of it, and if I tell you, I ain't telling anybody else. Get me?"

"Understood. Why don't you show us what happened."

The man, who refused to even give us his first name, led us back to the gap between buildings two and three.

"Right here," he said. "It happened right here."

He was at the correct spot, but I wasn't convinced. Any of the homeless people who were around when the body was discovered would have known the location of the murder.

"Yes," I said. "What did you see?"

"There were two people here. I'd never seen either of them before. They looked like they didn't belong here. Out of place—kinda like you. I was coming back from looking for pallets, and I almost walked between these two buildings. It was windy that night, so they didn't hear me, which was a damn good thing. I couldn't make out what they were saying, but it looked like a hell of an argument. They were standing close and getting in each other's faces quite a bit."

"Did you get a look at either of them?"

"No. I was trying not to be seen. I just had a weird feeling about the whole thing. One was a little taller than the other—I remember that."

"Which one was taller?"

"The guy that got killed, but not by much. Anyway, next thing I know, one of them slumps to his knees. A second or two later, I heard a sound like a twig snapping and the guy's brains are splattered all over the wall of the building. The shorter one took off like a gazelle. Ran that way, off to the north. Probably had a car waiting over there, but I wasn't about to follow to find out."

"Can you get a car over there?"

"Yeah. There's another way in. It isn't real obvious from a map, but you can get there if you're familiar with the area. Gotta get on a road that looks like a dead end, but isn't."

"What happened next?"

"I got the hell out of there."

"You didn't call for help or tell anyone?"

"Help? There wasn't no helping that man. He was as dead as they come."

"How do you know?"

"I checked his pulse. I also helped myself to a few bucks in his wallet. You're not going to tell the cops are you?"

"No. Not a word. When you were getting his wallet, did you see anything out of the ordinary?"

"No, not really, except for that weird card."

"Card?"

"There was a card with some strange lettering on it." He described the card found on both corpses.

"Like this?" I asked, showing him an image on my phone.

"That's it! Don't know what it said, but I figured I best leave it alone."

I reached into my pocket, handing the man a wad of bills. "Can I get you anything? Blankets? Wood? A lift to a shelter?"

"No," he said, pocketing the money, "just keep me out of it, whatever it is."

* * *

"I'm chilled to the bone," Mack complained, "but as much as I hate to admit it, I think this crazy little trip was worth it."

"He definitely saw the murder," I said. "The police have kept the details of that card away from the public thus far. The only way he could've known was to have seen the card. How tall was Rick Stevens?"

Mack tapped on her phone before answering. "Five foot, ten inches," she said.

"The killer was a bit shorter," I said.

"Yeah, yeah. I'm warming up to the theory. Oh! Stop here," she said, pointing to a restaurant. "They make an amazing breakfast."

"You don't want to try to get a bit of sleep? I'm exhausted."

"Nope. I'm going to start looking at the stuff Jennifer gave you, and you're going to help!"

"All right, all right! Let me call Kevin and let him know where we are."

"No need," she said. "He's right behind us. Bless his heart, he's been keeping an eye on us the entire night."

Dammit. I was being careless again. Fortunately, it hadn't cost us dearly.

* * *

A shower helped revitalize me, but before I could dig into the unpleasant task that awaited, my phone rang. It was Jerry Keynes.

"Jack, how goes it?"

"Still alive, in spite of myself."

"So I've heard," he laughed. "You asked me to start looking into Quantelle."

"Yes!" In all the chaos, I'd almost forgotten.

"As companies go, they're about as squeaky clean as you can get.

There are precious few instances of litigation being brought against them—for anything—and every single one has been settled out of court. No fines. No violations. Well-rated as an employer."

"I know you're not calling me to tell me you didn't find anything."

"The only thing even slightly out of the ordinary—and even this is grasping at straws—is their propensity as a company to carry company-owned life insurance on their employees."

"I knew about that, Jerry. One of the victims was heavily insured by Quantelle. Given what he did for them, I can't say that I blame them."

"The interesting thing about what I discovered is that Quantelle has now had two significant insurance payouts in the last eight months—your friend Barry, and before that, the fellow that was in charge of their overseas expansion efforts."

"Any idea what that policy was worth?"

"Ten million or more, according to my sources."

"Cause of death?"

"Massive heart attack."

"Anything odd about it?"

"Nothing, apart from the fact that the man was only forty-five. It was never investigated, if that's what you're asking, Jack"

"Even added together, twenty-five million is just a drop in the bucket to a company like Quantelle."

"I wouldn't be too sure about that," Jerry said. "They're not publicly held, so everything is just conjecture, of course, but there are those that believe they've hit the top of their domestic potential. They're innovative, no doubt, but they still have the inescapable expenses of shipping and labor, neither of which seem to be dropping."

"That would explain why they are looking to expand internationally."

"But international expansion is nowhere near as fast or as easy as domestic expansion. Even Canada brings some unique challenges. I'm not saying they're doing anything wrong, mind you. Every indication is that they're doing well, but I wouldn't be so quick to dismiss the impact of twenty-five million dollars, especially when it drops straight to the bottom line, expense free."

"Point taken, Jerry."

"But, that said, there is no reason to draw any derogatory conclusions about Quantelle. Their reputation is about as spotless as it can get."

CHAPTER TWENTY-ONE

"This may take a bit longer than hoped," Mack said, after superficially reviewing the information provided by Jennifer Adams. "For a small business, she certainly found ways to unnecessarily complicate things. She's got accounts here that make no sense to me whatsoever. Money's moving all over the place, but the core receivables and payables are fairly quiet. What a bloody mess!"

"That was Jenn," I chuckled. "She could take the simplest thing and turn it into an obscure mess in no time."

Mack's fingers gently massaged her temples. "What's on your mind? I can tell from your expression you're not focused on these journals."

"Do you think O'Neil was telling us the truth about Jenn's death?"

"I *know* he was," Mack said, beaming with confidence. "One of my sources confirmed it for me."

I ran my hands through my hair, trying to urge my tired brain into action. "She recognized her attacker, or at least sensed danger, and tried to run."

Mack nodded. "That is what the prevailing theory is, although that could change based on forensic data."

"It took a shot to the leg to slow her down. One thing I'll say about her, flaws and my broken heart aside, she always took good care of herself. She lifted weights and ran regularly. The last time I saw her, she still looked fit as ever, from what I could tell in our brief meeting."

She moved to the edge of her chair, her attention focused on me. "Continue."

"If our killer is ritual-based, he couldn't just run after her and kill her haphazardly. He had to be able to drive that bayonet in her stomach while facing her—just like the others. But why a shot to the leg? Why not just catch up and overpower her?"

She raised her eyebrow. "Not his killing style?"

I stood up, stretching. "If the profile Adnan sent me is accurate, we're talking about a man in his sixties. He might not be *able* to chase down Jenn Adams."

"You have a point there," she said, nodding. "The location of the extra stab wound is telling, too. It was violent and intended to produce immense pain and suffering—not to mention, of course, the unmistakable sexual overtones. A spurned lover, perhaps?"

"Entirely possible, but hardly helpful. I wasn't the first, or certainly the last, fool she left out in the cold. Hell, you want a list of suspects, start with every band she ever saw in concert and track down their bass player."

"Huh?"

"She had a thing for bass players, Mack. I have no idea why, but it seemed to be a repeating theme over the years."

"And how, exactly, do *you* know?"

I laughed. "Strictly third hand information. She kept in touch with a couple of my friends after we broke up."

Her lips curled into a wry smile. "Well, if you want to start interviewing bass players, have at it, but I'm going to get back to the books."

"Nah. These killings are linked, Mack. They have to be. We just haven't found out how."

"Maybe we'll find it in here," she said, tapping one of the journals. "Let's focus and try to get through the day."

* * *

"I hear you have the third body," Adnan Jasik said, as I answered his call. "So the poem has been fulfilled again."

"So it would seem."

"That signals the end. There are always three murders. Never more, never less."

"Perhaps."

"You sound less than convinced, my friend. Has the paper been tested?"

"Yes, supposedly, but the results are not available yet."

"That will tell the story."

"Adnan, tell me something. What does the poem actually say?"

"It is nothing more than a nursery rhyme, as you call it. It doesn't translate directly to English, but the tale is a story of three birds. The birds sit on their branch all day, mocking the other birds, stealing their food, making life generally miserable. One day, a new bird dares to sit in their tree. They mock the bird and threaten to steal its feathers. But the little bird refuses to leave, telling them to sit on their branch and sing beautiful songs instead of being mean. But the three birds are wicked, and they gang up and chase the new bird away. The winter that follows is rough, and none of the birds have enough to eat. This is when the new bird returns, but instead of a little bird, he is grown up—a hawk! He brings food, but won't let the three birds eat, because they were wicked to him. They offer to sit on the branch and sing for their food, but he chases them away. 'You had your chance to sing,' he tells them, 'but you chose to be wicked. Now eat the seeds you planted!' The three wicked birds fly away, never to be seen again."

"Interesting…"

"Of course, there are subtleties in the original language that are lost in the translation, but that is the idea."

"The cards only had a few lines of text, though. Your story is much longer."

"That's because, for people who understand the culture, only a few lines are needed. The rest of the story would have been taught by their mothers. Like in your American history, the first line of the

153

Constitution or the Gettysburg Address."

"I'm impressed, Adnan. I had no idea you were a student of American history."

"I am a student of the world, my friend. To survive in my line of work, one must understand cultures at their core."

"So, the serial killer is the hawk, and the three birds are the victims that have, somehow, done him wrong?"

"That is the theory, but it is without proof. After the third murder, our hawk always flies away."

"Maybe this time, the cat will catch the hawk."

"I hope you're right, but I'm not holding my breath. All the best to you, old boy!"

* * *

Try as I might, I could not stay awake. In spite of coffee and a short walk in the cold, I finally gave up.

"Mack, I'm sorry, but I can't stay awake. I'm going to head downstairs for a quick nap."

"That's all right. I need to take a break anyway and run a few errands."

"Errands?"

"Christmas shopping, oh forgetful one! The season's upon us, and I'd rather not be running around at the last minute."

Dammit. I was slacking badly in my shopping plans, too. It would have to wait for another day, though. I pulled a blanket over me and settled into the couch.

Dreams arrived quickly, but they weren't the pleasant fantasies of Angela Grady I had silently hoped for. Instead, they were memories of Jennifer Adams, twisted and morphed into the present. They roared with discord, frustration, and the inevitable feelings of inadequacy that she was always so effective at instilling. They raged on, twisting and turning through memories I would have preferred to stay dormant. Finally, I willed myself awake.

"You were having a nightmare, weren't you?"

The gentle voice of Angela Grady shocked me, causing me to sit upright, suddenly. I looked around, trying to make out where the voice came from. Her hand gently caressed my shoulder. I tried to move, wanting desperately to take her hand in mine, but found my limbs unwilling to cooperate.

"Yes," I whispered. "Nightmares about someone who broke my heart a long time ago."

"Perhaps," she said, "you need to allow yourself to shed a tear."

"For Jenn Adams? No, thank you. I'm not happy that she died the way she did, but I'll not shed a solitary tear."

She moved to the arm of the couch. "Perhaps then, about whatever is bothering you."

"Perhaps," I said, "but with some things, tears signal a finality, an ending I'm not willing to accept."

"All ends merely lead to a new beginning. You're bothered by more, though. I know that look in your eye."

"The case," I said.

"Oh yes. You're frustrated."

"More than ever."

"You have everything you need, my love. When the time is right, you'll see it."

"And you?"

She moved closer. "Do you like my earrings?" She pulled back her hair to show green shamrocks.

"Yes, very much."

She removed one, placing it on the end table. "A little something so you don't forget. Get some rest, my love. I'll see you soon."

I fought with all my might to stay awake. I fought to get up from the sofa and follow, but nothing happened. Broken, I closed my eyes, and sleep returned.

* * *

"Come on, Sleepy McSnorington, time to get up."

"Jesus, Mack, what time is it?"

"Dinner time," she answered.

"Was I really snoring?"

"Like an angry buzz saw," she said. "The folks from the United States Geological Survey stopped by. Apparently, you were screwing with their sensors. On the west coast."

"Mack!"

"Oh—and you have a call from NASA. Something about using you as a rocket engine."

"Mack!!"

"There's one other detail that might interest you."

"No, Mack, I'm not falling for it…"

"Seriously."

"Nope. I'm heading to O'Brien's for fish and chips, and you're not going to stop me."

"Just thought you might be interested in something I found."

"You discovered that my snoring opened a portal to a parallel universe? Or was I belching out some yet-undiscovered subatomic particle?"

"My, but we're snarky today! I, in my undeniable awesomeness, may have found a link between Rick Stevens and Quantelle. But, if you're still hungry for food from O'Brien's, my discovery can wait."

"How about we discuss how amazing you are *while* we eat? My treat."

"I'll be ready in five minutes."

I folded my blanket, returning it to its normal spot in my closet. On my way out, I glanced at the end table, briefly freezing in my track. A single, shamrock earring sat near the base of the lamp. Shaking, I picked it up, unable to do anything but put it in the table's small drawer.

* * *

"I think I'm losing my mind," I said, sipping my Guinness as I related my two bizarre Angela Grady experiences to Mack."

"For some of us," she said, "that theory has not been in doubt for many years. But seriously, I wish you'd go talk to someone. These dreams are, without a doubt, part of the grieving process. I wish I could help you with it, but I don't know enough about the subject."

"You think they were dreams?"

"I do," she said, her expression falling. "Everything you've described is consistent with what I've read about. Paralysis, sensory experiences, conversations—all are in the articles. Sometimes people think they're talking to ghosts, aliens, even God."

"Then how do you explain the blanket and the earring?"

"Do you really want to know? Because I'll tell you, but you might not like it, and I don't want you to hate me."

"Mack, I could never hate you. I need you to be my voice of reason, especially now."

"Okay," she said, raising her eyebrows. "Don't say I didn't warn you."

"Fair play."

"Where do you normally keep that blanket?"

"In the closet, just behind the sofa."

"And the earring? That's the one you found in Ireland, right?"

"I think so," I said, sheepishly. "I didn't look at it closely, but it looks the same."

"And you keep it where?"

"In the end table drawer."

"You were sleepwalking, plain and simple. People have been known to carry out complex tasks while asleep. It isn't a far stretch to think you fetched a few things from nearby."

I nodded, slightly dejectedly. Deep inside, though, I knew she was probably right.

"Either that," she continued, "or Angela turned temporarily ethereal to slip by your security system, undetected. If so, I would like to learn how to do that, because I'd really like to get a look at some of Quantelle's shipping records."

It was Mack's polite way to steer the conversation away from the subject of Angela Grady and my lingering hopes that she was, somehow, still alive. I smiled and nodded, allowing her to lead the conversation. What I didn't mention was that Angela wouldn't need to engage preternatural talents to slip past the security system. Upon my return from Ireland, I had secretly added a secondary access code to my security system, complete with a password that would only make sense to two people: Angela Grady and me.

"I'm still struggling with some of Jennifer's accounting," Mack said, jolting me back to reality, "but I'm starting to get the hang of it. I can't tell if they were up to anything fishy, but if they were, I'll find it."

"You mentioned a connection to Quantelle?"

"Well, not directly," she said, wincing a bit. "That's why I'd like to look at their shipping documents."

"So, exactly what *did* you find?"

"Rick Stevens did some consulting work for a company called ABX Industries. The only reason it stood out to me at all is because his bill rate was significantly higher to ABX than to anyone else. It turns out that ABX is an umbrella corporation created by some venture capitalists. One of the companies under their umbrella is Kala Shipping, Ltd. Guess who happens to own Kala Shipping?"

"No idea…"

"Lance Yannis and his wife Kate—the same Lance that works for Quantelle."

"Yeah. and he happens, conveniently, to be on vacation in a place with spotty cell phone coverage."

CHAPTER TWENTY-TWO

"Kala Shipping?" Ashley said. "Of course I've heard of it. It's the company Lance and his wife own. Kate and Lance—Kala. Get it? It's really more her thing than his, but nevertheless, they own it."

"So it isn't a secret?"

"Hardly! Lance disclosed it freely when he was hired, specifically to avoid any conflict of interest issues. Why?"

"Just checking on some loose ends. Is that your mother I hear in the background?"

"Yes," she giggled. "I think she wants to talk to you. Mom!"

"Hi there!" Eva Peretti bubbled. "Great day, isn't it?"

"Umm… it's cold and dreary…"

"I'm still vertical and not six feet under, so I'd say it's pretty damn good."

"Okay," I laughed, "that's one way to look at it. This is a bit awkward…"

"Spit it out," she said.

"Jillian, my researcher, isn't going to give me any peace until I talk to a grief counselor. I knew you'd been through something similar, and I wanted to ask…"

"I'll send the number right over," she replied, before I could finish my sentence. "I don't know why you'd feel shy about asking."

"I'm not sure," I said. "Some people might be put off by it, especially since we don't know each other all that well."

"Some people are offended by everything they see. I'm not one of them. I just hope it helps."

"I like the idea of us having coffee," I said, hesitantly. "This weekend is supposed to warm up a bit. I know a nice place that has some outdoor tables, perhaps with a jacket…"

"Thanks to my daughter's clumsy ways, my skiing schedule isn't going to be much of anything. Coffee this weekend sounds lovely. Saturday, two o'clock. I'll send you my address. Bring that hunk of a security guard with you. I think Ashley wants to see him."

Ashley's voice could be heard in the background. "Mother!"

I laughed. "We're pretty much inseparable these days. I'm sure he'll be along."

* * *

"I can tell you one thing," Mack said, looking tired.

"Oh?"

"Your friend Jenn was playing a little fast and loose with the accounting for Rick Stevens' business. It wouldn't surprise me if that was part of the reason she was trying to get out of town."

"She was hardly my friend, Mack."

"Just an expression, oh sensitive one. If the IRS got hold of some of this, I think they might want to have a conversation—the type that involves warrants, property seizure, and handcuffs."

"How far back do the records go?"

"The handwritten journals cover the last two years. The data on the flash drives go back seven years, give or take. That seems to be about the time Jenn took over the books."

"I think that was probably about the time they started dating, give or take. She tried to contact me sometime after she met Rick. I ignored it."

Mack's eyes narrowed. "You might not have responded, but you

160

didn't ignore it."

I sighed. "As usual, Jillian MacDonald, you're right. I read her email, several times over, and I remember every detail of the horrible thing. Hell, I don't know why she felt the need to send it to me, and I wish she hadn't."

"What was in it?"

"She'd fallen for a married man and wanted my advice. That's the long and short of it. I wanted to advise her to drop dead, but sending nothing seemed the politer approach."

"So Rick was married?"

"I don't even know if it was him she was writing about. She never pitched a name, and I certainly didn't care enough to ask. Now that I think about it, though, O'Neil did mention something about Rick Stevens having an ex and a daughter."

"You only thought to mention that little tidbit now?"

"Dammit, Mack, I'm sorry. Ever since O'Neil mentioned Jenn's name, my mind has been in a bit of a haze."

"Understandable. I'll have Tom see if Rick's erstwhile wife is of any interest. Now, back to the matter at hand."

"The finances?"

"Indeed. There are quite a few places where the numbers *look* like they add up, but under close scrutiny, there are some discrepancies. Like here," she said, showing me an entry. "Let's follow this chain of transactions through to the end."

She launched into an explanation of debits and credits that threatened to tear the thin fabric of my sanity into shreds. At the end, though, I understood the conclusion."

"There's money floating around this business that these books don't account for," she said, mercifully ending her thesis.

"How much money are we talking about?"

"Conservatively, a little over two million dollars, and that's just for the current year."

"Theories?"

"None, really. The most likely explanation is Rick's consulting business was being used to front and flow money from an all-cash business of some sort. Probably to hide income from the tax man—

that's the most common explanation. It could be money laundering. Some of the patterns are consistent."

"Jenn, at least when we were together, had a slightly skewed view of right and wrong, but that's from my perspective of course. It was the cause of friction between us on a couple of occasions, no doubt. We clashed on everything from private property rules straight through to fidelity in relationships, as ironic as that seems in retrospect."

"It seems that you two didn't have a whole lot in common."

"Looking back on it, we didn't. At the time, though, I was so enamored with her, I was willing to ignore damn near everything—even the little moral idiosyncrasies."

"Well, perhaps she graduated to bigger and better moral failings, so to speak. You were strong enough to walk away from her, albeit involuntarily. Maybe someone else wasn't able to maintain the same level of self-control. If she was cheating on you, who's to say she wasn't cheating on Rick?"

"Have I told you recently how amazing you are, Jillian MacDonald?"

"Hardly enough," she said, winking.

"Give me the information on Rick's ex. Have Tom start nosing around Kate Yannis' shipping business."

"And me?"

"In addition to being awesome, you can start reviewing Barry's computers."

* * *

It didn't take an expert divorce lawyer to interpret the case record surrounding Rick Stevens' dissolution: it was a long and bitter legal struggle, and one that he lost in spectacular fashion.

"Looking back on things," Sara Frazier, Rick's ex-wife, said, "the signs were there for a while. I shouldn't have been surprised, but when the whole mess started, I was on my heels. But not for long."

"I gathered that from the court records," I said.

"We weren't married when our daughter was born, but we'd been together for a few years and everything seemed to be going fairly well. We got married when our daughter was six months old. Rick's business was really starting to take off and life seemed pretty good. Then *she* showed up."

"Jennifer Adams?"

"Yep," she said, making no effort to hide the disdain that oozed from her voice.

"We have a bit in common, Miss Frazier," I said. "I'm another broken heart left in the wake of her ship. We dated for a while, and I was madly in love with her. The feeling wasn't mutual, although she led me around by my nose for a few months under various pretenses. All the time, she was cheating with someone else. I'm sorry to bring up old memories, but I'm trying to figure out who killed my friend, and Rick's death seems to be intertwined, somehow."

"Yeah, the police came knocking on my door when they found Rick's body. I'm sure they were running through their playbook of usual suspects. I was out of the country when the crime was committed. My boyfriend took me to Scotland to celebrate our second year together."

"Wow! Great present!"

"He's a gem. We worked together when I was dating Rick. We lost track of each other until a chance meeting in the supermarket. We chatted for ten minutes in the produce aisle," she laughed. "One thing led to another and here we are."

"How did Jennifer and Rick end up meeting?"

"Rick hired her to be his accountant."

"Oh, God," I groaned.

"Yep. Exactly when and where they met, I'm not certain, but she sweet-talked him into a job. Things spiraled downhill from there."

"What, exactly, did Rick do?"

"Rick called himself a corporate troubleshooter. If a company had issues, like a dysfunctional leadership team, he would find solutions to get them on the same page. He must've been pretty good at what he did, because he was always flying here and there. I always hoped he would take me on one of his business trips, but it never seemed to work out. Once our daughter was born, travel just wasn't on the agenda for either of us. He scaled back his trips a bit, too. At the time, I thought it was sweet that he would put our daughter before his work travel. In reality, I think the allure of Jennifer Adams was keeping him around. I don't have proof, mind you, just suspicions."

"Probably justified," I sighed. "When you were together, was Rick's business profitable?"

"When we first met, it was struggling a bit. He'd lost his house to pay back taxes to the IRS. He blamed his accountant. It seemed to be the truth, because once he started doing his own books, things picked up, and the tax problems were gone. Then *she* showed up."

"What happened?"

"When we divorced, I wanted the separation to be as painless as possible and equitable, especially since we had a daughter. Then the irregularities started to show up. Money that was missing, offshore accounts that I didn't know about, hidden assets, the whole nine yards. That's when I took off the gloves, Mister Costa."

"I reviewed some of the public records—it seemed to be quite acrimonious."

"That's an understatement. If he'd been honest, we could have settled it easily."

"You were awarded full custody of your daughter and he was given supervised visitation?"

"One afternoon a month. It was a harsh judgment, but at the time, it felt good to see him get his, so to speak. A few years later, I eventually allowed the visits to be unsupervised, then more recently, extended to the entire weekend."

"Is it fair to say that you two had mended some bridges recently?"

"It would never be the same, of course, but we had gotten to the point where conversations weren't constantly degrading into a fight. The same can not be said for me and Jennifer. We kept our distance, and I was perfectly happy to keep things that way."

"In the weeks leading up to his death, was Rick's demeanor any different?"

"The police asked the same question. Something was *definitely* going on with him. He didn't spell it out for me, but I'd known him long enough to pick it up from the tone of his voice. The weekend before he was murdered was supposed to be his time with our daughter. He called the week before and asked if we could swap for a future weekend. I agreed. In all the years, it was the only time he ever asked to reschedule."

"Do you have any theories about his death?"

"Nothing other than suspicions, but I'd bet money that Jennifer Adams was involved, somehow. She probably talked him into some sort of scheme and they got in over their heads. Rick wasn't a bad man, Mister Costa. Sure, he had his faults, like we all do, but his heart was fundamentally good. Maybe too good—he trusted people way too easily."

"And Jennifer?"

"A pretty face doesn't always mean a pretty heart. You should count your lucky stars that she didn't keep her talons in you. She had a nice veneer and could talk a good game, but she wasn't a good person. Not saying she deserved to die, but I'm not going to lose any sleep or shed a tear over her death."

CHAPTER TWENTY-THREE

"You think she's a suspect, don't you?" Mack said.

I settled into my normal booth at O'Brien's and sipped my Guinness. "Yes," I sighed. "I think we have to consider the possibility. I'm sure she's on George O'Neil's list."

"Sara Frazier is a single mom raising a daughter. Do you really think she'd jeopardize all of that?"

"Probably not, but I've seen stranger things happen."

"Is there any evidence that contradicts her claim that the relationship with her ex was actually improving?"

"No. The most recent filing seemed amicable, as did the one that preceded it—at least from what I could glean from the record."

"Why now? If she was going to get homicidal, it would seem that the peak of her rage would have happened around the time of the divorce."

"You're probably right. Apparently, she was out of town when Rick Stevens was killed, but she offered no alibi for Jenn's murder, nor was she particularly upset by it."

"Well," she sighed, sipping her Scotch, "I think it's a stretch, but probably worth at least a cursory look. Why the long face?"

"I've been thinking about my meeting with Jenn. I screwed up, Mack."

"How so?"

"When we met, I just wanted to be rid of her. I should have pressed her for answers. The more I think about it, the more I realize she probably held the key to understanding why Rick was murdered. She might have even known who was threatening him. Hell, she might have even known the murderer."

"What are you doing?" she asked, as I pulled out my phone.

"I'm going to hire Jerry to look into Rick's company. I want to know everything about it, what he did, who he worked with, everything. You and Tom are stretched thin enough already, and Zonk's busy working in a warehouse. Speaking of which, have you heard from him?"

"He's due to check in with us tonight."

"Excellent," I said, dialing the phone. Jerry Keynes answered almost immediately.

"Good to hear from you, Jack."

"I'm sure it is, especially since I'm calling you with an opportunity to make a bunch of money."

"I won't say no," he said, laughing.

"I want you to get me everything you can on Rick Stevens, Jennifer Adams, and Sara Frazier. Mack will send over the specifics on each of them."

"Any place in particular you want me to start?"

"Rick's business. So far, it's the only thread connecting things together. It's hardly solid, though. Rick did some consulting work for a shipping company owned by someone that worked with Barry Myers at Quantelle."

"Thread? That's being generous. More like a wispy fart in the breeze."

"I know it," I sighed, "but we still have three bodies and little to nothing connecting them, other than the signature of a serial killer, who might, in fact, be a myth."

"Do you know what the rumor around the police department is?"

"I've heard bits and pieces. What have you heard?"

"O'Neil thinks the Myers widow hired Rick Stevens to off her old man. When he chickened out, she found someone else to do the job…"

"…and to take care of the final loose end: Jenn Adams," I said, finishing his sentence.

"That's the scuttlebutt, at least."

"Any mention of evidence, or is it all conjecture?"

"They're being pretty tight-lipped, which tells me they're probably long on conjecture and short on facts, but you have to admit the theory is plausible."

"I don't have to admit any such thing," I protested, all the time silently agreeing with him.

"He's probably working on getting a warrant to dump her cell phone records, if he hasn't done so already. You're going to have quite a mess on your hands if he connects the dots," he chuckled.

"I'll worry about that when the time comes, *if* the time comes. In the mean time, send me your damned bill."

"You're always in such a hurry, Jack. Rush, rush, rush! You're probably going to hurry yourself into an early grave."

* * *

"What's the matter?" Mack asked, eating her salad. "I could tell the latter part of the conversation didn't go as expected."

I shared Jerry's news. "I'm a little surprised," I muttered, "that you didn't already know this little tidbit."

She stopped what she was doing to glance up at me with an annoyed expression. "I'm human, you know. Besides, my normal source of inside information is on vacation, and my alternates aren't as forthcoming as I'd like them to be."

"What are your thoughts?"

"It's plausible," she said, looking at me wistfully.

"Let's talk through it."

"Okay," Mack said, putting down her fork and playing along. "She's a sick woman with an uninspiring husband. She's thinks they're broke, and she's afraid they're not going to be able to pay for her medication, so she hires Rick Stevens to kill her husband for the insurance money."

"But she didn't know about the insurance," I argued.

"So she claims, but we found those policies in his desk drawer within a few minutes of looking. She's there all the time. Surely, she knew."

I smiled, acknowledging her point. "Okay, but how did she learn about Rick?"

"From Lance, her husband's co-worker. We know there's a connection there, we just don't know the nature of it."

I nodded. "What if Rick turned out to be all talk and no action? She would be forced to hire someone else—someone serious who would get the job done."

"And," Mack added, "she had to clean up the loose ends, ergo Rick and Jenn being eliminated."

"Which would," I said, sipping my Guinness and staring off into space, "explain why she's in such a damn hurry to get her hands on every cent she can. Professional people, even when their business is murder, want to get paid."

"It would also explain why she goaded and teased you into representing her. You're thinking the next tidbit on Barry's murder is around the corner, all the time she's having you do her dirty work for her. Because of confidentiality, you can't share a whisper of it. Clever, really."

"So why did Barry come chasing after me that night?"

"Maybe he got wind of the plot against him. Maybe Rick or Jenn tipped him off, and he was looking for help."

"Why not call the police?"

"I don't know," she sighed. "Maybe he was trying to protect his wife. As odd as it sounds, it wouldn't be the first time it happened."

I scratched my head. "I don't know, Mack. Maureen is many things, but stupid isn't one of them. Surely, she would know that the police would consider her the prime suspect and that they're going to check her phone records, unless..."

"What is it?"

"Bear with me a moment, Mack. I'm going to think out loud for a bit. What happens to the investigation if the police are unable to make any connection between Maureen and the crime using phone records?"

"They'll eventually be forced to look elsewhere if they run into a brick wall."

"Where do they look?" I asked.

"Well, for one," she said, "they'll be forced to consider the serial killer angle, especially if the press gets wind of it. That's only a matter of time, by the way."

"Exactly! How can she possibly be so certain that they won't find anything on her phone records?"

"She didn't use a phone," Mack answered, "but I'm not exactly sure what she could use as a substitute that wouldn't be traceable."

I took a deep sip of my Guinness, motioning for another. "What about all those radios and antennas Barry had? They reach all over the world, right? Are any of them limited to local coverage?"

"Yes, but she's not licensed, and all of the frequencies are open and in the clear. Anyone could be listening.. It would be awfully dangerous to setup a murder using what are, essentially, public airwaves. Before any of the radio communication could happen, however, they'd need to arrange a time, a frequency, and so forth. It isn't like she could get on the radio and broadcast that she's looking to hire a hit man. But," she sighed, "I suppose it's possible, assuming she knew how to operate the gear and could even get up and down the stairs."

"Unless, of course, she used Barry's phone to arrange future communication, instead of her own. If she coordinated it through someone at his work, it wouldn't look out of the ordinary to anyone examining the phone, including the police."

"But the police aren't going to get it, are they?" Mack said. "She gave it to you, her attorney, so it's protected by privilege."

"So it is," I sighed. "Well, it wouldn't be the first time I've been played, and probably not the last. But why me, though?"

"The most obvious reason is your money. It isn't as well-kept of a secret as it once was, you know."

"True."

"On the other hand, maybe you were a happy coincidence, or from your perspective, being in the wrong place at the wrong time."

"Story of my life, Mack."

"Oh, I don't know about that." She wrinkled her nose. "I was pretty happy to run into you when I did, and even happier that you turned out to be a reasonable man."

Many years earlier, Mack's computer skills saved me from what would have undoubtedly been a devastating case of identity theft. She accomplished it by essentially stealing my identity before the bad guys could. The maneuver landed her in hot water with the police, but thankfully, George O'Neil convinced me to listen to her story. I did, declining to press charges, and the best friendship of my life was born.

"Yes," I said, "that was a notable exception to the rule."

* * *

Tired, I had turned in early, only to be awakened by Mack.

"Get up," she insisted. "Tom's been attacked!"

I fumbled around for a moment, struggling to get oriented. Finally, I collected myself enough to get dressed.

"What happened? Is he okay?" I asked.

Mack tossed me my coat, "I don't have a lot of details, but they're taking him to the hospital."

The cold air shocked me mostly awake, but Mack's driving, through sheer terror, took care of the rest. It took me a little bit to realize that she was well in control, then I could relax a bit.

"Where did you learn to drive like that?" I said, as we made our way to the emergency room.

"I took a course a few years ago. Thought it might be a good skill to have, especially hanging around with you."

"You're probably right," I muttered, as the automatic doors slid open.

A long wait followed, dominated by frustration and unanswered questions. Finally, we were allowed to see him.

"You owe me a car, boss," he said, expressionless.

"Done," I answered, my eyes searching for clues to his condition. "How are you?"

"They tell me I'm lucky. A few scratches from broken glass is about the worst of it. I didn't sign up for this crap."

"What happened?"

"I was making some casual inquiries about Kala Shipping. I must've asked the wrong person the wrong question or something, because all hell broke loose on the way home. A car pulled around me to pass. Fortunately, I sensed something and hit the gas. That's when the shooting started."

"They shot at you?"

"With a damned automatic weapon! Probably the only reason I'm here to tell the story is that it happened in an area that I know pretty well from one of my past jobs. I managed to get into an industrial complex and lose them in the maze of alleys and buildings. The cops got there pretty quickly, because a security guard spotted us and called." He changed subjects abruptly, dropping his voice to a whisper. "The top button of my shirt is a camera and was recording the entire time. Get it, now!"

I complied, silently and quickly, before returning to his bedside. Within minutes, I understood his urgency.

"Your friend is lucky, John," George O'Neil said. "They shot the hell out of his car, though. My guys think it was an AK-47. Your friend's statement was less than helpful. Maybe you and Miss MacDonald can offer some insights that he was unable to provide."

"We're investigating on behalf of my client. Everything we have is protected by privilege. Now, if you're truly that passionate to see what we've collected, I can engage the District Attorney regarding blanket immunity for Maureen Myers. Otherwise, I suggest you focus your efforts on the subject at hand. Tom, did you give them a description of the vehicle?"

"I did."

"Did you describe the shooter to the best of your ability?"

"I did."

"Did you tell them the location and events of the shooting?"

"Uh huh."

"Then it sounds like our business here is concluded. Have a good evening, George," I said, inviting him to leave Tom's room.

"Asshole," he grumbled under his breath as he departed.

Tom motioned me back to his bedside. "What is it? Can I get you anything?"

"I quit," he whispered.

Dammit, I hate surprises.

CHAPTER TWENTY-FOUR

"Maybe he'll change his mind," Mack offered.

"He won't," I said. "I could see it in his eyes. "He's fine tracking down cheaters and insurance frauds, but he's not cut out for the uglier side of the business. I pushed too hard, and it damn near got him killed."

"He knows he's got it pretty good working for you. Give him a bit of time, John."

"I'll give him time, of course, but I have my doubts—he sent us his notebooks and returned his computers. I hope I'm wrong."

"Me, too," sighed Mack.

"In the meantime, we still have all the work we previously had, and now we have to figure out what it was that Tom was working on that struck a nerve. Dammit. I don't have time to bring anyone up to speed, and I'm sick and tired of writing Jerry Keynes big, fat checks."

An unexpected voice joined the conversation.

"I can help," Kevin Moriarty said. "I'm getting paid anyway, I'd feel better if I was actually earning it."

Mack and I exchanged surprised glances.

"I'll continue to do my primary job, of course. But times like this morning, I'm not really doing much. I might as well be productive."

Mack rattled off a series of impromptu interview questions, ranging from accounting to technology. Kevin seemed to handle them, but I would await Mack's appraisal. It arrived far quicker than expected.

"Make it happen," she said to me. "He knows his stuff, and we need the help."

"Well now, that was easy," I said, somewhat stunned by the sequence of events.

"What should I work on first, Mister Costa?"

"Seems like the most logical place to start is on Kala Shipping, but I suggest caution."

Kevin nodded, collecting Tom's computer and notebooks. "It'll take me a bit to get up to speed. Miss MacDonald, is it possible to get Mister Costa's security cameras on my monitors? I don't want to shirk my primary duties."

"Of course," she replied. "I'm already working on it."

* * *

It didn't take long before our gamble on Kevin Moriarty paid off.

"I think I've found the trail Tom was working on," he said. "It seems to correspond with what Miss MacDonald was able to retrieve from the lapel camera."

"Neither the audio or the video was very good, but it seems that Tom was asking some questions about a driving job in Florida or something like that," Mack added. "If you watch the video," she said, motioning to the screen, "this fellow here starts paying a lot of attention right about the time he mentions Miami."

I watched the grainy image and agreed with her assessment. A man, lurking in the background while Tom spoke to an overworked dispatcher, turned sharply at the mention of a freight company.

"He's interested all right," I muttered. "Any chance of enhancing the image?"

"You're looking at the enhanced version," Mack said. "Sorry. That's about as good as it's going to get."

I watched the video long enough to see the observant man disappear behind a door.

"Yeah. Something Tom said rattled him. Any idea what it was?"

"I've created a version with the enhanced audio synchronized to the video. Take a listen," Mack said.

Tom: "I'm looking for a driving job that will help get me back to Florida."

Dispatcher: "We don't have any open positions at the moment."

Tom: "Sorry. I heard that either you or your affiliate was hiring in Miami."

Dispatcher: "Who's that?"

The audio was interrupted by distortion, and I couldn't make out Tom's answer.

Dispatcher: "Never heard of them."

Tom: "Okay. Have a good evening."

"Dammit. What the hell was that distortion in the audio?"

"Tom was wearing his coat," Mack answered. "He must've moved while he answered. I've tried quite a few tricks to enhance it. Here's the best effort so far. Take a listen."

We played the clip over and over, but I couldn't make out anything but the first syllable.

"Sounds like it starts with the letter A, but after that, I can't tell what he's saying."

"That's our opinion, too," Kevin said. "We think he's talking about a company called AmeriBiz Express Freight."

"He could be saying that, but it could be any of a thousand other things," I said. "I assume there's another reason why you're focused on that name."

"There is," he said, switching images on the monitor. "Kala Shipping now has operations in three cities. One is here, of course. The other two are in Miami and Atlanta."

The screen changed to a satellite map.

"Kala Shipping isn't big enough to have a terminal like this," he said, pointing to a sprawling trio of buildings surrounded by trucks. "This is a major national freight carrier." He moved the map, centering on a smaller building.

"It still looks like a decent sized building," I observed.

"Kala only occupies a portion of it—about a third. Turns out that the other two-thirds is occupied by a company that is listed as ABEX on the map."

"ABEX is AmeriBiz Express Freight, I take it?"

"Yes, and in every city where Kala Shipping leases terminal space, ABEX shares the building. Here's the terminal in Atlanta," he said, changing the map. "And the one in Miami," commenting on the subsequent map view. "According to Kala's web site, they are looking to establish a hub in Texas in the first quarter of next year. I did a little digging and turned up permit applications for ABEX in Houston. Here's another interesting coincidence: ABEX, AmeriBiz, or whatever they want to call themselves, gets venture funding from the same capital group as does Kala Shipping."

"What we don't know," Mack interjected, "is what it means, if anything."

"Yes," I added, "it strikes me as odd that a venture capital firm would fund two mostly identical competitors that seem to be joined at the hip."

"Unless the two companies offer a dissimilar specialty," said Kevin. "If one specialized in refrigerated cargo transport, then there wouldn't be overlap, and the investment makes more sense."

I nodded. "Does Quantelle happen to have a presence nearby?"

"They do," said Kevin, moving the map, "but they are in many cities where neither Kala nor AmeriBiz operates. Plus, it's hardly unusual that the companies are located in relative proximity of each other. Freight and logistics companies tend to cluster around major highway intersections, rail yards, and areas with easy access to airports. All the locations we researched fit that description nicely. They could be guilty of nothing more than sound business practices."

"True, but if that's the case," I asked, "why did someone feel the need to shoot at Tom?"

"I'm still working on it," said Kevin.

* * *

Lost in all the excitement was Zonk's scheduled check-in. It came and went without incident, and he reported nothing out of the ordinary. That changed abruptly, signaled by a chirp from one of Mack's computers.

"Looks like Zonk has something to report," she said.

We had devised what was likely an overly-complicated and unnecessary communication protocol, all in an effort to protect Zonk from being discovered. Mack tried to explain it to me, but my eyes glazed over partway through, and she abandoned the noble effort. Nevertheless, I knew that the signal meant that I should expect a call.

I opened a drawer and selected the topmost cell phone. It was laughably low tech, but would serve the purpose. I turned it on, connected a recording device, and did the only thing I could do: wait.

It rang promptly on schedule, and I answered. Background noise told me that Zonk was, wisely, in a public location. We exchanged our prearranged pleasantries.

"Hi Mom," Zonk said.

"Your mom is here," I replied, "but can't come to the phone right now."

"That's aright. I'll talk to you until she's ready."

The conversation passed our agreed-upon protocol, so I dropped the pretense. "What do you have for me?"

"Not entirely sure," Zonk answered, "but something has happened a few times—three now, to be exact—that I wanted to report."

"Fire away."

"Three times now, we've been told to leave our shift an hour early and the shift that followed reported an hour late. The first time, it made a lot of sense. We'd had a great first half of the shift and ran out of work. They let us take off early because we really didn't have anything to do. The last two times have been different."

"How so?"

"First off, we're up to our eyeballs in work. There is no way they were letting us go early for that reason. The attitude is different, too. The first time, a bunch of us milled around, shooting the breeze and all. The last two times, we were escorted out of the building by security. They were serious about it, too. I did the best I could to linger without being obvious, and I could tell they were checking every nook and cranny in our part of the warehouse."

"Did they offer any explanation?"

"Not really. One of the security people said something about a safety situation. One of my co-workers theorized that it might be some sort of hazardous spill, and they needed to get us out of there so they could clean it up. That would make sense to me, except for the fact that we don't really deal in anything particularly hazardous. I suppose if one of the trucks on the dock had something leaking in it, that would explain it."

"I expect your co-workers will be asking questions. See if you can pick anything up."

"I'll try, but I don't want to appear too interested in it. Most of my co-workers stopped listening or caring when they learned we were getting paid for our full shift. And another thing…"

"Go on."

"Quantelle's chief of security, was hanging around the last two times it happened. I've not seen her past five o'clock since I started there, until the last few nights."

"Did they shut down the whole warehouse, or just your area?"

"Just our area, from what I can tell. I work in what amounts to the far corner of the building—an alcove of sorts. The layout isolates us, including the loading docks that serve our area, from the big warehouse floor."

"Is there anything special about the packages you work with that would warrant an alcove?"

"Not that I can tell. I've seen everything from computer electronics to musical instruments come across my scanner. That's really all I have to report. Apart from that, everything has been straightforward, and Quantelle seems to be a good employer."

"Thanks, and stay safe. Did you hear about Tom?"

"No. I've stayed away from everything that would connect us."

"Someone chased after him with a fully automatic AK-47. He's okay, but he's turned in his notice."

"Wow!"

"It wasn't expected, that's for sure. He was investigating a freight company co-owned by one of the people at Quantelle. Apparently, he struck a nerve."

"What was the name of the company?"

"One is Kala Shipping, the other is AmeriBiz Express Freight, although they sometimes call themselves ABEX."

"I've never heard of either, but I'm not always near the loading docks. I'll keep my eyes open and let you know if I see trucks from either of those companies."

"Sounds good, and if you hear a new voice, we've hired Kevin Moriarty until Tom comes back—if he comes back. You be careful, okay?"

"Of course I will."

CHAPTER TWENTY-FIVE

The promises of an unseasonably warm and comfortable day turned out to be optimistic. A misting rain and dreary skies were the order of the day.

"Nice house," I said as Eva Peretti answered the door. The large, brick, colonial-style house easily dwarfed my modest home.

"Thanks. Want to buy it?" she laughed.

"You're selling it? Why?"

"I'm thinking about it," she said, inviting me in. "With Ashley grown and out on her own, it's quite a bit more than I need, although I'd probably miss the pool in the summer."

"It's quite lovely, but I can see why it would be a bit much for someone living alone."

"I came from a suburb of Philadelphia," she said, giving me a tour of the ground floor. "I was one of seven children. I swear, our whole house would have fit into the garage, but we managed. All of us turned out all right, I think." She pointed to a picture on the wall. "There we are a few years ago at a family reunion. There's yours truly," tapping her finger on the picture. "I'm the youngest of the bunch and the only one without grandkids, but my parents always said I was the most deliberate and cautious one."

"Are these both your daughters?" I pointed to a nearby picture.

"That's Ashley, of course, and her older sister Jessica. Those were fun days, John. Ash and her sister were inseparable—still are. They talk on the phone all the time. Thank goodness for the internet! Without it, they'd both spend their entire pay check on their cellular bill."

"You don't look like you're too happy in this one," I said, pointing to a different picture.

"Oh, that was an awful week! That's Paul Vinton," she said, tapping on the image of a light-haired man standing to her left, "my ex. This was a business trip to Mexico, and I spent the majority of it enjoying the great view of my bathroom door." She laughed. "Don't drink the water!"

"What does your ex do?"

"He's a surgeon, but this trip wasn't related to his work in medicine. He's part of an investment group, or at least he was then. I don't know if he still does it or not—we rarely speak to one another."

"Sorry," I said, "I didn't mean to bring up unpleasant memories."

"Oh, no. Not at all. I keep this picture around to remind me that things don't often go as planned, but we can overcome the setbacks. When this was taken, I didn't expect to be living alone in this big house. But hey, I'm healthy, happy, have a great job, and am absolutely loving life. Paul can kiss my sweep bippie!" She chuckled. "Now, are you ready to get coffee?"

* * *

"You're an interesting man, John Costa," Eva said, sipping her cappuccino.

"I am?"

"You can afford any house you want, any car on the planet, yet you choose to live in a modest two bedroom home in a rather typical suburban area, and you drive a used sedan. How did you avoid the golf course crowd?"

"I guess I never learned how to spend money. My house holds my things and my car gets me around."

"My dad would have called you a *sensible man*, I think. He didn't care too much for Paul."

"Oh? Why not?"

"Paul always had money. His family was well off, so he wasn't familiar with the worries of paying bills, and fretting if there will be enough left over to have a good Christmas this year. When I was a kid, we never had any money. My dad drove a heating oil truck, and my mother worked as a housekeeper in a local hotel. Somehow, though, we always had everything we needed. I think it's a different world now. People don't just want what they need, they want more. Yet, they're never satisfied. It took a divorce and a lot of self-evaluation for me to figure it out."

"Well, whatever you're doing seems to be working."

"It was a long road, but I got here. Of course, having a house with a clear deed in my name and a healthy bank account doesn't hurt. But honestly, I'd trade all of it to have a cozy house full of family like I did growing up. You have family in Ireland, don't you?"

"Yes, all over, but the largest concentration is around Cork, where my mother was born."

"Do you ever go over to see them?"

"I visited about four years ago, but my life has been a bit of a whirlwind since then. Maybe when things settle down, I'll pay them a visit again."

"You should," she said, sipping her coffee. "What do you do for Christmas?"

"Usually very little, and nothing at all the last couple of years."

"You know those brothers and sisters that you saw in the picture? Most of them and their families will be here for Christmas. The place will be a madhouse full of Italians, but it will feel like a home, at least for a few days. If you think you can deal with a few hours of insanity, why don't you join us for Christmas dinner?"

"Oh, I wouldn't want you to go to any effort on my account."

"We always make way too much food. Bring your friend Jillian and that hunky body guard that follows you around. Ashley will just die!" She giggled.

"All right," I laughed, "we'll be there if at all possible."

* * *

"How was your date?" Mack asked, seconds after I walked in the front door.

I frowned. "It wasn't a date. We just had coffee and chatted a bit."

"Uh huh," she said, unconvinced. "Kevin, you saw the whole thing. Was it a date?"

"I'm staying out of this one," he said, slipping into the office.

Mack studied me. "What's bothering you? You two didn't hit it off?"

"No, it isn't that. We had a very good conversation. Hell, we're all invited to Christmas dinner at her house."

"Oh, something other than Chinese food this year? Sounds fun."

"I'm sure it will be nuts, but in a good way, and she's a remarkable chef."

"So what's the issue?"

"Just something I noticed when I was looking at a picture she had in her house."

"What was it?"

"There was a picture of her ex-husband on a business trip in Mexico. The other people in the picture were his business partners, but not involved in his medical practice. One of the people in the background was wearing a polo with a logo on it that looked awfully familiar."

"Oh?"

"It's probably nothing, but it bore a striking resemblance to the AmeriBiz Express Freight logo. I would have dismissed it, but Eva mentioned that the group in the picture was involved in investments. You think I'm nuts, don't you, Mack?"

"Yes, but not about things like this. Your intuition is pretty damn sharp."

"I guess that's a requirement when you have luck like mine, at least when it comes to women."

Mack frowned. "Don't tell me that Eva Peretti's on the suspect list, too?"

"I'm rapidly getting to the point where everyone is on the list, present company excluded. Maybe I'm wrong, but the logo sure looked like AmeriBiz. Same red ellipse, same white lettering, same oddly-sized letter x with a strange tail. The more this goes on, the less I'm likely to write something off as a coincidence."

"Does that mean we're having Chinese food for Christmas dinner again?" she said, looking dejected.

"No. I think we should attend Eva's party. If I'm wrong, we'll have a good evening and chalk all this up to unhealthy paranoia. If I'm right, then we might learn a few things."

"For the record," Mack said, "I don't think Eva is involved. She doesn't seem to be the type."

"No," I sighed, "she doesn't, but we've been stupendously wrong before."

* * *

"You're up early," Mack said.

"Couldn't sleep," I replied, offering her some coffee.

"Restless dreams?"

"No, just a restless mind. I've been reading through what Adnan sent us, feeling like I'm missing something, but I haven't been able to find anything yet."

"I worked on Jenn's books a bit more last night. It took me a bit to sort through all of it, but I was able to correlate some of Rick's income with his expenses. It ought to have been straightforward, but everything was so convoluted, it took a while to sort it all out."

"I'm not quite sure I follow you, Mack."

"Let's say that, as part of a case, we have to travel to the west coast. We would keep a log of the case, the expenses, and the income it generated. It would be easy to figure out where we went, our spending, and how much we earned in profit. All of it ties together."

"Sure. Makes sense."

"Rick's books didn't exactly work like that, but I think I've got Jenn's system decoded enough to understand it. From what I can tell,

Rick Stevens did a fair amount of travel for his business. Most of it was domestic, but about a quarter was overseas."

"That's consistent with what his ex told me."

"His pattern of travel and payment is pretty consistent, too. Most of his trips were three days. One day to fly out, one day there, another to fly back home. Once in a while, he would have a four day gig mixed in, but that was relatively rare."

"Yeah, he was probably one of those people that a corporation would fly in for a day or two to talk to their executive teams—the type who spouts bullshit laced with made-up acronyms, but with just enough common sense mixed in to make it sound like he was the fount of all wisdom. Sounds *exactly* like the kind of business that Jennifer Adams would be involved in."

Mack laughed, shaking her head. "I suppose that's one way to look at it."

"I know, I know," I sighed. "I really need to let it go."

"You do," she nodded, raising her eyebrows. "But here's the interesting thing in Rick's pattern of travel. I almost missed it because of the way Jenn recorded things. Over the last few years, he made a series of longer visits, where he stayed upwards of a week; even longer for a couple of overseas visits."

"Maybe he had some clients that wanted an extra dose of nonsense…"

A look of annoyance flashed across her face. "All but one were to the same four locations."

"Interesting… I suppose you're going to tell me where."

"I might, if you offer a suitable apology for interrupting me."

"Mack!"

"I really don't ask for much, in the grand scheme of things!"

"Mack!!"

"Oh, all right! Genius is never appreciated in its time. His extended visits were to Atlanta, Miami, Manila, and, ready for this… Sarajevo. When he went on these special trips, he was quite well paid, too. Jenn probably did some of her bookkeeping shenanigans to distort his income and, as far as we know, there might be more that isn't even on the books."

"How much are we talking about, Mack? I know some of those corporate lecturers make decent money, but you make it sound like…"

"His last trip to Atlanta came in at just under a half a million dollars, and that's just the part I can find in Jenn's books."

"I don't think he's being paid half a million dollars to lecture on teamwork, communication, and synergy."

"I don't either, and get this—he had been home from his last trip around a month when he was killed. His last trip was an extended visit—quite lucrative, too—but it wasn't to any one of the four usual destinations. It was to Houston, and was timed perfectly with the issuance of some permits to AmeriBiz Express Freight."

"That just can't be a damned coincidence!"

"No, I don't think it is," she said. "The only problem is, I can't prove the connection from Jenn's books. She did a wonderful job of hiding income sources."

"Well, if nothing else, it confirms two things for me. First, we're right to be looking into AmeriBiz and Kala."

"And the other?"

"Is that you're absolutely freaking amazing, Mack!"

CHAPTER TWENTY-SIX

"Paul Vinton ended his participation in the venture capital firm, ABX Industries, shortly after his divorce from Eva Peretti was finalized," Kevin said. "I don't know the specifics as to why they parted company or if it was done on friendly terms, but there's nothing out there to suggest that he's still involved with them. Are any of these the man you saw in the picture?"

The screen changed, displaying a grid of pictures. I stared at it for a while, challenging my memory. "That one," I said, pointing to a man's picture. "I'm pretty sure he was in the picture I saw at Eva's house."

"That would make sense," he said. "He's the founder and chairman of the board. ABX is one of his businesses. Do you recognize him?"

"No. Should I?"

"That's Swindon McCarter."

"The name rings a bell, but for some reason I'm picturing an older man."

"You're thinking of his dad, the Texas oil billionaire. This is his eldest son—the one who inherited the largest share of the estate."

"Sure. I don't exactly run in those circles."

"In the case of Swindon McCarter, you're probably better off. He's got the reputation of being quite the playboy, throwing extravagant parties, and for a rumored bevy of illegitimate children scattered all over the place. Word has it, he writes a big check and moves on."

"What about his business dealings?"

"Equally smarmy, from all indications. He dabbles in all sorts of things, and I suspect that ABX Industries falls into that category. It's hard to track down everything that they're into, but I could easily see it as a money sink for him."

"I didn't realize Paul Vinton had that kind of money," I said.

"He doesn't," Kevin answered. "I've been only able to track down a handful of investors from when he was involved, but my guess is he was the poorest of the bunch, probably by a factor of ten or more."

"It would be interesting to know what got him in that scene, and why he got out."

"I've got a call in to him. Hopefully, he'll shed some light on the situation."

"Good work, Kevin. Where's Mack, anyway?"

"She's out shopping for a dress to wear to Eva's party."

"Why the hell are you here instead of keeping an eye on her?"

"Relax, Mister Costa. My backup went along; she's in good hands. Besides, I've been given strict instructions to make sure that you go and buy a new suit today."

"I don't have time to shop for a suit. Besides, the one I have is perfectly good."

"She thought you might say that. I've been authorized to use force if necessary," he said, fighting a smile while he flexed his right bicep.

"I'm not going to win this argument, am I?"

"Not with her, you're not," he said.

"If we go to O'Brien's for lunch, we can pop over to…"

"I've also been given a list of acceptable stores," he said, before I could finish. He handed me a handwritten list. "Not to speak out of place, Mister Costa, but I think this party is important to her."

I wasn't exactly sure why, but if Kevin was right, I didn't want to disappoint my friend. "Well, if this is the list, I understand the urgency. All of these do fitting and custom alterations, and it won't be done in time if we wait. Is there anything else I should know?"

"I'm supposed to make sure you buy something appropriate for a celebration and not a damned funeral. Her words, not mine."

* * *

I smiled patiently as Mack's conspiracy unfolded around me. The only place that could fulfill our time requirements was both the last place on her list and the most expensive. Somehow, it felt like this was a surprise only to me—doubly so when Kevin produced Mack's list of "suggestions" on the style and fabric of suit. I protested briefly, but realized that I was fighting a losing battle. In the interest of lunch, and my own well-being, I capitulated.

Jolted by what felt like a stunning amount to spend on a suit, I made a dash for lunch at O'Brien's in the hopes of salvaging some small remnant of my original plans. Even that was for naught, though, as Maureen Myers summoned me in her own, special way.

"The first check arrived today, Rover. Come over and get your next treat."

"I was just about to get lunch. Can it wait?"

"No. I have an appointment for physical therapy in an hour. Now or never, Rover."

Dammit.

* * *

My lunch, an unpleasant, stale burger dispatched from a drive through, sat heavily in my stomach. I barely made it to the porch when I noticed another vehicle pull up in front of her house. Maureen's door opened.

"Here ya go, Fido," she said, handing me an envelope. "You almost missed your chance," she said, pointing her cane at the other car, narrowly missing my head in the process.

"What is it?"

"How the hell should I know? Barry mumbled some nonsense about giving this to you if anything happened to him, so I'm giving it to you."

"This could be important, Maureen! Why didn't you give this to me sooner?"

"Because I didn't trust you."

"Do you trust me now?"

"Not really, but more than before. Now get the hell out of my way. These nice people are going to take me to my appointment."

"You trust them, I suppose, even though you've probably never met them before."

"Well of course I do. They're wearing uniforms and have credentials," she growled. "You look like a panhandler looking for a handout. Well, you got one." She tapped the envelope. "Now, home you go."

I watched her make her way to the vehicle before turning to Kevin with, undoubtedly, a stunned, angry look on my face. "You drive, Kevin," I said, tossing him the keys. "For everyone's safety."

He stared as she drove away. "Hell is empty and all the devils are here. But Shakespeare never met Maureen Myers. That woman's an asshole!" he said.

"Though this be madness, yet there's method in't," I sighed.

* * *

Mack cast me a wicked smile as I walked through the door. "How was your day?"

"I was the victim of a vast and foul conspiracy. Where are my antacid tablets?"

"You really worry me sometimes, John," she said, wrinkling her nose. "I hope you've managed to find some time to get some work done, and that you haven't spent the entire day having fun."

"I can assure you, Jillian MacDonald, I have had absolutely no fun today. We will discuss your nefarious ways as soon as I find my antacid."

She raised her eyebrow. "Suit yourself," she said, motioning to the door leading to the music room. "Your antacid awaits!"

"Here," I said, handing her the envelope. "Special delivery from Maureen."

* * *

"Well, *that* certainly took a while," Mack said as I finally made my way to the office.

"The hamburger was part of your nefarious plot—of that, I have no doubt. When I find the proof, they'll be hell to pay!"

"And the insanity continues… This envelope is proof," she said, the smile drifting from her face.

"Maureen gave that to me. Supposedly Barry told her to give it to me if anything happened to him. I guess that eliminates any doubt that his death was random."

"She waited until now?"

"Don't get me started, Mack. What was in the envelope?"

"Puzzle pieces, more or less, but nothing that makes sense."

She handed me four sheets of plain paper. Each was divided into grids, similar to a modern spreadsheet, except the grid lines were drawn by hand with a pencil. The cells were filled with numbers, letters, and a few symbols. The rows appeared to have been filled in at different times, as some were in blue ink, others in black, and a few in pencil. It looked more like doodling than anything meaningful, and none of it made any sense.

"What am I looking at?"

"Your guess is as good as mine," she said. "I was hoping she gave you some sort of hint about it, so I'd know where to start."

"Come on, Mack! Where's your sense of adventure? You love a good challenge, and this looks to be exactly that!"

"That, I do." She glanced down at the top page and started to chuckle.

"What is it?"

"This might be nothing more than doodling and not have anything to do with our murders."

"Why do you say that?"

"Here," she said, pointing to the page. "This symbol looks like a little banjo. It repeats a few times." She turned to the second page. "Yeah, it's here, too, and on the third page…" The smile faded from her face. "No. This means something—it isn't just random doodling."

"Knowing my luck and Maureen's weird ways, this is probably just a session schedule written in some silly code Barry developed in his spare time. She's probably having a good laugh at our expense right now."

Mack smiled. "Complete with a bottle of bourbon and a pack of cigarettes, although…" her voice faded.

"Go on."

"There are certain elements about this grid that are consistent with a schedule, although the column that would normally hold the time is way too narrow. Still…" Her voice trailed away. "Do you mind if we skip the movies tonight? I've got a couple of ideas on this thing, and I'd like to get to work on it."

"Of course not, Mack. I'll be in the music room practicing if you need me for anything."

* * *

While playing, I allowed my mind to focus on something other than Barry's murder and quickly lost track of time. Mack's voice startled me.

"That's a pretty tune," she said. "What's it called?"

"Foxhunters," I said, putting down my violin. "It's a reel, a type of dance."

"I know what a reel is. I tried my hand a bit at Irish dancing when I was a kid, just like damn near everyone else on my block. As you might have guessed, I wasn't very good," she said, laughing quietly. "I don't understand the titles behind a lot of the music you play, but that one I can understand just from the way the music sounds."

"It has a sound that conjures images of old school fox hunting, I'll give you that. Now, I know you didn't come down here to talk about music. Was my playing bothering you?"

"Not at all. Actually, I didn't even realize you were playing until I came down the stairs. Usually I can hear you, but for some reason it was much quieter."

"Practice mute," I said, holding up a black piece of rubber. "It hugs the bridge, restricting its ability to vibrate; therefore, less sound."

"Clever," she said, "and appreciated. Not that I don't like your playing. Just sometimes, when I'm trying to concentrate and I don't want to wear headphones."

"No worries, Mack," I said, laughing gently. "Just let me know if I get too loud. What's on your mind?"

"Your friend Barry was a smart and creative man," she said. "You were right about one thing when it comes to these papers."

"Oh?"

"The good news is, I can definitely say that these papers are some sort of a schedule. It took me longer to figure that out than it should have, because I was thinking like a computer, instead of like a creative human being. I kept trying to turn these columns into dates and times, and it wouldn't work."

"But a schedule is made up of dates and times. I'm not following you."

"Of course it is, but there's nothing that says it has to be written out like digits on a computer screen. Here, take a look. The third column is the time."

I stared at it for a while, but didn't see anything except letters and symbols.

"The hands on a clock face," she whispered.

Then I saw it. "Oh, that's clever as hell!"

"Yep. The orientation of the first symbol is the little hand, the second is the big hand, and the third denotes morning or night. He used a similar idea to disguise the date in this column." Her finger tapped the rightmost column. "So there you have the good news. I understand the dates and times. The bad news is, I don't understand anything else on these pages."

"Barry was logging something, something important enough to warrant some sort of code that looked like random doodling. We just have no idea what it might be."

194

"I know a couple things it isn't. It isn't a copy of his amateur radio log. I cross referenced his electronic logs and his written logs against these dates and times, and didn't get a single match. It also isn't your session schedule."

"Oh, I was only joking about that."

"Well, I had to check. He used several musical instruments as symbols throughout. None more than this little banjo symbol, though. He must've really loved playing that thing."

I glanced over at his instrument, still in its case and propped in the corner. "Yes, I think he did."

"One of these days, you'll have to play it for me," she said.

"Okay," I chuckled, "but when I do, you might want to wear earplugs. I'm not a very good banjo player, and they're anything but quiet."

"Can't you use a mute?"

"They don't really make mutes for them, not that I'm aware of. An open back banjo is a bit quieter, but Barry's has a closed back and a brass resonator ring. That's why it's so damned heavy and loud! Consider yourself duly warned."

"Fair enough," she said, smiling. "Good night, John." She gently kissed my forehead.

"Good night, Mack."

CHAPTER TWENTY-SEVEN

"You certainly do find such interesting people to surround yourself with, Jack," Jerry Keynes said, "and get yourself in the middle of such epic messes."

"What now, Jerry?"

"The test results on the notes came back late yesterday. My source on this is well-placed, so I don't have any reason to doubt what's being said. Not that what I'm going to tell you is going to help, but you should know. The stock of paper found on the first two victims, Rick Stevens and Barry Myers, was the same, but different from the control sample from Sarajevo."

"So we've got a copycat."

"Perhaps. Or perhaps something else is going on. The tests from the note left on Jennifer Adams matched the Sarajevo sample perfectly."

"Wait... What?"

"Oh, it gets better, Jack. A source inside the medical examiner's office told me that they have refused to conclude that all three murders were committed by the same person. There are, apparently, some inconsistencies. Exactly what they are, my sources didn't know, or wouldn't tell me." He laughed. "Your buddy George O'Neil is about to become one of the unhappiest people in town."

"Why's that?"

"A local reporter has gotten wind of this whole unpleasant business and is starting to ask questions. He's a real bulldog—a bit given to sensationalism, but with really good instincts. He can smell that something's not right, and I don't expect him to ease up on it until he gets answers. Remember that case a few years back where a poor fellow died from toxins he encountered at work?"

"Yes I do, but the details are hazy. Something to do with industrial chemicals?"

"That's the one. Everyone thought the guy was exposed to poisons at work, but the reporter didn't buy the story, and stuck with it until the truth came out. Turns out, the poor old fellow had a wife that wanted him dead. Now, do you see my point about marriage, Jack?"

I laughed. "I'll keep that in mind, in the unlikely situation that a woman wants to discuss matrimony. What's the reporter's name? I'll know it as soon as you say it."

"Vincent DeLuca. Vinny D, live on the scene!"

"Oh brother! Well, maybe O'Neil will be unhappy, but this might be the break we need. Everybody is being so damn tight-lipped right now, we're having a hard time making any progress."

"Don't feel bad. I don't think you're alone in that category. In spite of their technology and resources, my sources tell me the police are absolutely flummoxed. What's that expression you use, the one your mum used to say?

"At sixes and sevens?"

"That's the one. Makes no sense, but it seems to fit. I'm still learning a few things about the first victim. I'll call you when I have anything worth sharing."

"Sounds good. This DeLuca guy—is he trustworthy?"

"Yeah, in spite of being a bit obnoxious at times, he's one of the good guys. Just don't tell him I said so."

* * *

I hadn't made it two steps into the office when Mack descended on me.

"Vinny D, live on the scene!"

"Are you auditioning as a reporter now?"

"No, but I'm also not auditioning as an answering service. He's already called three times this morning."

"Well, he doesn't waste any time. Jerry said there was the possibility of a call."

"Please tell me you're going to call him. I look absolutely *terrible* in orange."

"What does orange have to do with anything?"

"Because one of the two of you is going to die at my hand if that phone doesn't stop ringing."

"Oh, is that all you're worried about? I'm pretty sure the local jail they'd take you to uses blue outfits. I think that would go with your hair nicely." Her green eyes nearly turned bright red as she pointed to the phone. "All right!" I said, "I'll call him."

"Good," she said, "because I have something interesting to share."

"Oh?"

"Nope. Not until you make him go away."

"Taking a page out of Maureen's playbook, are we?"

"Fetch, Fido," she said, doing her best imitation of Maureen's throaty voice.

Glaring at her, I settled into my chair and dialed the number Mack handed to me.

* * *

Unlike his intense television persona, Vincent DeLuca spoke in a deliberate, soft voice on the phone. To his credit, he had done his homework and had some impressive sources. He knew damn near as much about the case as we did, and likely a few things we didn't.

I was able to deflect and avoid his questions about Maureen Myers, citing confidentiality. When I tried to redirect him to George O'Neil, his frustration surfaced.

"Captain O'Neil directed me to talk to you. He said you were engaged in an independent investigation of the crime."

"Oh, he did, did he?" In my imagination, I was preparing a special place in hell just for George O'Neil.

"Look, maybe we can help each other. I understand you had a relationship with the third victim, Miss Adams."

"We were acquainted, yes, but we hadn't spoken for many years."

"Acquainted isn't the term my sources used."

"All right, already! We dated for six months, but when it ended, it ended. I can understand why George O'Neil brought it up when she died, but I don't understand why my long-dead relationship with Jenn matters to your story."

"You met with her recently, didn't you?"

"I can neither confirm nor deny that said meeting took place."

"That isn't helpful, Mister Costa."

"I'm not trying to be helpful; I'm trying to get you to leave my assistant and me alone."

He continued, still pleasant, but unabated. "Did you know her boyfriend, one of the other victims?"

"I never met him. I really don't think..."

"Did you know that he was under investigation, as was Miss Adams? Specifically, for irregularities in reporting quarterly taxes and foreign income."

"Okay," I sighed, "you have my attention Mister DeLuca."

"Good. Now maybe we can help each other. I have a source that was close to both Miss Adams and Mister Stevens. Were you aware that for several months leading up to his death, they had been arguing frequently?"

"No, I didn't. Your source didn't happen to know the cause of the friction, I suppose."

"No specifics," he said, "but I was told it had something to do with his business and some overseas issues."

"Did it have anything to do with trips to Manila and Sarajevo? He broke his normal travel patterns when he visited those cities. The trips were longer, and significantly more lucrative."

"As a matter of fact, Mister Costa, it did. Rick had gotten into something, and was trying to get himself out of it. My source didn't say what it was, but I was left with the impression it wasn't ethical."

"In talking to Rick's ex-wife, I got the impression that Rick might have been in trouble. She blamed Jennifer Adams."

"So you think I'm looking in the right place? I mean, we've got three bodies on our hands, and the police aren't talking."

I sighed. "Your investigation makes sense to me, but I'll be honest with you. One of my investigators went nosing around in the wrong place and ended up getting his car shot up. It might have been a coincidence, but someone out there isn't happy that we're asking questions."

"I heard that call come in on my police scanner. That was you?"

"One of my people, but Mister DeLuca, I'm telling you these things in confidence. I expect them to be kept that way."

"Hey! You hurt me, Mister Costa! I've never given away the identity of a source. I even spent three month in the slammer on a ridiculous contempt of court charge because I wouldn't talk."

"What judge?" I asked.

"Mortonsen."

"Old bastard," I laughed. "About time someone stood up to that that crusty old crook."

"That was me! What the hell was your man doing in the vicinity of Dyle Road, anyway?"

"Inquiring about a job driving a truck."

"That's unexpected," he said.

"If you prove yourself reliable, I might even be nice enough to tell you why. On the other hand, if you screw me over, I'll buy the station you work for, fire you, sell it, and repeat the process for the next station that hires you. Do I make myself clear?"

"Crystal."

* * *

"I see you survived your brush with fame," Mack said, nibbling on her pizza.

"For better or worse, I traded some information with him. He's got some useful connections, that's for sure. It does make one wonder how he was able to find out that Rick and Jenn were under investigation for tax and foreign income irregularities while we remained in the dark."

She wrinkled her nose. "Ingratitude will get you nowhere. Besides, you're always forcing me to stay within the law. If you'd let me bend a few from time to time, you might not need to rely on people like Vinny D!"

"I also might end up seeing you once a week during visiting hours at the nearest federal penitentiary. For what it's worth, you'd be wearing orange."

"Now that you put it that way…"

"See? I really am looking out for you, Mack."

"As you should! Do you want to hear something interesting?"

"Of course," I said, leaning forward in my chair.

"I still can't decipher the stuff on Barry's documents, but I was able to correlate some of the times he recorded with Rick's extended visits."

She grabbed another slice of pizza before changing the display on one of our large monitors to show her work.

"Here are Barry's entries from three o'clock in the morning. Without fail, two days later, Rick's in Atlanta. And another thing, this column," she moved her mouse pointed in circles around the column in question, "is always the same."

"No it isn't," I protested.

"It is. It just doesn't look it at first glance. He used the same letters and symbols, they're just reordered or reoriented depending on the month. The same correlation happens for Miami."

She changed the view on the screen again.

"Four in the morning on Barry's sheet, five days later, Rick's in Miami. Same re-arrangement scheme in this other column. Unfortunately, we have no idea what it means, but its hard to call it a coincidence."

"What about Rick's overseas travel. Any correlation there?"

"Still working on it."

"Whatever it is, Barry felt it important enough to encode, and to send it to me."

"Let me ask you something," Mack said, her expression turning serious. "How well did you know Barry?"

"Why?"

"I don't want to tarnish his memory, but is there any chance he was involved in whatever unsavory stuff Rick was supposedly doing? We don't have fire yet, but there seems to be more and more smoke every day."

"I wasn't good friends with Barry or anything, but from what I knew of him from playing music together, it strikes me as unlikely."

"What about Jenn?"

"What about her? I think my feelings on the subject are well known." I was guilty of barking my answer, but it wasn't a subject I felt like rehashing.

"Not those feelings, Grouchy McHolds-a-Grudge... Do you think she's likely to be involved in something unsavory?"

"I'd say she's more likely to be engaged in legal shenanigans than Barry, if that's what you're asking."

"What about murder?"

I paused for a moment, collecting myself. The question was blunt, but fair. "No, Mack, I don't think so. Lying, cheating, stealing? No doubt. Not murder. At least I don't think so."

A FEW SIMPLE MURDERS

CHAPTER TWENTY-EIGHT

"Well, I have the official explanation for our shortened shifts at work," Zonk said, checking in as per our schedule.

"What is it?"

"A malfunctioning carbon monoxide sensor in the alcove."

"Do you believe it?"

"It's a plausible explanation, on the surface of things, but that doesn't explain why the security chief was there. I haven't seen her since, but the test will come next week. My shift is ending ninety minutes early, and the shift that follows delays their start by the same, but only in my section of the building."

"What's the reason this time?"

"Routine maintenance. Also plausible, but it strikes me as poor planning if that's really the reason. We're making the last big push toward the holidays, and the quantity of orders we're handling is climbing. I can understand fixing something that's broken, but routine maintenance should be scheduled around busy times, not in the middle of them."

"How's your cover holding? Any reason to believe they suspect you of anything?"

"No, but they probably will if I go through with my plans for the next outage."

"What do you have in mind?"

"I think I know of a place where they won't check if they sweep through the alcove. If I can hide there undetected, I might be able to get a look at what's going on. Knowing my luck, I'll spend three hours hiding in cramped conditions to watch them work on a conveyor belt or something."

"I'm not sure I like this idea."

"Well, I have the bodyguard you hired looking out for me, of course, and I do a decent job of taking care of myself."

"Tom thought that too, until someone started firing at him with an AK-47."

"I'll be careful."

"You're going to do it, regardless of what I say, aren't you?"

"No," he sighed, "but I don't feel like I'm contributing anything other than paranoia and speculation. Will it make you feel any better if I secretly put out a couple of Miss MacDonald's tiny cameras and stream the whole thing?"

"I'd feel better if you did that and *didn't* stay there. At least then we'd know whether or not it's worth the risk for you to stay the next time, if there's even a next time. This could be normal operation for Quantelle, and we could be looking in the wrong direction."

"All right, Mister Costa, you make a good point."

I could tell that Zonk was disappointed, but I wasn't in the mood to take risks, especially not after what happened to Tom.

"I'll arrange for Mack to get the cameras configured and delivered to you. Be careful, okay? No heroics."

"I understand."

* * *

An unfamiliar face answered the door at Ashley Vinton's apartment. I'd not seen the slender, brown-haired woman before, but she seemed to recognize me. Silent and expressionless, she motioned for me to come in, her eyes studying the parking lot behind me.

"Meet my bodyguard," Ashley said, from the couch beyond. "Isn't she a wonderful conversationalist?"

The woman's expression didn't change, and she remained silent. Her short, brown hair surrounded a weathered face that bore hints of Semitic origins.

"John Costa," I said, tentatively introducing myself.

"I know who you are," she replied, but offered nothing else in response. She moved into a corner chair from where she could watch the room and the parking lot beyond.

"She's a bit scary," said Ashley, adjusting the position of her leg, "but she seems to know her stuff, and I'm glad she's on our side. I've been able to pry a few things out of her, like that she's ex-Israeli military."

"That speaks for itself," I said, raising my eyebrows. The woman's expression didn't change.

"Speaking of bodyguards, where is yours, Mister Costa?"

"He's waiting for me in the car. I wanted to minimize, um, distractions."

She blushed. "That obvious, huh?"

"Yep," I said, smiling. "Are you feeling up to answering a few questions about your employer? It shouldn't take long."

"Of course. It isn't like I'm going anywhere," she said, tapping the cast on her leg. "My mother keeps sending me food, which is wonderful, but I can't do much in the way of exercise. By the time all this is done, I'm going to be fat!"

I chuckled. "Your mother means well."

"I know it, and I appreciate it, but I have to maintain the veneer of self-reliance. If I don't, she'll be over here all day fussing over me. Now, you had questions?"

"There were back-to-back shutdowns in one section of Quantelle's warehouse recently. Is that a common occurrence?"

"It happens," she answered, "and for any number of reasons."

"Such as?"

"Broken equipment, any hazardous condition, preventative maintenance, or if there isn't enough work to support a full shift."

"Carbon monoxide?"

"Sure. I don't think I recall it ever actually happening. If enough rolled in from the trucks at the docks, the sensors would trip. Our heating system runs on natural gas, so we maintain sensors throughout the building."

"Do you know if it's common to have routine maintenance scheduled during a peak time?"

"Quite the opposite," she said, emphatically. "Our maintenance crews do everything they can to minimize disruptions. Wait a minute…" Her eyes twinkled. "You've got someone working on the inside, don't you? You think there's something going on at Quantelle!"

"Yes to the first question, I don't know to the second. Ashley," I said, turning very serious, "it is imperative that you keep this to yourself. Not a word to anyone."

"Of course."

"Nobody. You talk, and I'll make sure Kevin Moriarty's next job is in Saskatoon!"

"Uncle!" she said, pretending to zip her lips shut. "Not a word."

"Would next week be a good time for maintenance?"

"Dear God, no, unless something threatened a complete shutdown of an area!"

"That's what I thought. Is there any way to tell if there's an impending maintenance issue?"

"I can try logging in and checking the maintenance schedule."

Her bodyguard shook her head. I understood and agreed with her reasoning.

"No," I said, "I don't want you to do that. You're supposed to be at home, recovering, and detached from the daily goings-on. If there is something afoot, I don't want any attention drawn to you, and a login to check much of anything beyond email would do exactly that."

"Good thinking," she said, "but I really, really find it hard to believe that Quantelle would be involved in anything. You've never worked there, Mister Costa. It just isn't the sort of company that would do anything even slightly wrong."

"We *were* attacked, you know, and I'm fairly certain someone on the inside facilitated the attack."

"You're right. I guess my loyalty is misplaced."

"Maybe," I said. "If you don't mind, I'd like my assistant to call you regarding access to Quantelle's maintenance schedules."

"Of course."

I handed her a card. "That's Kevin's number, but he'll only answer when he's able, so don't take it personally if the phone goes to voice mail."

It was all I could do to keep up with Ashley as she rattled off a string of details about Quantelle's security systems and access. Eventually, I resorted to recording her using my phone.

* * *

"Mack, see what you can do with this."

She reviewed the notes and listened to the recording.

"I can't do anything with it," she said.

"Why not?"

"Because you never let me break the law. These recordings give me everything I need to get into some of Quantelle's systems, but I would be doing so without authorization. You, of all people, should know!"

"Is there anything that could be construed as a good, healthy stretch?"

She sat back in her chair, stretching. After a moment, a smile came to her face.

"I have an idea," she said, "but it's going to require you to do something."

"What do you need me to do, Mack?"

"Find an excuse to spend the rest of the day somewhere else so you're not tempted to ask any more questions."

* * *

Laura McConnell pulled me aside. "Who's your new friend?" She tilted her head toward my usual table.

"That's Eva Peretti. I met her daughter while investigating Barry's murder. I'm going to try to talk her into coming to hear us play at our next session."

"Oh, this is serious," Laura said, winking.

"We'll see," I said. "How's business?"

Laura and I had known each other for many years. She was the first person I hired when opening O'Brien's, and it turned out to be one of my few strokes of genius. A graduate student at the time looking to fund her education, her strong intellect was unmistakable. Coupled with a sparkling personality and natural customer service skills, she was an ideal candidate to manage the establishment. I only expected her to stay for a year or two, but hoped that her business acumen would establish a solid foundation for the business to carry on without her. She did that and more, attacking the challenge with a work ethic rivaled only by Jillian MacDonald. Unexpectedly, she stayed, finding a string of excuses not to graduate. I repaid her efforts and loyalty by giving her the business and a healthy rainy day fund should the business start to founder. Freed from the shackles I had unwittingly fitted on her, she had taken O'Brien's to new heights, all while maintaining the comfortable, inviting feel of a traditional Irish pub.

"This is a record holiday season for us," she said. "Are you going to stay for the band?"

Laura, when she renovated and expanded the business, added a stage for live music, cleverly positioned so that patrons on the other side of the centrally-located bar could still enjoy an intimate conversation.

"No, we're just going to have a bite to eat. Eva's having family over for the holidays, and she's got a lot of preparing to do."

"Will you be here for the traditional Christmas Eve toast?"

"Of course! I wouldn't miss it!"

* * *

Eva chatted nearly nonstop during dinner, to the point I worried she wasn't going to eat any of her food. Somehow, though, she managed to do both. It was obvious that she was somewhat daunted by the prospects of entertaining her entire family, and the nervousness manifested in endless dialog.

"I don't know why I get so worked up over it every year," she said. "I'm probably setting unrealistic expectations for myself, but I always worry I'll let my family down."

"Don't they help you with the preparations? It seems rather much to put all of the burden on one person."

"They help where they can, but the lion's share falls on me."

"Is there anything I can do to help?

"If you're serious, I just might take you up on that offer."

* * *

The prospect of assistance seemed to calm her nerves and by the time dessert arrived, our conversation was relaxed and fun.

"One of these days, I'd like you to come hear us play Irish music. We're here every Wednesday, if you're not busy."

She smiled. "I'd love to! Are you on the stage?"

"No. It's a session. We get together and play tunes, informally. Right over there," I said, pointing to the empty table in the corner surrounded by chairs.

I rose, taking her over to the table with me.

"I always sit here," I said, resting my hand on one of the chairs. "Barry always liked that seat over there. Nancy, another fiddle player, usually sat next to him." I stopped, abruptly.

"What's wrong? A sad memory?" Her eyes searched my face, obviously concerned.

"No. Sorry. I didn't mean to zone out like that. Something just occurred to me…"

"I need to get back to my preparations anyway," she said, kissing me on the cheek. "I know that look; I get exactly the same way when I'm focused on something."

CHAPTER TWENTY-NINE

The punishment for calling Maureen Myers late in the evening was swift and horrible.

"Are you calling to whisper sweet nothings in my ear," she rasped, "or do you want to know what I'm wearing?"

"Actually," I said, trying to suppress my natural gag reflex, "I have a question about the case."

"Boxers or briefs?"

"Excuse me?"

"I want to know if you let that Italian passion of yours breathe freely, or if you cage it, like a wild animal, pacing, wanting to break free."

"I don't even know what to say, Mrs. Myers. Your question isn't even close to being appropriate."

She laughed, deep and smoky. "You're not my type, anyway. Not young enough! What's on your mind, Fido?"

"Barry's banjo…"

"A night like this, and you're thinking of a damned banjo? No wonder you're single! What about it?"

"Where did you get it?"

"How the hell should I know. He bought the damn thing!"

"No. After Barry died, how did you get it? Did the police bring it to you?"

"One of the musicians brought it over the next morning. A woman—I think she plays the fiddle."

"Nancy?"

"That's the one. Why?"

"I'm curious as to why it wasn't collected with his other belongings and taken in as evidence."

"The only thing that damned banjo is evidence of is Barry's bad taste in music and instruments. You know, I found the receipt for the thing while going through some of Barry's crap the other day. Do you know how much he paid for that awful-sounding thing?"

"I looked it up on the internet, Mrs. Myers. I recall the average value was a little under four thousand dollars."

"Well, my idiot of a husband paid almost five thousand dollars for it. He couldn't get it from a music shop. No! He had to go buy it from a boutique instrument builder. If he was going to pay that kind of money, at least he could've bought something that sounded good. Like an accordion."

"Good night, Maureen."

"You didn't answer my question!"

"I'm not going to. I'm not your type, remember?"

* * *

"Hi Nancy, it's John Costa. Sorry to call so late."

"Oh, Mister Costa! No problem, I stay up late nearly every night these days. I guess it's part of getting older. What can I do for you?"

"You took Barry's banjo to Maureen, right?"

"I did. Is everything okay with it? I was very careful handling it."

"It's fine. I'm curious, though, as to why you ended up with it instead of the police."

"It was sitting there, so I asked them what I should do with it. They asked if I knew how to get it back to his family. I did, so they told me to take it. They took down my name, information, and the details of the instrument. Did I do the wrong thing?"

"No. You're fine, Nancy. It didn't occur to me until today that Maureen had it in her possession so quickly after his death. I wondered if the police had somehow missed it, but it's good to know that it wasn't. You sat next to him that night, didn't you?"

"I did, just like always."

"Did you notice anything different in his behavior that night?"

"No, not really, other than leaving to try to catch you. I told all this to the police, though."

"Do you mind telling me? I know it's probably an unpleasant memory, but I'm trying to sort out what happened."

"Well, let's see… you led that set of three tunes. I think you spent as much time blowing your nose as you did playing. Then you got up and left after wishing everyone well. A minute later, Barry put his banjo down. I thought he was going to the restroom, but then he mentioned your name and took off out the front door. He might have said more than your name, but if he did, I couldn't make it out."

"Did he seem in a hurry?"

"Not at first, but once he was done with everything, he mentioned your name and made a beeline for the front door. He didn't run, but he walked quickly. I thought maybe you'd left something, and he was trying to get it to you. Just like I told the police."

"What do you mean, *done with everything* ?"

"He put his banjo back in its case, covered it, and closed the latches. He took good care of that instrument. If he needed a restroom break, he never left it sitting out."

"Other than chasing after me, was there anything else unusual about his behavior that evening?"

"No. He didn't say much, of course he never did. I do remember he was trying a new type of pick. His playing seemed a little quieter than normal, but that's the musician in me talking."

"Thanks, Nancy," I sighed. "Have a good evening."

"Sorry I couldn't be of more help. Will you be at the next session? We've missed you!"

"I'm going to try."

* * *

"Mack, am I allowed to ask questions yet?"

"No, Quizzy McCurious, you're not. I'll let you know exactly when. Oh, your new best friend called."

"Oh God, not Maureen Myers wanting to know what kind of underwear I prefer."

She looked at me, aghast. "Please tell me I didn't hear your correctly."

"No," I said, "you heard me right."

"I don't even want to know. What you do in your free time is your business."

"Mack! There isn't enough whiskey in the world…"

"I would never judge you."

"Mack!!"

"No," she said, mercifully relenting. "The call was from Vinny D on the scene!"

"What did he want?"

"He wanted to know what kind of underwear you prefer."

I glared at her, fighting back laughter. "All right. You win. Well played, Jillian MacDonald."

She bowed. "He didn't leave a message, other than to call at any time."

I skulked out of the office, not wanting to risk any more humiliation.

* * *

"I have someone who's willing to talk to you, Mister Costa," Vincent DeLuca said. "Someone close to Rick Stevens—with some interesting things to say."

"What's the catch?"

"No catch, just a trade."

"One could argue that a trade is, in fact, a catch."

"I suppose. But I've got someone willing to tell you a few more details about Rick and Jenn, stuff you're not going find looking at ledgers and expense reports."

"What am I trading for that?"

"I want to know what you were investigating on Dyle Road. Why was your man applying for a job driving a truck?"

I sighed. "All right. If your source proves to be worthy, I'll share what we were investigating over there."

"How do I know you'll come through with your end of the bargain."

"You don't."

"That's the best you can do?"

"Pretty much. But you, of all people, should know my reputation."

"Yeah, you're a damned boy scout. I guess if you can't trust a boy scout, who can you trust?"

"There you go. How and when do I get in touch with this source of yours?"

"You'll get a call at this number. If you don't hear from them by this time tomorrow, assume there's been a change of heart."

* * *

I really wasn't too eager to share my investigation with Vincent DeLuca, but he had managed to dig into an aspect of the case that we hadn't had the time or staffing to pursue. My fears eased greatly when my phone rang several hours later, just as I was settling in to bed for the night.

The caller was a man, who identified himself only as Vinny's source. He seemed nervous, and I did my best to put him at ease. Eventually, his reluctance faded.

"I've known Rick since high school," he said. "We both grew up in Miami and amazingly ended up getting jobs here within six months of each other. Rick was working in the Human Resources field at the time, before he discovered his true calling."

"The corporate speaking thing?"

"Yeah, that. It was kinda rough at first, but they were working hard at it."

"They?"

"His wife, Sara. She really supported him, at least until Jenn Adams came along. I warned him about her, but he wouldn't listen."

"You didn't like her?"

"I've seen her type before, and I knew Rick had a blind spot to people like that. He was a good dude, but a bit of a rube."

"What do you mean?"

"He meant well, but he got talked into things, stupid things. Well, she came in and gave him a song and dance about growing his business, expanding, better cash flow, the whole bit. I wanted him to wait, check her out before doing anything. By the time I got to say a word, he'd already hired her. Hell, he was probably already banging her. Why he'd do that with a wife like Sara at home, I'll never understand."

"Go on."

"Well, at first, it looked like I was wrong. His business took off, but at the same time, his marriage was disintegrating. No surprise there. One thing led to another, and he split up with Sara. The divorce got damned nasty."

"I talked to Sara about it. It seemed like in more recent years, they'd gotten on more equitable terms."

"True. He never said anything to me, but I think he started to have regrets. He wanted to spend more time with his daughter, maybe scale back his business a bit."

"I'm betting Jenn didn't like that one bit."

"Sounds like you know her."

"More than I'd like to admit."

"She wasn't the least bit happy about that. She started to schedule even more travel, as if she wanted to make it more difficult for him to see his kid. Then it happened."

"What did?"

"She cut some sort of deal with a group of overseas business people. Big bucks, but Rick didn't like the sound of it."

"What sort of deal was it?"

"She was going to help these people get their products into the United States, work with customs, and so forth. Rick wasn't too happy about it, but he went along with it because he was Rick and she was Jenn. Jenn got her way with him, every time. Just like when they first got together, the deal started out okay. The money was incredible, but I could tell that there was something bothering Rick. He'd come over and drink. A lot. He was never a heavy drinker before that. He'd never talk about it, even with me. Mister Costa, we always talked about everything."

"Getting things through customs doesn't exactly sound like Rick's bailiwick. What made him think he could do it?"

"Jennifer Adams. She'd tear him down, then build him back up. By the time she was done with him, he'd be putty in her hands."

"Do you think what they were doing was illegal?"

"Just a few days before he died, Rick told me that he'd had enough. He was going to leave Jenn. He also asked me if I knew anybody that worked for the FBI. Now why would he ask a question like that if what they were up to was legal?"

"Good question."

"Another thing: we used to love going back to Miami to visit. It was something we did every year. We'd each take a week off of work to fly down, see family, old friends, eat lunch at Versailles in Little Havana, visit South Beach, and generally enjoy our time back home. Once Jenn got him in with the damn Bosnians, he never wanted to go to Miami. Hell, he went there for business all the time. I suggested that we combine one of his business trips with a quick vacation, and he damn near bit my head off!"

"Wait—you said the Bosnians?"

"Yeah. The foreigners the Jenn got him mixed up with were Bosnians, that much he told me."

"Did he mention anything else about them?"

"He never said it in so many words, but I'm pretty sure they scared him. I don't think they were good people, and it wouldn't surprise me at all if they had something to do with his death."

"Do you have any idea where I can find them?"

"No, not a clue. I'll tell you something else: until this mess is over and Rick's killer is locked up, I'm sleeping with my damned forty-four magnum. You ought to do the same."

CHAPTER THIRTY

"As much as it pains me to say this, Mister DeLuca," I said, "your source was incredibly helpful, and I'm going to hold up my end of the bargain."

"See? I told you we might be able to help each other."

"It seems that you were correct. There's a company called Kala Shipping, Ltd. that has a terminal along Dyle Road. Kala is co-owned by an employee of Quantelle Logistics."

"Quantelle—they're the place where your friend, one of the victims, worked, right?"

"The same. I was trying to establish a connection between Rick Stevens and Barry Myers. The best we've been able to come up with is that Kala Shipping operates under an umbrella corporation called ABX. ABX is nothing more than a venture capital consortium, which by itself isn't particularly interesting. However, we discovered that Rick Stevens did some work for ABX, and whatever he did, he was highly compensated for his trouble."

"That's a pretty thin connection."

"I know. You don't need to remind me. It turns out that Kala seems to be joined at the hip with another freight company owned by the same investment group: AmeriBiz Express Freight. They almost never go by that name, though. Their logo reads ABEX. Everywhere there's a Kala terminal, ABEX is right there in the same building renting space. In addition to being here, Kala has terminals in Miami and Atlanta."

"ABEX is right there, too," he added.

"You've got it."

"So your man was nosing about the Kala terminal, and someone started shooting at him on his way home?"

"Not quite. He was inquiring about a driving job with Kala that would help him get back to Miami. They told him Kala wasn't hiring, but when he mentioned ABEX, their ears seemed to perk up."

"You know that Rick was from Miami, right?"

"I do now, thanks to your source. I hope you've got him somewhere safe."

"You're damn right I do. Do you think the Miami connection is coincidental?"

"Not for a minute."

"I think maybe I'll go make a few inquiries, maybe pay Kala Shipping a visit."

"I'm not sure that's such a good idea."

"I'm not an idiot, Mister Costa. I'm going to go in with cameras rolling, but not to investigate Kala Shipping. I'll go in under the pretext of investigating the shooting. Better yet, I'll do it under the pretext of a gun control story. Maybe our cameras will catch a face that someone recognizes. You never know."

"You do what you want, Mister DeLuca, but please, for the love of God, be careful!"

"So one of them takes a potshot at me. Won't be the first or the last time, I'm sure. Besides, we've all gotta die of something, right?"

* * *

Christmas was rapidly approaching, and with it, the inevitable rush to buy presents. Mack's list, was, as usual, centered around computer equipment, but seemed abnormally complicated and cryptic.

Fortunately, I had Kevin with me to translate. Although not at Mack's level of skill, he could at least point me in the right direction.

"I don't mind buying this stuff," I groused, trying to decipher the subtleties of one of her requests, "but sometimes I wish she'd just be happy with jewelry."

"Here's what you want," Kevin said, pointing to a gadget locked in a glass case. "She'd never be happy with jewelry, and you'd be upset with yourself if you went that route."

"Why do you say that?" I said, trying to get the attention of a sales associate.

"Because what makes her special is that she *doesn't* ask for jewelry, and what makes you special to her is that you're willing to come to this store, in person, and get exactly what she wants, instead of chickening out and getting a gift card."

"Or jewelry?"

"You've got it."

The salesperson finally broke free from another customer and came over to help us.

"I want to buy that," I said, pointing, and showing her the entry on Mack's list.

"Someone must be on the nice list this year," she said, smiling broadly. "This is the absolute top of the line." She opened the case and retrieved the item. It seemed too small to carry such a hefty price tag. "Anything else you need my help with?"

"We only have one other thing left on the list," I said, showing her the remaining entry.

"That'll be over here. Definitely on the nice list!"

She wasn't kidding. The sticker shock of the previous gadget had barely worn off when a new round hit. She slid open another locked cabinet, retrieving an item from the back of the topmost shelf."

"This is the latest processor innovation," she said. She followed with a torrent of acronyms, a few of which I pretended to recognize. "We recommend liquid cooling if you're going to overclock this processor."

I searched Mack's list, but saw nothing related to cooling.

"If I get the stuff you're recommending, and my friend doesn't need it, can I return it?"

"Of course," she said. "Let me show you some options."

"Honestly, I'm probably not going to understand what you're going to tell me. Can you just point me to the best one that's available?"

"It really isn't that simple," she said. "We have two kits that get good reviews. This one is easier to install, but honestly doesn't cool as well. This one is more of a challenge to install, but does provide better cooling performance."

"I'll take the challenging one."

"Are you sure?"

"Oh yes," I said, smiling.

Kevin chuckled.

* * *

The mail arrived early, and with it, the first large delivery of Christmas cards. Tired from my shopping excursion, I poured a cup of coffee and settled into the sofa. Some of the cards I recognized immediately as being from friends and family. The rest, I suspected, were from various businesses thanking me for my patronage throughout the year.

The first two I opened were, as expected, the greeting card equivalent of form letters. I didn't recognize the writing on the third envelope, and there was no return address, but the missive bore all the traits of the previous two. The card was generic, complete with a simple holiday greeting, but was not signed. A business card tucked within fluttered to the floor. I picked it up to read it, and my blood ran cold.

"Mack!" I put the card on the table, instantly regretting that I had touched it.

"What is it?" Concern decorated her voice as she ran into the living room.

"Don't touch it. I probably already ruined any forensic evidence from it, if there ever was any, but take a look at the writing on it."

Two lines of neatly written Cyrillic lettering stared up at us. Shaken, I grabbed my phone and took a picture.

Mack was already a step ahead of me. "The writing is different than on the cards of the victims, but I have no idea what it says."

"Knowing my luck, it probably means *you're next*. I just sent it to Adnan. Hopefully he can sort it out for us."

"Are you going to call O'Neil?"

"After we know what it says. Get a baggie and some tweezers. Maybe they can recover some prints from it or something."

She nodded, but we both knew it was a long shot at best.

* * *

"I recognize that writing," Adnan Jasik said. "I got a similar card last year."

"What does my card say?"

"The translation is not perfect, of course, but the general idea is: *time to be the hawk.*"

"Time for whom to be the hawk? Is it talking about me? The writer?"

"The way it is written, it could mean either."

"Adnan, if I may ask, what did your card say?"

"Again, within the limits of translation, it said, *birds can be dangerous*. Not too helpful, is it? Have you checked the paper for the distinctive watermark?"

"No," I sighed. "I put it in a baggie in case the police want to test it."

"You'll find nothing, and they won't be interested. There is no way to prove where it came from, who handled it, and so forth."

"What about testing the paper?"

"That would be interesting, and we could have a handwriting expert compare the two samples, your card and mine. At least we'd know if they came from the same person, whoever that might be."

"You think it's from the serial killer, don't you?"

"I do, but I have no proof. It could be a warning, it could be boasting from the killer, or it could be an instruction. Only God and our killer knows for certain. But this—this is only a theory."

* * *

As predicted, O'Neil wasn't particularly interested in the letter.

"You have no idea if that letter came from the killer or not. There's nothing in there that tells me it is anything but a crank. Hell, Vinny D probably sent it just to annoy you."

"Oh yes. I'm sure that's what it is. Remind me, at some point in the future, to thank you properly for dropping him into my lap."

He laughed. "Someone's got to keep you on your toes. I'm sorry. I can tell you're disappointed, but I can't tie up precious resources to process that letter, only to find that it has your fingerprints on it, fibers from your carpet, and dust from the letter carrier's truck. I'll put you through to someone to file a report if you'd like."

"George, we have three bodies on our hands, and nobody's been arrested. The press is starting to get word of it. How's it going to look when they learn that we might have ignored a piece of evidence."

"Evidence? My monthly cable bill is better evidence of a crime than this!"

"I was afraid that's how you'd feel about it. I'm going to send it off for analysis."

"Hey, it's your money, John."

* * *

I made arrangements, at tremendous expense, to send the mysterious card overnight to the same lab that analyzed the missive sent to Adnan Jasik. Drained, I settled into the love seat in the music room. Mack's voice startled me.

"You feeling up to playing a tune for me?" she said, handing me a pint of Guinness.

"Thanks, Mack! I'll play a bit, if you grab my fiddle for me."

She nodded, but instead of my violin, she brought the case containing Barry's banjo. "Can you show me how to play this thing?"

I looked at her, shocked. "You want to learn how to play the banjo?"

"Maybe," she said.

"Why?"

"Getting an early start on my New Year's resolution."

"What is your resolution, anyway?"

"To find new and improved ways to annoy you."

We laughed, but as I stared at the banjo case, the humor faded.

"What's wrong?"

"Barry really loved this thing. Nancy told me that he carefully packed it away before chasing after me the night he died. Maybe if he'd just left it on the chair or the table instead, he would have caught up to me, and he'd still be alive."

"It obviously meant a lot to him."

"Yeah," I said, opening the case and removing the instrument's cover. "I think he had some custom work done on it, judging by how much he paid for it. Look at it—absolutely meticulous."

"It's a beautiful instrument."

"Here, I'll play a few notes on it. Hopefully, you'll quickly abandon all thought of learning it."

I removed the instrument from its case. I realized I didn't have a pick handy, so I started searching through the case's compartments.

"That's odd," I said. "Nancy mentioned Barry was experimenting with a new pick, but all these are the same. I would have expected to see both old and new."

I played a few notes, surprised by the sound that emanated from the instrument.

"What's wrong?" Mack said.

"It should be brighter and louder. A lot louder."

"Is it the pick?"

"I don't think so. Do you mind bringing me one from the table over there?" I motioned toward a table on the other side of the music room. On it rested some picks, used on the rare occasion when I played my guitar.

Mack nodded and returned with a variety of picks. None produced a significant change in the sound. I started examining the instrument. Nothing looked out of the ordinary, but tapping on the head produced a dull thump instead of the bright ringing sound I expected. It felt taut, as expected, and looked to be in pristine condition.

"Something is damping the motion of the head," I said, "like a mute."

"I didn't think there was a way to mute a banjo."

"Other than putting it in the fireplace, there isn't, unless…"

"What is it?"

"I've heard stories of people stuffing a hand towel or something similar behind the head to quiet down a loud banjo, but that would require partial disassembly of the instrument."

"Can you open the back?"

I shrugged, turning the instrument over and examining it. I didn't notice anything at first, but as I studied it more, I found what I was looking for. The workmanship was meticulous, and I realized why Barry had paid a premium for the banjo: a portion of the back unscrewed, allowing easy access to the inside.

Peering in, it was as I surmised. A small towel had been stuffed into the cavity to dampen the sound.

"This is why it doesn't sound right," I said, removing the towel. Fortunately, I happened to peak inside before closing the back. "Mack, there's a sheet of paper in here!"

I retrieved the paper and handed it to her. She glanced at it, immediately jumping up from her seat.

"The banjo concert can wait! Come on, we've got work to do!"

CHAPTER THIRTY-ONE

"What is it?" I asked, sprinting into the office.

"The Rosetta Stone," Mack replied. "This will help me decipher what Barry was writing on these papers."

"Dammit. I'm so stupid! That banjo has been under our noses for a while now, and I didn't even open the case."

"You couldn't have possibly known what was in there. Until Maureen gave us the sheets, it would have looked like a sheet of meaningless doodles. Hell, we might have thrown it away, not knowing any better. Now stop beating yourself up and get busy helping."

"Okay, I said. What do you need me to do?"

"Make a fresh pot of coffee and order pizza. This is going to take a while."

* * *

I spent the next couple of hours hoping to feel useful, but there wasn't anything I could do. Eventually, she released me to get a few hours of sleep.

I made my way to the master bedroom and turned in.

Exhausted, I fell asleep quickly. It had only been slightly over an hour when I woke up, inexplicably. Staring at the ceiling, I waited for my eyes to focus.

Moonlight streamed in through the curtains that covered the sliding glass door that led to my balcony. The extension, cantilevered off the back of the house, wasn't something I used often, preferring the larger area of the back patio below to the narrow balcony.

The angle of the moonlight caught the partial outline of a person, lurking outside the door. Although the intruder was tucked closely against the side of the house, I was sufficiently familiar with the shadows the balcony and its railing cast to know that something was out of place.

Momentarily, I pondered if this was another strange dream where my imagination would make the figure materialize into Angela Grady. Slowly, so as not to be noticed, I moved my right arm. Unlike in my dreams where paralysis prevented movement, my limb responded flawlessly.

Feigning the normal tossing and turning that a sleeper might do, I rolled over onto my right side, turning my back to the window. Unknown to my uninvited visitor was the fact that in this position, I had an unobstructed view of the porch in my dresser's mirror. My orientation also afforded me access to retrieve my hidden firearm.

From my improved vantage point, I was able see that my ruse had worked. Emboldened by the fact that my back was turned, my visitor slipped out from his hiding spot. He was slender and moved gracefully—likely my attacker from the warehouse, I thought. A gun, looking artificially long thanks to the attached suppressor, waited in his right hand. His left hand retrieved a hammer that telescoped to about eighteen inches in length. Its head, heavy, with a pointed end, served a clear purpose: to break the glass on my door.

I smiled. What my would-be assailant didn't realize was that during my ill-fated Irish odyssey, I had installed a few upgrades. The terrorist organization I was investigating at the time had demonstrated both a world-wide reach and an interest in achieving my death. In response, I installed bullet resistant glass throughout. The door to my small balcony not only had upgraded glass, but a reinforced frame. His small hammer and his handgun, even at point blank range, didn't stand a chance.

He turned and swung the hammer with high velocity. Much to his surprise, the door deflected his blow without the slightest difficulty. He hesitated. As he realized what was happening, I jumped out of bed and turned on the light that illuminated the balcony. Briefly panicked, he looked around before jumping to the ground below.

I flung the door open, only to hear screams and the sharp clatter of Kevin Moriarty's taser. I sprinted downstairs and out the back door where I found the man curled into a fetal position, rendered helpless by the electrical shock delivered by the device.

"Costa, get his gun," Kevin ordered.

With my own firearm aimed directly at the man's chest, I moved quickly, vigorously kicking the gun away. What fight was left in the attacker faded. Kevin cuffed the man's hands and called the authorities.

* * *

The attacker had quickly morphed from a menace to a forlorn figure as he sat, helpless and disheveled, in my entryway. His silence, however, was the last thing we wanted.

"He'll talk if I break his leg," Kevin said. "We could say it happened when he fell."

"Yeah, Captain O'Neil would buy that story without even taking a look. He might even break his other leg just for getting dragged out of his warm bed on a cold night. Do you want the sledgehammer?"

Mack emerged, unfazed, from the music room. "At least put down some plastic if you're going to use the sledge. Last time, it took a week for me to get all the little splatters of blood out of the carpeting."

I could tell the man wasn't buying our ruse, but when Kevin emerged from the garage tossing around a heavy sledgehammer like it was a child's toy, I could see his resolve weakening. It faded altogether when he saw that the handle and head contained dried blood stains.

"Jesus, what the hell are you thinking?" he said.

"I just need the name of who sent you, and you can spend the rest of the evening in a nice, warm jail cell instead of in the hospital. You see?" I said, pointing to the bloody hammer. "The last person didn't even make it to the hospital."

I allowed my anger to bubble to the surface. Wide eyed, and jaw clenched, I moved my face within a few inches of his.

"You know the nice thing about being rich?" I growled. "You can get away with anything—even murder. Now give me the goddamned name!"

"Rakic!" the man cried. "Ivan Rakic!"

"How and where do you meet him?"

"I don't! He calls me when he needs me."

"Wrong answer! Break one of his feet," I said, turning to Kevin.

"No!" the man screamed.

"Then try again to improve your bullshit answer," I growled.

"I only met him once," he said, his voice shaking. "We met in the back of a trucking place on Dyle Road."

"Which one?"

"ABEX. Red logo, white letters."

"Kevin," I said, calming, "take this lying piece of crap out front and get rid of him. You know what to do."

"You got it, boss," Kevin grunted.

"Wait!" the man cried. "I don't know what he's got going on, but when scaring you at the warehouse didn't work, he got really pissed off. Something's happening next week. I don't know what, but he kept insisting you had to be out of the way by then."

"Amazing," I said, staring at him, still holding my crazy expression. "Take care of this piece of crap."

"I told you everything!"

"Good for you. Why," I said, clenching my jaw, "do you think I'd let you live after you tried to break into my house and kill me and my friends? My reputation? That's bought and paid for, too."

Kevin dragged the man out the front door and into the waiting hands of George O'Neil and a medical team.

"That was pretty intense," Mack said, looking impressed.

"Thank you," I said. "I came up with the idea when Kevin mentioned the sledgehammer when we were in the garage a few days ago. I'm glad I didn't clean it! It's been on my to-do list for a couple of months."

The dried blood on the hammer was very real and completely mine. It was left over from a fight to the death with a rotten fence post. In fixing the post, mostly to prove to Mack that I could, I managed to slice my hands. The injury was more annoying that anything else, but it bled profusely. I kept the stained hammer as a battle trophy of sorts.

* * *

George O'Neil ran his hands through his hair. "Exactly what the hell happened here?"

"A man trespassed on my property, tried to break into my home, and shoot me. It was only through great personal restraint and the quick thinking of my bodyguard that he didn't get shot."

"What the hell did you three do to him? He's out there confessing everything he's done since he was in high school."

"Perhaps the man has experienced an epiphany, George, and has decided to reform his life."

"What the hell is this about a bloody hammer and a murder."

I laughed. "The hammer's right here, and the blood is mine. The victim was buried in my yard months ago. The third fence post from the corner is the unfortunate soul that I almost dispatched to the hereafter. You can interview it while you're retrieving the intruder's gun. Mack has video of the horrible events if you're interested."

It was all George O'Neil could do to maintain his serious demeanor as he watched Mack's subtitled recording of my epic battle with the fence. It ended with me showing my bloody hands to the camera, and carrying the sledgehammer by its head, held high in the air in a victory stance.

"He seems to have found a way around my security system," I said, turning serious, "so we may or may not have footage to share with you."

"We have it," Kevin said. "The sensors picked him up when he got on the roof."

"How the hell did he get on the roof?" I asked.

"From the big tree in the neighbor's yard," Kevin answered.

"The man has some serious acrobatic skills to pull off a trick like that."

"Why didn't the alarm go off?"

"It did," he said, "I just muted it before it went nuts. If it alerted and he ran away, we wouldn't be able to question him. When he got down on your balcony, I didn't have a non-lethal way to neutralize the threat, so I had to wait until he was within the fifteen feet the wires on my taser will reach. I knew that damn blast door you've got installed up there would keep you safe," he said.

"I assume you're going to want to press charges," O'Neil said.

I nodded.

"Any idea why this man would attack you?"

"You know, George, we were asking ourselves the same question. We think he is a disgruntled accordion player hell-bent on revenge. Either that, or AmeriBiz Express Freight is a front for some illegal activity, and I've asked one too many questions. But, personally, I'm leaning toward the accordion theory."

CHAPTER THIRTY-TWO

"Of course!" Mack said, as she worked on deciphering Barry's papers.

Between giving statements and O'Neil's investigators tromping around, we'd had little chance to concentrate on the case at hand.

"I take it you've discovered something."

"This is definitely a log of shipments. We already knew about the date and time columns, but here are columns for the origin, the destination, and the carriers, both inbound and outbound. I'm not sure what the purpose of this column is," she said, highlighting a narrow column near the right-hand side of the log. "It seems to be a number when I decode it, but I have no idea what it means."

"Weight?"

"I thought that, too, but the numbers are all small, ranging anywhere from three to fifteen. It could be tons, I suppose, but I thought most shipping documents were more meticulous about recording weight."

"A count of something? Number of boxes? Number of palettes?"

"Probably, but I have no idea what. I also need to do more

work on this column here," she said, highlighting the widest column. "It looks like the same code, but there's something different about it. When I decode it using the same formula as the others, I just get nonsense. I'll keep working on it."

"Okay. Any sign of our favorite carriers on this sheet?"

"There's not a single mention of Kala anywhere on here, but AmeriBiz Express is all over the place. About a third of the shipments show AmeriBiz as the inbound carrier. All but a few of them show AmeriBiz as the outbound carrier."

"Okay…"

"And look," she said, highlighting a row, "at the duration. Never more than an hour and a half."

"So what are you telling me?"

"Shipments are arriving at Quantelle, something happens, and then another shipment leaves a couple of hours later and virtually always on an AmeriBiz Truck. And get this: some very interesting patterns are emerging."

"Yes?"

"Regardless of the origin or the inbound carrier, the destination is always one of four cities: Atlanta, Miami, Houston, or Los Angeles. One hundred percent of the shipments to Miami and Atlanta were on AmeriBiz."

"But Mack, how do we know this has anything to do with Quantelle. It seems obvious, since logistics is their core business, but is there anything definitive linking them?"

"I'm glad you asked that," she said, positively beaming. "I asked Ashley to send me the layout of Quantelle's shipping docks. Every single dock number on Barry's log matches to one in Quantelle's alcove area. Their naming scheme is a little unusual, but it still could be a coincidence. Here's why I think it isn't."

The screen changed, highlighting two rows early in the log.

"Ashley confirmed that Quantelle renumbered the alcove docks to better match the system used to number the rest of the docks. Barry recorded the new number, but also noted the old number and they're identical. This *has* to be at Quantelle."

"Interesting. Any theories?"

"Theft is the most logical explanation, but I'm not sure it holds up under scrutiny. According to Ashley, Quantelle has had items stolen from the warehouse, but for a company their size, their loss rate is pretty low. When it happens, it's usually small, valuable items—like the time when an employee tried to stuff two solid state drives in their coat pocket and walk out. Security caught them easily. If there was theft on the scale to warrant the use of trucks, they would certainly know about it, but nothing like that has been reported."

"I can tell from your expression that you have an alternate theory."

"Counterfeit merchandise."

"Talk to me."

"Okay—let's say I've got quite a bit of knock-off merchandise, badged with a fancy label, but not the real thing. I could sell it on the internet, but that's risky and time consuming. But what if there was a place full of the real thing?"

"Quantelle…"

"Exactly! If I had someone on the inside, I could, with proper coordination, swap out the real stuff for the copies. Now I've got a truckload of the real thing, and Quantelle has the fake. They probably don't even realize it, because their inventory counts still work—their person on the inside makes sure it all works. Meanwhile, I'm free to sell the real stuff at full price, and Quantelle gets stuck dealing with whatever fallout the knockoff creates, assuming anyone really notices. If anyone *does* notice, the selling company takes all the heat, not Quantelle. They're behind the scenes. They plead ignorance, the insurance carrier covers the loss, and everyone's happy."

"Damn."

"I would do it when nobody's around: during maintenance, a long shift change…"

"A defective carbon monoxide detector…" I added.

"Bingo," Mack said. "I can't prove it yet, but hopefully soon. But you're not allowed to ask about that."

"I won't. So, who are the players in your little scheme?"

"I'd need someone from security."

"The head of the department would be a decent choice, don't

234

you think?"

"Undoubtedly. I'd also need people that know the systems, both from the inventory and the shipping side of things. Someone would need to direct the targeted products to the alcove bays at the right time, then someone to make sure that the inventory gets swapped correctly, and the counterfeit stuff gets back in circulation with nobody the wiser. Probably wouldn't hurt to have a couple of people to actually do the work of loading the trucks, and so forth."

"It makes sense, Mack. Jenn and Rick were involved in some sort of business venture related to importing and getting things through customs."

"Or around customs."

I stretched, staring off into space. The theory had merit, but something was bothering me. "I get that there's money to be made, but enough to kill for?"

"People have been murdered over a few dollars, John."

"True," I said, shifting in my chair. "Here's another angle to consider: corporate espionage."

"An interesting idea," she said, running her fingers through her hair. "Let's hear what you've got."

"What if the goal isn't to make money off the real items. What if the goal is to discredit Quantelle?"

Mack grinned. "Oh! I like it!"

"Swap real product for counterfeit, just like you said, then have some secret shoppers buy the items, knowing that they're likely to get the fakes. The shoppers make a stink about it, but to the press, not to their vendor. A reporter like Vinny D gets the story, and Quantelle has a public relations nightmare on their hands."

"And," Mack added, "the competition has already accused Quantelle of cheating. Now they'd have the proof needed to lure customers away."

"With everybody buying things online and wanting them to show up five minutes later, a few big defections would probably ruin Quantelle, leaving all that business—probably billions of dollars—just waiting to be claimed."

"Of course," she said, "there's a far more pedestrian explanation:

drugs."

"True that," I sighed. "Whatever's going on, the people doing it are playing for keeps."

* * *

"Oh my God!" Eva exclaimed as she opened her front door. "I can't thank you enough for agreeing to help me get the place ready. Oh, and you brought your friend! Too bad Ashley isn't here."

"I've been banished for the remainder of the afternoon," I said, smiling. "Mack's got a lot of work to do, and apparently I was distracting her."

"Doesn't your other friend want to come inside, too," she said, glancing toward the second large, black SUV parked in her drive. "It's a cold day, and I've got hot cider on the stove."

"No," I said. "Someone tried to break into my house recently, so we've increased our security significantly in response. He'll keep an eye on things from the outside, if that's all right. I hope your neighbors don't report him for loitering."

"Most of them are gone for the holidays anyway, off someplace warm; and those that remain don't even act like they know who I am, so I think your man will be just fine. He's not leaving without cider, though!"

"All right," I laughed. "We'll make sure he gets some."

Pleasantries aside, she put me to work assembling the massive artificial tree that would dominate the entryway.

"It fit in one box when I bought it," she joked, tugging the smaller of the two boxes it now occupied up the basement steps. "They had people at the store to help us load it, but you should've seen Ash and me trying to get this thing in the house. Oh crap! Where did I put the base?"

"It isn't in one of these boxes?"

"No. The original one broke, and I had to get a replacement. Now, where did I put it?"

The mystery kicked off a search that started in the basement, passed through several storage closets, a quick peek into a crawl space, and ended in the garage. Eva's car occupied one of the three available spaces, while a smaller, covered car waited in the far bay.

"What's that?" I said, pointing to the car.

"Oh," she laughed, "my victory trophy—Paul's sports car. I'm sure he used it to impress his little bimbo, and I'm equally certain he went out and bought another one after the divorce was final. Seeing the disappointment on his face when the judge awarded this baby to me... Well..."

She removed the cover. The sleek, stunning Italian roadster looked like it was going fast, even when parked.

"Wow! Nice!" My imagination drifted to images of Eva Peretti cruising the Autobahn.

"You want it?" she said. "I've never even driven the damn thing. Right after Paul delivered it, I had a mechanic come over and do whatever they hell they do to cars to prepare them for storage. At the time, I thought Ashley might have fun with it a few years down the road—I even offered to pay the insurance—but she's never shown any interest in it. I'll sell it to you if you're interested."

"Oh, I don't think so."

"It's quite an upgrade from that boring thing that you drive," she said, winking.

"It might be fun to drive sometime, but this really isn't my style. It seems to match your personality, though."

"Oh, don't let the bubbly stuff fool you. At heart, I'm just a simple Jersey girl who stumbled her way into some money."

"Jersey? I thought you were from Philly."

"Yep, suburb of! Just one that happens to be on the other side of the river. Oh! There it is."

She pointed to a shelf. I reached up and retrieved the replacement base.

"Let's get some of that cider," she said, "it's chilly out here!"

We retreated to the kitchen where Eva poured mugs of warm, spiced cider. I found myself staring at the picture of her ex-husband with his business associates. "That's Swindon McCarter, isn't it?" I said, pointing to one of the people in the image.

"I see you've done your homework! Yeah, that's him, the

damned bum."

"Not a fan?"

"He's a snake oil salesman if there ever was one. He talks a good game, complete with that charming Texas drawl of his, but he's as phony as can be. If that man had a moral compass, it would spin around until it either burst into flame or pointed right back at him."

"You blame him for your divorce, don't you?" My question was unfairly blunt, but Eva didn't seem upset by it.

"No. I blame my ex-husband's lack of moral fiber for it, but this idiot set the stage where it could play out. One thing about growing up when and where I did and being a member of my family: we knew how to spot a phony a mile away. My parents were good judges of character, John; nobody could take advantage of them. That's probably how they managed to save up enough so that we'd always have Christmas, even if it was a rough year. I knew this guy was trouble the minute I met him. Anyway," she said, raising her mug, "here's to good riddance to the lot of 'em!"

CHAPTER THIRTY-THREE

"I didn't have the heart to tell Ms. Peretti that her ex-husband is still mixed up with Swindon McCarter." Kevin said, as we drove home from what turned out to be an entire afternoon of decorating and party preparation. "He cashed in his investment with ABX to pay for the divorce settlement. What I found of particular interest were Paul Vinton's reasons for choosing to divest of ABX instead of other investments. Any of a dozen would have satisfied the judgment against him, yet he chose ABX. Interested in why?"

"Jesus, Kevin, you're getting as bad as Mack with the damned teasers. Of course I bloody want to know!"

"He left after the arrival of some new investors into the ABX family, specifically a trio that hailed from the Balkans. He sent over their names, and I've got Jerry researching them, along with Ivan Rakic. I asked Paul if he had heard of Ivan, but he claims to be unfamiliar with the name."

"What, in particular, about these three men turned Paul off?"

"He wouldn't elaborate beyond saying that they were pressing to make investments he wasn't comfortable with. It was right around the same time that ABX invested in AmeriBiz and Kala, which I don't think for a minute is coincidental."

"Nor do I. Sounds like these three came in and tried to start calling the shots. I bet that produced a lot of friction, especially when dealing with someone with an ego like Swindon McCarter. It isn't too surprising that Paul left. I imagine others did, too."

"Well, whatever transpired didn't sour the relationship between them for long. Two years later, Paul was back, investing in another branch of McCarter's various endeavors."

"Speaking of McCarter, in your research, did you find any investments he made with direct competitors to Quantelle? If Quantelle is exposed for sourcing counterfeit goods, the competitors are bound to profit mightily. It sounds well within Mr. McCarter's personality to force the issue, don't you think?"

"No doubt. It wouldn't be the first time he destroyed a competitor's company through espionage, or so the rumors say. Unfortunately, I haven't been able to find any investments in anything remotely related to logistics other than Kala and AmeriBiz. If he's invested in the competition, his holdings aren't significant. Those two little trucking companies aren't poised to step in and fill the gap if Quantelle collapses."

My theory of corporate secrets and subterfuge was sexy, but my intuition told me that the reality was likely less glamorous. "We should probably pursue the drug angle. It seems more along the lines of trucking companies and automatic weapons than my espionage theory."

"I can do that," he said, as he pulled into my garage.

* * *

"This pretty much cements it," Mack said, as I walked into the office.

"Cements what?"

"How utterly amazing I am!"

"Not to mention being completely modest," I said.

"My modesty is one of my many better qualities," Mack said, winking. "Take a look." She pointed to the screen. "There's a perfect correlation," she continued, "between the entries in Barry's notes and events at Quantelle."

"You got in?"

"Of course not," she chided. "That would be against the law, and this is the point where you stop asking questions."

"Got it," I said.

"On the left is a log entry from January, and on the right is the corresponding event at Quantelle. In this case, the shifts ended early and started late due to a lack of work. Quite plausible, but nevertheless, it syncs perfectly with Barry's notes. And here's another one—a broken drive on one of the conveyors in the alcove. Also plausible, except the drive was replaced less than a month before and passed inspection on an earlier shift the day of the log entry. Here's a hazardous spill," she said, changing the screen showing another correlating entry. But that's not even the best part."

"Oh, do tell, Mack!"

"My sources were kind enough to share with me shift schedules. There are a lot of names, of course, especially since people tend to come and go in that type work. All of the events that Barry logged took place on shifts later in the day, always after dark. The way Quantelle arranges their shifts, this could span any of three different shifts. Needless to say, this is a huge list of names. However, when I looked at it a little differently, the list shrinks dramatically. I looked for names that repeated, regardless of their normally assigned shift."

"So you were, in essence, looking for people who were changing shifts in correlation with the events Barry logged, right?"

"You've got it. That cuts the list down to a total of twelve names. But there's only one name that *always* appears during these logged events: Lance Yannis."

"He's on vacation, too. How convenient!"

"I've got people looking for him."

"That sounds rather sinister, Mack."

"It isn't like it sounds," she laughed. "I've collected numerous samples of emails he sent from his phone. We know his cellular phone number, and we know what carrier he's with. If that phone signs on and hits any system that my friends and I are watching, we'll know."

"Friends? Other hackers?"

"I prefer to call myself a system security specialist, but yes. I'm part of a network of hackers that work on solving crimes."

"You mean there are more like you out there?" I said, feigning horror.

"Oh yes, we're everywhere!" she answered, wide-eyed and making an unflattering face.

"I don't even want to know how you found out about this network."

"That was easy! I founded it. The trick is filtering out the good guys from the bad guys pretending to be good."

"Just like life…"

"Yep," she sighed. "Take a look at this." The screen changed.

"You got security footage, too?"

"You're forgetting the rule about asking questions…"

"I mean, how thoughtful of our anonymous sources to send us unsolicited, security footage."

"That's the spirit! I narrowed down the search to just the times leading up to, during, and after the events in the logs, focusing on the cameras in the alcove. This is the main entrance that leads out of the area, and you can see the people leaving, just as expected. Now look."

The screen changed.

"I don't see anything."

"That's exactly the point," she said, smiling broadly. "This is when they were supposedly fixing the broken conveyor belt. Here's where they should be working, but there's not a soul to be found."

"What the hell?"

"Don't feel bad. It took a while for me to see it, too. Maybe this will help."

The screen changed again. The cameras were the same, but there were people in the area working.

"Don't look at the people," she said, eying me, expectantly.

It took a few more comparative viewings before I saw it. "The clock!"

"Good eye! It doesn't look quite right, does it?"

"No…"

"That's because you're looking at the same five minutes of video repeating itself over and over again. It's pretty well done, but the patterns on the clock give it away under close examination."

"So what does it all mean?"

"These video files have been altered. Instead of the real video feed, someone fed the system a looped video of people working. A quick glance would show people performing repetitive tasks and likely be unnoticed by security."

"Dammit. According to these videos, absolutely nothing happened during the times Barry logged. We have no idea what the cameras *really* saw."

"Unfortunately, that's the long and short of it. On the bright side, I have a decent idea who manipulated the security system footage."

"Who might that be?"

"Brenda Simmons, the head of security. Her employee ID card was used to access the warehouse doors during all the events."

"Sadly, this isn't particularly usable either. She could claim her presence was merely coincidental, and that she was doing her job. Impressive work, though. The altered video files confirm what we've suspected: *something's* going on at Quantelle; we just don't know exactly what."

"But we know a few of the people involved," Mack offered.

"Yes, we do. Let's see what we can learn about Ms. Simmons."

* * *

"Dammit!" I slammed my fist against the desk. "The lab just confirmed that the paper and the handwriting on the card I received matched Adnan's sample. The paper's the same as what was found in Yugoslavia, and I handled the damn thing destroying any forensic evidence."

"You couldn't have known," Mack said. "I would have done the same thing in the same situation—it's human nature to pick up something that falls."

"I know, but it doesn't make me feel any better. I'll tell O'Neil, so he can tell me that it's irrelevant."

At my request, the lab included Adnan Jasik on the email where they shared the test results. As expected, he called within a few minutes of receiving their findings.

"Your letter was authentic, then," he said.

"So it would seem. Unfortunately, it is like damn near everything else we've learned: useless."

"I have been chasing this killer for many years, but I think if my uncle hadn't been such a scoundrel, I might be looking harder for his killer."

"I was hoping to wrap this up before Christmas. Say, have you heard the name Ivan Rakic before?"

"Why?"

"I had a fellow try to put a bullet in me the other night. My security measures stopped him, and we were able to get him to talk to us. That was the name of the man that sent him."

"If it is the same man I'm familiar with, his nickname is Ivan the Terrible. What does he look like?"

"I haven't met him yet, so I don't know."

"The man I'm speaking of masquerades as a business man, but that's only a cover. His real business is anything that will make money quickly and in large amounts. What he's known to be involved with includes drugs, stolen secrets, prostitution, weapons, and counterfeit currency, just to name a few. He's brash and violent, but slippery when he needs to be. He has his people do a lot of his dirty work, so he stays out of trouble. Interesting his name should come up, though. Not much has been heard from him for a number of years now. There are some who think he's dead."

"Can you send me his picture?"

"Sure. The copy I have is a decade old, but the key features won't have changed. Costa, if it's really him, and he tried to kill you once, he'll try again. Ivan the Terrible isn't known for giving up, or for changing his mind."

* * *

"Word has it," the man on the other end of the phone said, "that you're asking quite a few questions about my venture capital endeavors, Mister Costa. Now, there are some folks out there that might wonder if your inquiries are less than amicable, but I pride myself on looking for, and finding, the best in humanity. I find those struggling ventures that are going to bring people jobs and prosperity, and I give them a helping hand. So I can only conclude that your interest is along these veins, and not something unpleasant."

The Texas drawl made it obvious that the caller was none other than Swindon McCarter. A few moments later, the caller removed all doubt.

"Swindon McCarter here, Mister Costa, and I'm damn glad to make your acquaintance."

From the tone, pacing, and folksy friendliness of his voice, it was easy to see how he could woo prospective investors.

"Funny you should call me," I said. "You were on my list of people to call today."

"Well, then I would call this sequence of events fortuitous."

"I'm not certain how familiar you are with me, but…"

He interrupted. "Oh. Mister Costa, I know all about you, my friend: lawyer turned private investigator; millionaire who tried to give away his fortune when he learned some of it was ill-gotten."

"Then you undoubtedly realize that my call isn't about becoming one of your cadre of venture capitalists."

"I know it," he said, "although I must admit that you'd be an interesting person to have as a business associate."

"In the course of an investigation I'm conducting, two company names keep popping up. They're companies that received venture funding through ABX, which, I believe, is one of your interests."

"While ABX is certainly one of my holdings, as you undoubtedly know, I'm not involved in the day to day operation…"

"Kala Shipping, Ltd. and AmeriBiz Express Freight," I said, pressing and interrupting without apology.

"As I was trying to say, Mister Costa, I don't get involved in the…"

"They're both freight companies, Mister McCarter. Don't you find it odd that a venture capital firm would fund competing businesses?"

"I'm certain that the investment team had their reasons, but as I said…"

"Would you be surprised to learn that these two companies always share terminal space?"

"I'm sure I don't know…"

I could hear a subtle change in the tenor of his voice. Stress was overtaking the folksy drawl. I turned up the heat.

"I think there's a good chance that something illegal is going on, and those two companies are involved. Now it could be a case of a well-intended investment that went poorly, or it could be malfeasance all the way to the top. Frankly, I don't care which, but I'm going to find out."

I had baited the trap, and an angry Swindon McCarter fell right in. "I can buy you and sell you, Costa! I'll swamp you like an ocean liner swamps an insignificant dinghy!"

"But when that ocean liner has a gaping hole in its hull and water's rushing in, that dinghy looks mighty good. In the panic, who knows what the passengers will do to get there. They might even insist that the captain goes down with his ship."

"I don't respond well to threats, you little pissant worm! I've got nothing to hide and nothing that's of concern to you."

"Oh, it isn't me you have to worry about, Swindon. It's my friends in law enforcement, my friends in the press, and the computer hacking community that I'd worry about if I were you. I'm just the captain of an insignificant little dinghy that's letting you know there might be a problem in your hull. Nothing more."

I hung up the phone before he could answer.

"The gentleman doth protest too much, methinks." Kevin said, smiling.

"Mack, block his number for a few hours. I want to let him stew for a while."

246

CHAPTER THIRTY-FOUR

"Your friend Barry was an absolute genius, John," Mack said, staring up from behind her desk. "I mean that, too; not in the way the word gets bantered about these days, but for real."

"Oh?"

"I finally started making some progress on his computers. He had them locked down and for good reason. I never thought logistics could be interesting, but I'm rethinking that."

"What's on there, Mack?"

"Probably a billion dollar idea, if it can be proven to work, that's all."

"You're serious, aren't you?"

"Completely. I'm only about a quarter of the way through this system, but it's damned impressive. The part I'm looking at now is an Artificial Intelligence engine to process what is coming in from the collectors, the aggregation engine, and the correlation system."

"I'm going to sit here and pretend I understood that."

"From what I can tell," she said, "the system is collecting trend information by looking for keywords. The collectors take the keywords, and troll around on the internet looking for them. There they go to the aggregation engine. When they reach some sort of statistically meaningful level, it sends them off to the correlation system. I haven't had much time to look at it yet, but I think the general idea is that it looks for relevant combinations of keywords. From there, the data goes to the logistics processor where it plans capacities and flows based on the trends the system predicts. In other words, the system is predicting product demand six to eighteen months out, based on random chatter from people on the internet."

"Sounds a bit like science fiction."

"Well, in his code, Barry referred to this as *Generation 2* of his technology, so maybe Quantelle is doing a bit of this now. But if this thing works, it could be a real game changer. Not just for getting products during the holidays, but for everyone. Maybe it can correlate travel tendencies with the flu season, so we know where we're likely to need the most vaccine. Or getting food into areas where famine is likely to strike before it hits."

"Barry did this? My friend, Barry?"

"Every line of the code, from what I've seen so far. There's only one problem."

"What's that, Mack?"

"We don't know if it works. The core logic of the AI system is built on the assumption that the chatter of people is less than random— a collective consciousness, so to speak."

"Like Jung's concept of synchronicity?" Kevin asked. "The notion of meaningful coincidences?"

"Wasn't there a song about that in the eighties?"

They both turned and stared at me silently, before continuing.

"There have been people trying to use this kind of trending information to predict major events, like terrorist attacks, for a few years," Mack said, "with varying degrees of success. If Barry's notes are accurate, this system takes it to a whole new level."

"If it works," I said.

Mack nodded.

"You know," I sighed, "we might never get to find out."

"Why's that?"

"It might never see the light of day. Quantelle's likely to claim that it uses their intellectual property. Maureen's likely to claim it as hers, and I don't see either side backing down."

"Well, if it matters, Barry states very plainly in the code that his system isn't a derivative work, and he's applied for patents for it."

"That might help Maureen's claim. Any luck on the remaining translation?"

"Not yet. I'm hoping that the answer is somewhere on one of these systems."

* * *

"Johnny! Vinny D here!"

"Good afternoon, Mister DeLuca."

"For Christ's sake, call me Vinny. You sound like one of my damned grade school teachers when they were about to ream me out in front of the whole class."

"All right, Vinny, what can I do for you?"

"I think you're on to something with those trucking companies. I went over to Dyle Road under the pretext of doing my story on gun violence. Everyone was more than happy to talk to me, except two places: Kala Shipping and ABEX. They shut me out cold!"

"I'm not surprised. I *will* be surprised, however, if that's the sole reason for this call."

"I've turned up someone willing to talk to you, but completely off the record."

"What do you want in return, Vincent?"

"Call me Vinny, please! At some point, I'm going to need to get a usable story out of all this. My producer is getting a little tired of waiting."

"Well, you're likely to have to wait a bit more. In the mean time, though, you might ask yourself the question, *where do Kala and AmeriBiz get their capital?* " When you answer that question, you'll find it's a venture capital firm named ABX. ABX, you'll find, is the brainchild of none other than Swindon McCarter. Give him a call, and ask him some questions. Shake him up, but gently."

"You want *me* to shake up Swindon McCarter? He's the guy that does the shaking. Hell, he eats guys like me for lunch. He could eat my whole damn station for lunch!"

"Don't tell me I've placed my faith in the wrong investigative journalist. You're Vinny D on the scene! Now get on the scene, and make Swindon sweat a little bit, as only the press can do."

"What the hell am I going to say to even get him to take my call?"

"I don't care. Use your imagination; make something up, but tie it to those two freight companies."

"You're going to owe me one hell of a favor, my friend."

"If my intuition is right, you're going to be in line for the exclusive of a lifetime. Just be careful so you're around to break the story."

* * *

Vinny's source refused to give even his first name, and revealed only that he was a veteran of truck driving.

"I've been driving truck for twenty years, and I've never been treated anywhere like they treated me a ABEX."

"AmeriBiz?"

"That's the one. They label their trucks ABEX, but all their paperwork says AmeriBiz; go figure."

"So what was your experience with them?"

"Just about a year ago, I had just left my previous company and was looking for jobs. I put my info out on the internet, and they gave me a call. It sounded like a good deal, so I gave it a try. At first, everything ran smoothly. It was mostly short haul stuff. I picked up freight at both airports and took it to the terminal. The pay was good, and I needed the money, so I kept doing it. After about a month of this, I got a call from one of their dispatchers, a foreign lady, asking if I was available for a longer run."

"To where, if you don't mind me asking."

"Atlanta. I was to pick up a truck at the terminal, head over to a warehouse off of Ramey Drive, load up, and drive to Atlanta, with as little stopping as I could manage."

"What happened?"

"Well, everything started out okay, but when I got to the warehouse, their security people told me there was some sort of a safety issue, and I was to park my truck and follow them."

"Was the security officer a woman, by chance?"

"No. There were two of them; huge guys, and the one had some sort of a foreign accent. I swear they were packing heat. I wasn't about to get into it with them, so I did as I was told. They walked me around the corner to where the other docks were and had me wait in a drivers' lounge. There was another security person waiting for me there. She was nice enough, but I could tell she was keeping a close eye on me."

"What did this woman look like?"

"Brown hair, just to her shoulders. Kinda plain-looking, if you know what I mean."

"You didn't happen to catch her name, did you?"

"No. She was wearing an ID, but I couldn't read it from where I was. I needed the money pretty badly, so I just sat there and read a magazine until they told me it was safe. We walked back over, and I found that my truck had already been loaded. I hopped in and got underway."

"They loaded your truck while you were waiting?"

"Yeah. Whatever safety problem they were having must've gone away pretty quickly. Anyway, I got to Atlanta without any problems. When I got to the yard, instead of directing me to a bay, they just had me park in a lot and unhook. They gave me my paperwork, and I bobtailed back home. After all that, I figured I ended up hauling an empty trailer all the way to Atlanta, given the problems we had at the start of the trip. But I wasn't a foot out of the gate when I happened to notice someone else hookup to my load and take it around to the back of the warehouse. Odd, too, because that was the Kala side of that terminal, not the ABEX side."

"Anything else odd about the trip?"

"Not really, apart from the fact that I got paid major dollars to haul an empty—at least double what I'd make anywhere else. I did a couple more months of local work and one more trip to Atlanta for them before they stopped calling me in."

"The second trip to Atlanta—how was it?"

"Easy money. This time I picked up a shipping container at the warehouse and was on my way. The second time, Atlanta was a turn and burn."

"What does that mean?"

"They had a load ready for me to bring back. As soon as I unhooked my load, I went and got the next. No time to waste—got right back on the road and headed north!"

"Why are you talking about this now?"

"Well, two reasons. That reporter came around asking about guns and shootings in the area. I'm telling you—that ABEX terminal down there is like a damned arsenal. I swear everyone that works there is packing heat. Secondly, I just got a call to do another Atlanta run tomorrow night—3 AM pickup, as usual."

"Did you take the job?"

"Nah. The money would've been nice, but I've signed on with a different company, and they have me heading to Boston."

"Safe travels to you. I'll make sure the reporter has a little something extra to put in your stocking at Christmas."

"Merry Christmas!"

* * *

"Good news!" said George O'Neil. "We like your boy for all three murders."

"My boy?"

"The fellow that tried to attack you. His name is Chester Rosenbloom, although he goes by Chet Rose. Ever heard of him?"

"Nope."

"He used to be an acrobat until he decided that crime paid better. He's been in and out of various penal facilities over the past fifteen years, but this is the first time for him in the big leagues, so to speak."

"What's his record?"

"All small stuff, robberies, mostly. He was involved in a jewel heist about seven years ago in Houston. He did all the legwork getting in and out of the place. When the cops showed up, his buddies left him holding the bag."

"Do you like this guy for all three murders?"

"He's all but confessed to them…"

"*All but* confessed?"

"We're working on it. You're sounding like a lawyer again."

"I thought there were dissimilarities to the point where the medical examiner refused to conclude that the three victims were killed by the same killer."

"Now you're sounding like *his* lawyer. The M.E. didn't rule it out, either. The biggest stumbling block is the angle of entry of the bayonet wounds and the force with which the wound was delivered. Barry Myers was killed by a powerful stabbing motion. Rick Stevens' wound was delivered with less energy. Jennifer Adams' was somewhere in the middle. Look, Costa, all of those details aside, the same person *could* be the killer, and when this guy confesses, we've got him."

"You sound like you're in a hurry to make an arrest."

"The Mayor sure as hell is," he grumbled.

"What about Ivan Rakic?"

"Oh yes. Ivan the Terrible. We searched our state and the neighboring two and couldn't find any evidence of anybody by that name living in the area. Even expanding our search nationally didn't help. Interpol lost track of Ivan a few years back, but there's no record of him entering the country, and none of the NSA surveillance programs have picked him up as being here. More than a few of them think a rival killed him. Your assailant keeps going on and on about him, but we think he's just making it up."

"I don't."

"You wouldn't, Costa. You never met a murder that you didn't think was a damned international conspiracy."

"This is anything but a few simple murders, George! Something much bigger is going on, and Quantelle Logistics is somehow in the middle of it."

"Can you prove any of this?"

"Not yet, but I have word that something is happening tomorrow night. Can you at least look into it?"

"You know as well as I do that suspicions aren't enough. If I show up at Quantelle, they're going to send me on my way and be well within their rights to do so. Give me something solid to go on, and I'll get warrants together. Right now, the best I can offer is to have a few extra units in the area."

Dammit.

CHAPTER THIRTY-FIVE

"Yes, Mister Costa, I promise. I'll set the cameras and then get the hell out of there."

"I mean it, Zonk; now say it again."

"Cameras, then get out."

"What are the chances you're going to get caught doing it?"

"If I thought I was going to get caught, I wouldn't do it. The trick is going to be aiming the darn things. Normally, when a security camera is positioned, the installer has a small monitor with them, or they're on the line with someone watching the screen."

"Can't we do that?"

"We can, but I'd rather not have them online any more than is absolutely necessary. We've got the cameras configured to use Quantelle's guest wireless network. Hopefully, nobody's watching, or if they are, they mistake the cameras for phones connecting to the network and ignore them. Of course, there's the possibility that they'll shut off the network while they're doing whatever it is they're doing. If that happens, we're screwed."

"Well, we can't control what we can't control. Do the best you can, but get the hell out of there when your shift ends, just like they want you to. We're dealing with people who play for keeps, Zonk. Don't forget that."

* * *

"This is incredible," Mack said, staring up from her monitor.

"Barry's program?"

"Well, yes, that too, but I was finally able to figure out the rest of the cipher."

"Really? Great job, Mack!"

"One of Barry's computers was different. It didn't have any software development tools, or anything related to his research. It looked like an ordinary computer, the kind one might use for web surfing and email. There was just one problem: the size of the disk and the free space didn't add up. Turns out, he had created an encrypted partition that didn't show up unless you knew the password."

"You figured out the password?"

"No. Too much trouble. The program he used to create the partition was older and had been compromised a few years back. I used the widely-known exploit to get in."

"Seems odd for a man like Barry, someone you have called a genuine genius, to use something with a known weakness."

"The creation of the partition was relatively recent and probably related to the events we're investigating. I expect he wanted it to be found, but only by someone who would know the software's weakness."

"What if the wrong person found it?"

"They might miss it completely, or try guessing the password. Too many failures, and the partition destroys itself."

"Then it's good fortune that it was you that ended up with the computer. What's in this partition?"

"Nothing much…"

"Mack!"

"A few files."

"Mack!!"

"All right, already! He started to notice some inconsistencies in his warehouse system. At first, he thought it was an error in his program.

But then he discovered the truth. He kept sort of a digital diary—check it out."

10/23: Wasted a week running algorithmic diagnostics after detecting some flow inconsistencies on some orders running in area XA-1. Discovered XA-1 was offline for 2 hours, 10 minutes, but the condition was not logged to the master flow control software. Reported issue to floor manager who assured me it was an oversight and would be corrected.

1/11: After two more incidences of flow inconsistencies with no meaningful response from the floor manager, I have escalated the issue to my manager. I don't care if they need to take some bays out of service, but the predictive flow module will make erroneous routing decisions if the areas are not taken off line in master flow control. Otherwise, we risk missing fulfillment targets when orders are misrouted to the alcove.

"Here is the moment where Barry decided that there was a bigger issue," Mack said, changing the image on the screen.

2/21: It is now painfully obvious that the issues in the alcove are intentional and are being ignored by management. If this is an attempt to discredit my system so that they can avoid paying me my bonus, it will not work. Installed monitoring software and bypassed flow control alerting for the alcove.

3/18: External data collection blocked by firewall changes mandated by security department. Hiding the results on my company computer until I can figure out what's going on.

"It goes on much the same until these entries:"

5/22: Narrowed the list of participants. We may have a bigger problem.

6/24: I think someone is running their own business inside our business and using the docks to do it. If they take the system off line, it will effect the reports and people will start asking questions.

"Take special note of this one, John."

7/18: Tried to pay the alcove a visit tonight, but was turned away by a huge security guard that sounded like he came from Russia. Report was of a hazardous condition, but I checked the flow engine, and nothing hazardous was routed to the alcove. This is unbelievable.

"Your friend had his suspicions," Mack said. "He even tried getting into Quantelle's security system, only to find his access to it was blocked during the times in question. All he could do was to continue to record the few pieces of data he could get."

"Mack, his logs included carrier, origin, and destination information. How on earth did he get those?"

"This entry explains it."

9/4: Device scanning reveals rogue printing equipment attached to our network during the odd times. Fortunately, this

contingency was included in the monitoring
software I deployed. They are clearly printing
shipping documents. I have updated my logs to
show the data I have collected.

"Here's the last entry in his journal," she said, scrolling past
many lines of text. "He didn't date it, but the timestamp on the file
shows the last update to be less than a week before he died."

I was finally able to break the
encryption used on one of the older print jobs
I intercepted. It was either a photocopy or a
scanned version of a driver's license, only
the picture didn't seem to align with the
details of the document. Age was
significantly different than expected. I will
be bringing this to the attention of our head
of security first thing in the morning. I will
also ask John Costa at the next session for
his advice, if he is willing to offer it.

"Less than a week later, he was dead," I muttered, staring off
into space, anger building.

"Yep," Mack said, resting her arm gently on my shoulder. "The
strange happenings in the alcove were throwing off the routing system
he built. Your friend did all the right things: he reported the issue to the
floor manager, escalated to his boss, and then to the head of security."

"One of them is in on it," I said, finishing her sentence.
"Whatever the hell it is."

* * *

"For the record, John, I think this is a terrible idea," Mack said.

"I have to agree with her, Mister Costa."

"Can I get Zonk's video feed on this thing?" I said, holding up
my laptop.

"Yes," Mack sighed.

"I'm to use my mobile hot spot and our security thingy, right?"

She rolled her eyes. "It isn't our security thingy. It is our virtual private network and yes, you need to use it to get the video."

"Look, I know you two don't agree with this, but I'm going to be there when Zonk leaves tonight."

"Zonk already has the protection of a professional, Mister Costa," Kevin protested.

"Yes, one who is undoubtedly skilled, but will be hopelessly outnumbered and outgunned if something were to happen. Zonk's a kid. He talks a good game, but he's inexperienced. He's my friend, and I'm not going to let his safety to chance, especially after what happened to Barry."

They exchanged glances.

"Kevin. You of all people should know. Henry V, right? *In peace there's nothing so becomes a man as modest stillness and humility. But when the blast of war blows in our ears, then imitate the action of the tiger.*"

He sighed. "Yes. Henry V. Act 3, Scene 1. *Once more unto the breach, dear friends, once more.* I'm with you, Mister Costa."

* * *

"Damn, it's cold," I muttered. The cloudless night was the year's coldest on record. We had parked our vehicle, Kevin's massive black SUV, in the warehouse parking lot at Quantelle Logistics, doing our best to tuck it in with other larger vehicles. Less than five minutes had elapsed since we shut off the engine, and already I wanted to dip into the thermos of hot coffee.

"Fire up your hot spot and get things connected," Kevin said, oblivious to the cold.

Following Mack's instructions, I was quickly online. My backup phone rang, on queue.

"Okay," Mack said, "I see you guys. We just need to wait for Zonk and we're set. Should be any minute now."

The wait was cold and felt eternal, but in reality, it was only a few minutes. I used the opportunity to catch up on a few emails, including the picture promised to me by Adnan. I stared at it, searching my memory for why what I saw on the screen looked familiar and smiled. Before I could say anything, a slight click in the audio signaled Zonk had joined our conference call.

"Hi Dad," he said, "I'm all done, and I'm headed out. Are you here to pick me up yet?"

"Yes, I'm here. I hope I came to the right spot."

I turned to Kevin, who nodded in response. Zonk's choice of words, a prearranged code, told us that he was being watched.

I eyed the employee entrance carefully, breathing a noticeable sigh of relief when it opened a stream of workers trickled out. Zonk was among them, still carrying on a fictitious conversation on his phone. His bodyguard emerged a few seconds later. It wasn't until Zonk climbed into the back of our vehicle that I started to relax.

Before the door closed, his bodyguard said, "Follow me."

Kevin nodded, and we left the parking lot as part of the convoy of employees leaving for the night.

A few turns later, we were in an adjacent parking lot.

"Quantelle's cameras don't bother to look over here," the other bodyguard said as he climbed into the vehicle. "I was worried that if we lingered in the lot, they might get suspicious."

"God, I hope this works," Zonk said, looking at the clock on his phone. "I programmed the cameras to start about a minute from now."

"Good thinking," I said. "That way you're out of the building when they come online."

"Yeah, except that I've never used the feature before. I really hope I didn't screw it up. We might not get another chance; they seemed abnormally stressed out tonight."

"That's probably my fault," I said. "I've been poking the bear lately. Okay, Zonk. Moment of truth."

I opened the laptop and clicked per Mack's instructions. The program opened, but there was no video.

"Give it a minute," Zonk said, looking nervously at the clock. "The clocks on the cameras might not be in sync, and they take a minute or two to start and get connected."

"I still show signal from the Quantelle guest network," the

bodyguard said. "They haven't shut it off."

"One of the reasons we picked this spot," Zonk said, "is that we can connect to Quantelle's network if we use a special antenna." He motioned to the gadget, resembling an elongated soup can, in his bodyguard's hand. "If they block our cameras' outbound signal at the firewall, maybe we can still see them through the network."

"Will we still be able to record?" I asked.

The question was quickly rendered moot when the screen came to life.

"Here we go," Mack said.

"You two watch the screens," the bodyguard said. "Kevin and I have your backs."

"Damn," Zonk grunted, pointing to one of the cameras. "I wanted to point this one a little more to the left. It's only catching half of the last bay."

"It's fine, Zonk. You did a great job. Between the two cameras, we've got a decent view."

"Show time," Mack said. "Tonight's first star on the red carpet… Brenda Simmons!"

We watched the screen as the head of Quantelle's security, accompanied by two large and obviously armed men, made a slow pass around the alcove.

"They're looking for anybody left behind. See, Zonk? That's why I wanted you the hell out of there!"

"God, I hope she doesn't find the cameras," he whispered.

The security chief's path brought her ever closer to the first, and best, of our two cameras. She grew larger in the monitor, until her face dominated the screen. She frowned and then reached toward the camera.

CHAPTER THIRTY-SIX

"Dammit," I groaned.

"Wait," said Zonk, smiling. "She fell for it."

Brenda Simmons' scowling face moved away, and the camera remained intact.

"What just happened?"

"I gave her something to find," Zonk said, his relief obvious. "The few times I've seen her, she struck me as terribly anal, so I left an empty soda can to draw her attention away from where the camera is hidden. I figured she couldn't pass it up."

The security chief completed her scan. Finally, I heard her voice come over the speakers of Kevin's vehicle.

"We're clear. We're clear. Let's go."

A heavily accented voice replied. "Copy. We go. We go."

"The cameras have sound?" I asked.

"No," Mack said. "Quantelle holds FCC licenses for three frequencies, but the radios that you and Ashley described to me had only two channels. The licensed frequencies are public record, so I programmed one of Barry's radios to listen to Quantelle's third channel. That's what you're hearing."

Before I could compliment Mack's intuition, one of the loading dock doors opened. A delivery truck pulled up and the back opened. A flurry of activity followed as the contents of the vehicle were unloaded and wheeled quickly to a nearby office.

"Clever," said Zonk. "They're using one of the old forklifts to unload and move things, just like they did with the one that attacked you. The good lifts are all in service, so nobody will be any the wiser."

"Any idea what that equipment is?"

"Not entirely sure," Mack answered, "but I'd bet money that at least two of them are printers."

"That would explain why Barry mentioned printing in his journal. Damn, they're moving fast!"

Whatever they were doing, it was a well-practiced and choreographed routine. The last of the equipment was loaded into the office, and the door closed, leaving two large men outside on watch. Another twenty minutes passed before I heard Brenda Simmons' voice again.

"Gate, this is XA. Do you copy?"

"Copy, XA," a man's voice replied.

"Is red dot ready?"

"Negative. No red dot."

"Copy. No red dot."

Brenda popped out of the office and said something to the two men. They nodded, and she returned, closing the door behind her.

"What the hell is red dot?" I asked.

"Probably an ABEX truck," Mack answered, "given the design of their logo."

Another bitterly cold and stressful fifteen minutes passed before the radio alerted us again.

"Gate to XA."

"XA. Go."

"Red dot has arrived."

"Clear for bay one."

"Damn," Zonk said. "That's the bay with the partially obstructed view. I'm sorry, Mister Costa."

* * *

As luck would have it, when the loading bay door finally opened, our view was nearly useless. Between the camera angles and the position taken up by the two hulking guards, we could only see hints of what was transpiring on the dock.

"There's a lot of traffic in and out of that truck," Mack observed. "Zonk, is there an office next door to the one where they loaded the equipment? Whatever they're unloading now has to be going there, otherwise we'd see it on the cameras."

"A conference room, yes, and there is a door to the offices from inside the room."

"What the hell are they doing?" I growled.

I was getting frustrated. Part of me wanted to storm in there and find the truth, but the sane part of me knew we wouldn't stand a chance. I resigned myself to another cold wait.

Fifteen frigid minutes later, I heard Mack's voice. "Interesting," she said.

My eyes scanned the screen, but saw nothing out of the ordinary. "What is it?"

"I'm getting alerts that Lance Yannis' phone just came back online, and it's not out West. It's somewhere here in the city. I'll see if I can get a better idea of his location."

"Why am I not surprised?"

Another quarter of an hour passed with no update on Lance's phone, but it quickly took a back seat to the happenings inside the Quantelle warehouse. The office door opened, and we finally had a good look at what was going on. It made us sick.

"Jesus, Mack, get O'Neil on the phone, now!"

"Already on it," she said, her voice shaking.

"Human trafficking," muttered Kevin, as he peered over my shoulder. "Dear God," he said as a disheveled young woman appeared on the screen, walking slowly toward the waiting truck, "she's only a teenager."

"Come on," I said. "We've got to stop this! We've got to get in there and help them."

Kevin rolled down the window of his vehicle and mumbled something to the other bodyguard. "If we go in there now, we'll be shot before we get ten feet into the property."

"It's worth it! O'Neil's going to have police on the way. Maybe if we slow them down…"

"No." Kevin said, resolutely. "Our best chance is to intercept that truck. They have to leave some of their people behind to load up their equipment and cover up any evidence. If we're lucky, the truck will be unguarded."

It made sense, and the images on the screen told me that we'd never get to the warehouse in time. The doors on the truck closed, and the loading dock door descended shortly thereafter.

"Do it!" I shouted.

Kevin started the engine, and the SUV roared out of the parking lot, all of us holding on for dear life as he tested the limits of the vehicle's stability. Behind us, Zonk's bodyguard followed.

"There are two ways in and out of the loading docks," Zonk shouted, straining to be heard above the roar of the engine and squealing tires.

"Which way?" Kevin shouted, as a two-way intersection loomed at the end of the parking lot.

"Zonk!" I screamed.

"Right!" He shouted.

Kevin slammed on the brakes and spun the wheel, deftly sliding the massive vehicle around the corner.

"If I'm wrong," Zonk said, "we may never catch up to that truck."

"Why did you pick the direction you did?"

"This way is rougher, so it's used less. The other way, there's a chance our truck would've been in line to get out the gate. I didn't think that was a risk the traffickers were willing to take."

"Good call!" Kevin shouted. "There it is!"

A white truck, adorned with the red ABEX logo and pulling a shipping container, turned onto the road in front of us.

"He looks to be alone," Kevin said, noting the absence of any other vehicles exiting the lot.

"We've got to stop him before he gets to the freeway, and we certainly can't let him get to the ABEX terminal. That place is a damned arsenal, according to my sources," I said to Kevin.

"I've got it floored!"

"Mack! Get our location to O'Neil. We're going to try to stop this truck, but we're going to need cops. We're alone for now, but I don't know how long that's going to last."

"On it," she replied. "Exactly how the hell are you going to stop a semi?"

"Leave that to us," said Kevin, speaking into his two-way radio. "Hang on."

We overtook the truck, turning sharply into its lane and braking. The driver sounded his horn as he slammed on the brakes. Simple physics took over. The truck's weight carried it forward, and it slammed into the back of our vehicle, crushing it, and sending glass shards flying.

I was driven back into my seat, then forward, my motion stopped abruptly and painfully by my seat belt.

"He's running!" someone shouted.

Disoriented, I staggered out of the vehicle, only to be pulled down to the ground by Kevin. "His friends are coming," he said, pointing to a vehicle speeding in our direction.

Out of the corner of my eye, I caught a glimpse of the driver sprinting into the nearby woods. Oblivious to the impending danger, I ran after him.

"Costa!" Kevin shouted, but I paid no heed. Gunfire erupted behind me, but I maintained my pursuit.

The narrow grove of trees gave way to a field. Illuminated by the orange streetlights from the nearby freeway, I saw the driver making his escape. I sprinted with everything my legs would give. As we neared a thicket, I lunged, wrapping my arms around his legs and dragging him to the ground.

We scuffled, his interest mostly to break free. That changed, though, when it was obvious that I wasn't going to permit an easy escape. He started to reach for his waist and the weapon that undoubtedly waited for him there. I changed tactics in response, moving to secure his arms. We locked hands and battled for leverage.

The tackle had left me, fortunately, in a superior position as I worked to pin his arms to the ground. Worried that he might try to use his larger size to roll or flip me, I needed to end the scuffle. Unable to free my hands to punch him, I resorted to another option. I allowed my torso to lower and before he could respond, I delivered a vicious head-butt directly to the bridge of his nose. Bone and cartilage failed under the force of the blow, and blood gushed from his broken face.

A second one wasn't required. His surprise gave me the time I needed to break my hand free and draw my weapon. His struggles ceased immediately.

I stepped back, still winded and shaky from the confrontation. The driver sank to his knees, his hands interlaced on his head at my instruction. My hand still shaking, I wiped sweat and blood out of my eyes and retrieved my phone. Using it as a flashlight, I studied the kneeling man.

"Nice to finally meet you, Lance," I said, "or do you prefer to be called Ivan Rakic?"

"How did you know?"

"A friend sent me an old picture of you. You've shaved your beard, your hair is different, but your eyes—they're the same. When you ran from the truck, I knew whoever was driving was aware of their cargo. A regular driver, someone who didn't know, would have had no reason to run."

"We've been doing this right under the nose of the police. I can't believe you tracked us down when they couldn't."

"I had an advantage that the cops didn't. They have to get search warrants, have probable cause, and all that silly stuff that I talked about when I was in the courtroom. But I don't have such restrictions. You see, when you killed my friend, you got me involved. When you tried to kill me, you got me angry, and I'm not the type of person you want to make angry."

"Your friend got too close; I didn't have any choice. Not only did he discover our business venture, he was close to figuring out who I am. He was contacting people back home and getting too close. A shame, because I liked him. I tried to convince him to look the other way, but he was so worried about his foolish software looking bad he wouldn't listen."

"So you lured him into the alley that night?"

"I was there to kill you both if necessary. You lived because you left the pub alone."

"What about the note and the bayonet?"

"Smoke and mirrors to get the police to waste their time looking for an old Bosnian myth. We just needed a few more weeks, and then we'd be out of here. The fact that Barry got as close as he did told us it was time to move on. Your involvement only amplified that."

"Where did Rick Stevens fit into all this?"

"He worked for us, but I have an airtight alibi for my whereabouts when he was killed. I know who did it, and it might be worth something to you."

"It's worth nothing to me. I set out to find who killed my friend, and I've done that. The rest is up to the cops."

"The cops have the wrong person. That much I'll tell you for free."

He knew me well enough to understand that I couldn't let it go. The injustice would eat at me, mercilessly.

"I'm not in a position to make any deals, but I can make a recommendation. Or I could shoot you between the eyes right now and put an end to all of this."

"You wouldn't."

"I'd make it look like you drew your weapon, and I was left with no choice. The video would only serve to prove my claim."

"Video? What video?"

"Mack," I said, "I'm putting you on speaker. You're getting all this, aren't you?"

"Perfect picture, decent audio," she replied.

"Can you make the video look like he tried to draw his weapon, Mack?"

"Piece of cake," she said, confidently. "Just make sure you're at least seven feet away, like the last time we did this. It'll be easier to edit if he's a little less full in the frame. But make it snappy. O'Neil's going to be there in about three minutes."

I put the phone down and summoned as much anger and hatred

to my face as I could muster. Moving deliberately, I stepped back from him a few paces.

"That looks to be about seven feet. Stand up," I barked.

He complied, hesitantly.

"I guess you find all this worth dying for, and my conscience isn't going to have a moments' pause after I kill you. But because I'm so damned nice, I'm going to give you one last chance to tell me everything."

He smiled. "Not worth it, my friend. I'll take my chances with your lenient justice system. Jennifer Adams killed Rick when he started to get cold feet. He was a stupid, weak man, anyway. She told him we were importing gray market electronics, and he believed her for the longest time. Those girls in the truck—worthless. Whores, likely to die on the streets. What does it matter if it is here or back in the Balkans."

"Why did you kill Jenn?"

"I didn't, and I don't know who did. Rivals, perhaps. I wouldn't kill her—she was a good business partner. A little crazy, but good."

"Costa!" a familiar voice shouted.

"Over here, George."

O'Neil emerged from the grove, accompanied by four uniformed police officers.

"You certainly get yourself into the most interesting messes, John," he said.

"I do, don't I?"

"Good work," he said, offering me his hand. "Come with me; you need to see this."

270

CHAPTER THIRTY-SEVEN

A dozen disheveled, terrified girls huddled together as paramedics worked to bring them blankets and check their condition.

"We have no idea who they really are," a policeman said, "all of these documents are likely forgeries. They don't even know to answer to the name that matches their pictures."

Upon seeing us, one of the girls, the tallest and likely the oldest among them, approached me. She hesitated, but O'Neil motioned her to continue.

"She's the only one who has talked to us so far. She may be the only one that speaks enough English to understand." O'Neil turned to the girl and spoke in a voice far more gentle than I thought the man capable of. "This is the man who found you."

She stared at me, silently, and I could do little more than return her gaze. Finally, she moved close to me and whispered, "thank you." Trembling, she embraced me. I held her close until the paramedics walked her to a waiting ambulance.

* * *

I sat on the bumper of O'Neil's car until the paramedics were done treating my compatriots. Apart from abrasions and a few cuts from flying glass, we all had emerged surprisingly unscathed. Zonk's car and Kevin's SUV were not so fortunate.

"We had to use them as shields until the police arrived," Kevin said, pointing to Zonk's bullet-riddled car.

"Good thing you weren't in them," I said.

"About my car, Mister Costa…" Zonk said, hesitantly.

I smiled. "I'll get you a new one."

"How many cars is this?" asked O'Neil.

"Four," I sighed. "Mine, Tom's, and now these two."

"Exactly how many did you destroy in Northern Ireland?"

"Which time?"

"I rest my case," O'Neil said, laughing.

"Dammit," I said. "I promised Vinny D the story. In all the confusion, I forgot to call him."

"Don't worry about it," O'Neil said. "He's already on the scene, and has been since nearly the outset. It's like someone very close to the situation tipped him off—someone named Jillian, I expect. Do you want to talk to him, because I'm sure he's dying to talk to you?"

"No, I think I'll catch the whole thing on the evening news tomorrow. Mack can get you everything you need in terms of evidence. I'm going to bed."

He extended his hand, which I accepted. He pulled me into an unexpected embrace. "You are the most stubborn, bullheaded son of a bitch I've ever met, and God help me for saying this because you're a damned lawyer, but you've got the best heart of anyone I know." He slapped my back with his hand. "Merry Christmas, my friend."

"Merry Christmas, George."

* * *

Sleep was my plan, but the universe had other ideas. Drew Scanlon, Quantelle's president, was on the phone before I got home, already in full damage control mode.

"We're already putting measures in place to make sure that

nothing like this ever happens again," he said. "The ownership and senior management of Quantelle is horrified that something like this took place without our knowledge at one of our facilities."

"I'm thrilled to hear that, Mister Scanlon, but I'm very tired tonight and just want to get some sleep."

"We are having a press conference first thing in the morning, and we'd be honored if you would attend and issue a joint statement with us."

"I've never met the owner of your company, Mister Scanlon, but I've heard he's a good man. You, on the other hand, get whatever is coming to you, which should be your walking papers and a stack of lawsuits that reaches to the heavens. This happened on your watch—plain and simple. No statement, no press conference, and no spin doctor is going to change that. Had you been more forthcoming in sharing the details of your internal investigation, little more than a sham in retrospect, I might be more willing to consider your offer. As it stands, though, I'm not."

"I can understand your position, but…"

"Did you know that Barry Myers reported the irregularities to both Sam Thomas and Brenda Simmons repeatedly?"

"Mister Thomas has been terminated from his position, and we're recommending that criminal charges be filed against him."

"If that happens, I'll defend him, and I'll win. Then I'll recommend he sue you for defamation of character, for starters. He's many things, and I don't care for the man, but he's too big of a coward to take this thing on his shoulders. I'd bet money that he escalated the issue, probably directly to you, and you chose to ignore it, for whatever reason. No, Mister Scanlon, the buck stops with you."

I hung up the phone before he could reply.

* * *

"Would you believe that Brenda Simmons has a criminal record?" Mack said, sipping a Guinness as we waited for the evening news.

"At this point, I'll believe anything. How on earth did she ever get hired as Quantelle's head of security?"

"According to Ashley and confirmed by Clarissa Jones, Drew Scanlon hired her personally and bypassed a lot of the usual controls in the process. Apparently, he did that a lot."

"Quantelle grew quite a bit under his watch," I said, sipping my Guinness, "but that was mostly due to Barry's software. I'm sure Drew Scanlon took all the credit."

"I guess the owner fired Scanlon immediately after the press conference, or so my sources tell me. He's pledged to use the money from the life insurance policy Quantelle held on Barry to help as many of the victims as possible. He called earlier," she said, "but you were sleeping, and I didn't want to wake you. He'd like to talk to you, but will understand if you don't call. For what it's worth, he sounded like a decent man."

"I'll think about it. Oh! Turn up the telly—here's Vinny's story!"

Vincent DeLuca, for the first time I could remember, had the lead story on the evening news. Usually sandwiched between the weather and sports, his frenetic stories tended to be high on energy, occasionally confrontational, but lighter on substance.

Tonight was different.

His treatment of the story was calm, factual, and professional. Coverage started with footage of a dozen people, Brenda Simmons at the head of the line, taken out of Quantelle in handcuffs. His cameras managed to catch a brief gunfight at the AmeriBiz terminal before Kate Yannis, who was, in reality Ekaterina Rakic, and others surrendered to the police. The story concluded with a number that people could call to donate items and money to support the victims. Even the anchors seemed stunned when the segment ended.

For News Channel Twelve, this is Vincent DeLuca reporting.

* * *

Vinny was on the phone to me at the first commercial break. "What did you think of the story, Mister Costa?"

"You did it very well. It was factual, timely, and touching—exactly what's missing from the news these days."

"Network is running with it for the national news. Me! Vinny D! National news!"

"Not Vinny D nationally," I said, "but Vincent DeLuca—that I can believe."

"I owe you a lot, Mister Costa. I may never get a chance at a story like that again."

"Maybe not, but there's lots of good stories out there. Like for example, there are some good people that have fallen on hard times living in the old foundry. Do a story on them; find out what they *really* need and show people a way to give it to them."

"Other reporters have done that story. We do something like it every year around Christmas."

"No. *You* do it. Do it like you did our story and do it *now*. At this moment, you have the ear of the public, but we're a fickle lot. Use it to do something good—something meaningful."

"You know what? I think maybe you're on to something. I've got to run—they're calling me to do the national lead-in. Merry Christmas, Mister Costa!"

"Merry Christmas, Mister DeLuca, and please, call me John."

* * *

I hung up the phone. Surrendering to sheer exhaustion, I stumbled to the music room and curled up on the sofa. Dreamless sleep collected me almost immediately.

The room was dark and the house quiet when I woke up. I looked around and found the green numerals of my clock. My eyes slow to focus, I squinted, trying to read the numbers. Somewhere around 2:00 AM, I thought. As I stared, something passed between me and the clock, momentarily blocking my view. Startled, I fumbled to get to my feet.

"It's okay, Johnny," the gentle voice of Angela Grady said, turning on the light. "I didn't mean to scare you."

I flopped back into the sofa. My muscles were unwilling or

unable to move, but my heart was pounding.

"I watched the story on the news tonight," she said. "It's everywhere by now. I'm sure our friends back in Ireland are proud of you."

"I wasn't mentioned in the story."

"I'm sure a little birdie told them about your involvement. I'm so proud of you, Johnny. You've given some people hope at Christmas that, otherwise, were facing death."

"Maybe since I have no hope, I can give it to others."

"No hope?" she said, frowning. "Why?"

"Because the woman I love is dead, and all I have left are hallucinations and pointless dreams."

She sat down next to me, the gentle scent of her perfume teased my nose. "Give me your hand," she said.

"I can't," I said. "I can't move in dreams like this. I'm paralyzed."

"Yes, you can. Give me your hand."

Much to my surprise, my arm worked. I slipped my hand into hers.

"There," she said, pressing it against her chest. "Warm, solid, and my heart is beating. Can you feel it?"

I nodded, tears forming in my eye. "How did you get in?"

"You gave me the code."

"Why do you keep coming to me like this? If you're alive, why not stay?"

"I can't right now. Please trust me—I want to, desperately, but I can't. But soon, John; next Christmas; under the mistletoe, the kiss we've both wanted and missed."

"Why not kiss me now?"

"My heart can't handle the strain, my love. But I wanted to pay you one more visit before I leave for a while, because you need hope. Hope lives, Johnny. Now rest, my love, and enjoy the season."

She turned off the light and vanished into the darkness. Try as I might, I couldn't resist the sleep that followed.

* * *

"All right!" I shouted, stomping to the top of the stairs, "who's the damned comedian?"

"What on earth are you talking about," Mack said.

"This isn't funny!" I held out a small, square box, wrapped in Christmas paper.

"I still don't know what you're talking about."

"Neither do I, Mister Costa," Kevin said.

"Look at the label, Mack," I said, handing her the present.

She read it, and the confused expression left her face.

"I can be pretty cruel when I have to be, John, but not like this. I wouldn't give you a present and pretend that it was from Angela Grady. You had another dream, didn't you?"

"Yeah," I said, sinking into the nearest chair. "It was so damned real, too. But dreams or phantasms don't leave presents. This isn't an illusion or a figment of my imagination!"

"No, it isn't," she said.

"Look at the damn security system. See if anyone accessed it using the bypass code. Check the cameras for activity."

Mack nodded, although I detected a bit of reluctance. "There's nothing in the logs, nothing on the cameras. Wait a minute," she said, moving to the edge of her chair.

"What?"

"There are about fifteen minutes missing from the system, right around 2 AM. I really don't have an explanation."

"I have one," I said, "Angela's alive."

"John," Mack said, "she's not. I'm sorry to be so blunt about it, but maybe that's what you need to hear. I've read the reports, and I've seen the autopsy photos."

"Where did you get those?"

"Your friends in Northern Ireland sent them in hopes that they might help you get closure and move on. There's never a good time, but maybe this is the *right* time. The images aren't pleasant, so I'll leave it up to you."

"Documents and pictures can be faked. You, of all people, should know that."

"Yes, they can," she sighed. "Do you want to see them? Yes or no."

I took a deep breath. "Show me."

Mack nodded and turned her attention to her computer.

"Mister Costa," Kevin said, "do you care if I speak my mind?"

"Please do, Kevin."

"There's another possibility: you bought the gift, you deleted the footage from the system."

"I didn't buy the gift, Kevin. I'd remember that."

"Grief can cause some episodes of unusual behavior. It is rare, but possible. Since you came back from Ireland, have you lost time? Have you ended up somewhere without knowing how or why you got there?"

"No, I don't think so. That can happen?"

"Yes," Kevin said. "If it's happening, you need to get some help. Even if that isn't it, you've experienced a traumatic event and a crushing loss. You need to deal with your grief. Sorry if I'm speaking out of line."

"No. I can find dozens of people willing to tell me what I want to hear. Mack, let's see those pictures."

She paused. "They're gone! I really don't understand how this could have happened. My local copies, my cloud copies, and the files from the download location are all gone!"

We looked at each other, but nobody offered an answer.

"Anyone care for a whiskey?" I said.

"Yes!" they answered.

CHAPTER THIRTY-EIGHT

"Hard to believe," George O'Neil said, "that Ivan and Ekaterina Rakic were living under our noses all this time—birth certificate, driver's license, social security number, school records, you name it. International criminals, and we missed their presence for years!"

"Kinda scary."

"They had a pretty clever setup, unwittingly provided by Quantelle's isolated alcove and disconnected senior management. I wouldn't be surprised if their plans included infiltrating other locations, especially given Quantelle's recent success."

"Human suffering, at the speed of modern logistics. Absolutely sickening."

"We've been working with the FBI to dismantle their trafficking ring. They would bring young women in through Miami, Washington, D.C., and New York on the promise of citizenship. Some were destined for the west coast. Those passed through Atlanta and Houston on their way to Vegas and L.A. Once here, they were fed drugs and turned into prostitutes. God knows how many."

"Hard to believe that it happens in our country in this day and age."

"You know, with all our technology, we're closing a lower percentage of murders than we did fifty years ago. A lot of the victims are sex workers at truck stops. They're forgotten by society. The girls in that truck have a chance now, thanks to you."

"It wasn't just me, George."

"Neither Ivan nor his wife have admitted to murdering Jennifer Adams. The good news is, Chet Rose is talking to us now that Ivan's in custody. Bad news is that he has an iron-clad alibi for the night of Jenn's murder, so we've only got him for the attack at your place and that bit at the warehouse. One of my theories was right, by the way?"

"Which one? I've heard quite a few of them."

"The attack at the warehouse was a diversion arranged by Brenda Simmons. They were after those notes Barry took. They couldn't let us get to his desk, in the off chance they were there. Chester was supposed to kill you, but lost his nerve."

"I think Ivan set Chester up to take the fall for the whole bit. So who do you think killed Jenn?"

"We're still working on it, but we've got a few ideas. Hey—are you going to be at O'Brien's tonight for the toast? It's a tradition, you know."

"Honestly, I was thinking about staying home. I'm a bit tired."

"You do and I'll send a police cruiser around to pick you up."

"Kevin might have something to say about that."

"So the rumor's true."

"Yeah, it is. Tom's not coming back, so I hired Kevin away from Jerry Keynes."

"He's going to be pretty bored chasing philandering husbands and insurance cheats all day."

"Maybe, but Jerry's work takes him all over the world. Mine is generally closer to home and, therefore, closer to Ashley Vinton. I'm sure the two of them won't be bored, especially not after that cast comes off."

"So, back to my original question, Costa. You coming, or do I need to use unnecessary force?"

"I'll be there, George."

* * *

Laura McConnell had the pub exceptionally festive as we arrived for the traditional Christmas Eve toast. The tradition started as drinks amongst co-workers prior to closing for the holiday. Over the years, it morphed into an event that also included regular patrons, often bringing their families for the brief celebration.

There were far more people at O'Brien's than I expected, but the reason became quickly obvious. A portion of the establishment remained open and serving patrons, while the rest was dedicated to the traditional celebration.

"A lot of people don't have anywhere to go on Christmas Eve," Laura explained, "so the staff and I decided to stay open and throw a bit of a party for them, too."

"It looks wonderful," I said, "and I'm sure the party is appreciated."

"We're getting ready for the toast," she said. "It's going to be over in the session area this year instead of at the bar. Too many people!"

We made our way to the back corner of O'Brien's. The normal crowd was there, along with most of the session musicians and, of all people, Maureen Myers. She sat in the corner sipping her bourbon.

It took the powerful voice of George O'Neil to get everyone quiet. He introduced Laura and returned to his table.

"This is my first Christmas in charge of O'Brien's," Laura said, "and I want to thank you all for your help and support these past ten months. We have a special memorial this year," she said, pointing to the table in the corner. "Our good friend, Barry Myers, passed away recently. We all know how much he loved our weekly Irish music session, so we've attached a plaque in his honor and memory to the table where he played."

She paused, allowing the applause to die down.

"And now, please join me in O'Brien's traditional toast: *Peace and blessings, and happy holidays, my friends! Slainte!* "

The simplicity and brevity of the toast was my fault, having been assailed to deliver it at the inaugural celebration whilst not quite sober. I never expected the tradition to stick and certainly not my simple words to endure; yet somehow they had.

* * *

"So they put a plaque on a table in Barry's honor," Maureen rasped. "Somehow, it seems fitting—similar personalities."

"Merry Christmas, Maureen," I said, trying to gracefully exit her presence.

"I understand you have some news for me, Rover."

"I'll be returning all of Barry's property," I said, "minus one computer, which the police need for evidence. There's some software on there that belongs to you, although Quantelle might challenge your claim to it. If the software does what it claims, you could be incredibly wealthy."

"Well, you can sink your teeth into them for me, Fido! You'll have fun."

"No, Maureen. That's a job for your new lawyer. I quit."

"You're not getting off that easily, Rover!"

"Yes, it's absolutely that easy, Maureen. I've had enough of being treated like I'm trying to rob you, being toyed with for evidence you should have turned over to me right away, and called every name in the book. For your information, my name is John; not Rover; not Spot; not Butch; and not goddamned Fido."

"Get back here, Costa."

"Kiss my ass, Maureen. Oh, and happy new year. Come on, Mack, let's get the hell out of here."

* * *

"I'm sorry, Mack," I said, rushing to get dressed, "I was so tired when we got home from O'Brien's last night that I didn't get your present wrapped. Then I overslept and they're still not ready. Can we do Christmas when we get back from Eva's party?"

"Of course," she said, "just get a move on! We don't want to be late."

I persevered, eventually getting my tie suitably knotted on the fourth try.

"I feel hopelessly overdressed," I said.

Kevin, attired in a tuxedo, said, "The only way to atone for being occasionally a little over-dressed is by being always absolutely over-educated."

"Oscar Wilde?"

He nodded.

"Okay," Mack said, "you two can trade clever quotes in the car. We've got to get going!"

She didn't even give me time to compliment her on her dress, which was nothing short of stunning.

* * *

"Wow!" Eva said as she opened the door, inviting us in. "All three of you look like a million bucks! Mack, I love the dress! Come on, I'll introduce you to everyone."

Exactly as Eva promised, the place was a madhouse, but inviting and friendly. Her guests ranged from infants to a spunky couple, introduced as her aunt and uncle, well into their eighties. The only guest not in perpetual motion was Ashley, who observed the goings on from a comfortable chair in the corner of the spacious family room. She was soon joined by Kevin, who waited on her hand and foot, for the remainder of the evening.

I tried to help Eva, but she was having none of it. "John, you're my guest, and I'm not going to put you to work," she said, motioning for me to return to my seat at the table. Defeated, I returned to my place.

Much like our impromptu dinner at Ashley's, Eva's Christmas dinner was flavorful perfection, easily outdoing the best restaurants in town. I found it difficult to pass up the numerous dishes that traversed the table. By the end of dinner, I barely had room for coffee.

Getting up to stretch, I found Eva motioning me to the kitchen. Amazingly, it was the only place in the house that wasn't abuzz.

"See?" she said, pointing to a blank spot on the wall. "I put the picture of my ex away. Time to move on."

I nodded.

"I just so happened to have hung some mistletoe above it," she said, looking mischievous and pointing to the sprig dangling over my head. "I've got a third cousin, once removed—or something like that—who's in the FBI. You better uphold the law, counselor, or he'll track you down."

"I think this is a clear cut case of entrapment," I said, moving closer.

"Guilty!" she said, gently cupping my face in her hands as our lips met. The gentle kiss endured, slightly longer than protocol demanded for friendly osculation.

"I was worried," she whispered, "that you wouldn't be ready yet."

"I'm not sure I am," I replied.

She smiled. "I understand, but I like the fact that you're willing to try."

"I like you, Eva," I said. "I think we should keep trying, but slowly, without pressure."

"That's a good idea, John. You know, when I said I wanted to go for a drive this coming spring in the sports car with you, I meant it. I like having you in my life, and I want you to stick around."

"Same. Do you have time for one more kiss, or is the house likely to implode in your absence?"

"I think we can risk it," she said.

* * *

I secluded myself in the music room to wrap Mack's presents. All was going smoothly until my phone rang. I didn't recognize the number, so I ignored it, but the caller repeated the call immediately. I debated turning off my phone, but on the third iteration, decided to answer it.

The voice was that of a woman with a heavy accent that resembled Russian.

"I know you are probably celebrating Christmas, Mister Costa, but I would like to tell you a story. Do you have a moment?"

"Who is this?"

"An insignificant storyteller that hopes you will find her story intriguing. Perhaps you are curious about the death of your woman. You are certainly wise to have left her all those years ago."

Chills ran through me. "You have my undivided attention."

"This is the story of a young girl who grew up in Yugoslavia. Her father worked for the Stasi. You've heard of them, no?"

"I have."

"Then war came, and her father was taken prisoner. Bad men sold the girl into slavery and prostitution. It is a sad story so far, isn't it?"

"It is. You were the girl, weren't you?"

"I was. My father taught me to fight, but I made the mistake of trusting these men. They shot me full of drugs and beat me until I complied. They sold me to soldiers who did terrible things to me. One raped me with the handle of his bayonet, and nobody heard my screams. But my father also taught me never to give up. One day, I broke free. I was lost and hungry, but I found my way to where my father was. Eventually, I devised a way to free him. When he learned what those men had done to me, he vowed to kill them. I took the same vow. Together, we tracked them down and delivered the justice that the world was unable to. But that was only the tip of the iceberg. Three bad men led to three more bad men. Always, there are more. You have seen this, no?"

"I have."

"Just like that girl became the hawk, so did you."

"Not quite the same."

"Different methods, true, but you stood up for the defenseless, just as I do. Is death really an unsuitable punishment for such men—and such women?"

"There is no doubt that it is suitable," I said, "but that is not a choice that falls on us."

"Oh yes," she said, "the law will deliver justice, you say. All your years in the courtroom, can you really say the law serves justice?"

"No," I sighed, "I can't say that."

"You're an honest man, Mister Costa."

"But without the law, where would we be? Survival of only the ruthless and wicked?"

"Perhaps the ruthless and wicked can, at times, do what the law can not. I wanted that horrible woman to suffer. Most men are pigs," she said, disdain dripping from her words, "but a woman that sells her sisters into a life of pain, slavery, and death, is the lowest."

"Did she know you were going to kill her? I met with her before her death, and she was scared."

"I saw you there that day, in the mall, talking to her. That is when I knew you were a good man. You were cold and strong against her, just like the hawk against the three birds. Yes, she knew, and she tried to hide, but I have been finding her type for many years. It was easy."

"So you hunted her down?"

"Like the pig she was. She tried to fight me, but my father trained me well. When she ran, I shot her in the leg. Then, I made her suffer, like the soldiers made me suffer. She screamed, but her soul knew the sounds would never be heard. That night, she knew what it was like to be forgotten. That is what I felt; that is the hopelessness the girls in the truck felt until you saved them. An animal shouldn't be made to feel like that! Jennifer Adams' choices made her life worthless; I did what your society and your justice are too weak to do."

"Why are you telling me this?"

"Because you and I, we are hawks. Different feathers, perhaps, but hawks nevertheless; and hawks hunt, Mister Costa."

"You understand that I'm obligated to report this call to the authorities, right?"

"You do what your conscience dictates. You have a good friend in Ireland, a man named Adnan, no?"

"I do."

"He, too, is a good man. Do you know what my advice for him was?"

"Birds can be dangerous."

"He searches for the hawk, but only casually, because the birds are the real danger. Perhaps this is good advice for you, too."

"May I ask you one more question?"

"You may."

"Why three? If there are so many bad men in the world, why stop at three?"

She paused. "Because in the story, there are three."

Her explanation was chilling, delivered with childlike simplicity.

"So you deliver justice, no trial, no jury, straight to execution. What if you execute the wrong person?"

"I never do."

"But if you did?"

"Maybe then, I would be one of the birds. Or perhaps it would be time for the hawk to fly away."

"If you are counting Barry as a bad man, perhaps it *is* time for the hawk to retire. Barry's evidence was the reason my associates and I were able to stop that truck."

"No, he was not one of the birds."

"But that would mean that there are only two…"

"Remember the story: The hawk hunts; the hawk kills the three birds; the hawk rests. Blessings to you and your friends."

The line went dead. I sighed, collected myself, and called George O'Neil. It was not the call I wanted to make on any day, least of all on Christmas.

"There's going to be another murder, George…"

CHAPTER THIRTY-NINE

"Who was on the phone?" Mack asked, as I emerged from the basement carrying presents.

"Just a wrong number, Mack. Just a wrong number."

She eyed me suspiciously, but didn't press the issue.

"Here are your presents," I said, handing her a stack of boxes. "Kevin, this one is yours."

"You didn't have to, Mister Costa," he protested. "I didn't know we were exchanging presents, so I'm not able to reciprocate."

"No worries. The gift isn't much of anything. You're kinda new to the team, so I didn't have a lot of time to figure out what you really like."

"I only got you one thing," said Mack, sheepishly, "although it's heavy and in a big box." She pointed to a large present tucked into the corner of the room.

"You guys go first," I said, settling into my chair.

"The complete works of Oscar Wilde!" Kevin said, holding his present above his head and smiling broadly.

"You're almost always quoting Shakespeare," I replied. "Time to add a little Irish wit to your repertoire."

"I'll get started on it right away," he said.

"Holy crap!" Mack said. "I was only kidding when I wrote this stuff down," she said, looking at her collection of computer gadgets.

"Well, you wanted it, so I got it for you."

"You even got the water cooling system! Great choice! Thank you."

"I love you, Mack. You're the best friend I've ever had. This is the least that I can do."

"Okay. Open yours!" she said, eagerly.

"I'm going to open this little one first," I said, holding up the mystery gift.

Mack and Kevin exchanged glances.

"If Kevin's theory is right, I get to see what I got for myself. Maybe I did the whole thing while sleepwalking."

I opened the small box, pretending to be amused, but inwardly, I was terrified. Another smaller, white box was within, which I also opened. Pushing away some cotton, I retrieved a gold chain. On it hung half of a coin.

"What is it?" Mack asked.

I stared at the coin a moment before answering. "Half of a two pence coin on a golden chain. The coin is from 1978, the year Angela was born."

An awkward silence followed.

"Okay," I said, collecting myself. "I'll open yours now, Mack."

"You don't have to do it now, if you're not feeling up to it?"

I looked at her, surprised by her words. "I'm fine."

"Really, you don't."

"The lady doth protest too much, methinks," I said, my expression turning to amused suspicion.

I walked over to the present, removing the paper without hesitation. It revealed another box and within that, another wrapped box.

Mack struggled to suppress laughter as I unwrapped the next box and opened the case within.

"You got me an accordion?"

"I have it on good authority that Maureen Myers likes accordion music…"

"Mack!"

"A lot of Italian tunes work well on the accordion. Maybe you can play it for Eva…"

"Mack!!"

Made in United States
North Haven, CT
24 February 2024

49162428R00182